Tinderella Wants a Fella

MATT KELLY

Published in Australia by
Moo Bear Media
PO Box 451, Chelsea VIC, 3196
www.mattkellyauthor.com
27 287 415 373

First published in Australia 2019

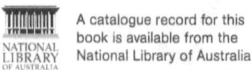

A catalogue record for this book is available from the National Library of Australia

ISBN: 978-0-6484109-2-8 (paperback)

ISBN: 978-0-6484109-1-1 (epub)

Cover design by Faaizah Ali

Layout and book typesetting by Sophie White

Printed by Kindle Direct Publishing

Disclaimer:

The characters and events in this novel are fictional and not based on real life people or real-life events. This publication is not endorsed, approved or connected to Tinder™ in any capacity. The author has never been an employee of Tinder™.

PRAISE FOR *TINDERELLA*

"In a culture where – even in 2019 – the rom-com genre is still viewed as a woman's domain, it's refreshing to see a young Australian male writer wearing his heart on his sleeve. And Matt Kelly certainly does that. Step aside, Mr Repressed-Man-Of-Few-Words-Aussie-Bloke, it seems love in the age of Tinder has found a far more emotive new voice."

– Sarrah Le Marquand, editor-in-chief of *Stellar* magazine.

"*Tinderella* captures the angst and absurdity of modern dating. Kelly takes you on the courtship rollercoaster and amuses with the internal chatter of the hopeless romantic as she embarks on the universal journey in search of love. The ride will lift the heart."

– Emily Bourke, ABC journalist.

"I was totally absorbed. *Tinderella* has just provided you with your wedding vows."

– Jules Moloney.

"I found myself loving, hating, laughing and despairing at different stages along the journey. A charming love story you'll be keen to tell your friends about."

- Kate Watts.

"Kelly has managed to uncover the inner thoughts of every woman looking for love, including the awkward moments we can only laugh at. Keep an eye on this boy."

- Amelia Phillips.

"A very honest tale that makes you feel like you're reading a true story of a friend. So often I caught myself smiling at the sincerity, authenticity and relativity of the protagonist. *Tinderella* sure has moments most people who have ever been in a relationship can relate to."

– Kate Rowswell.

"The search for love is a timeless concept that *Tinderella* playfully explores in the context of the modern day. I found myself eagerly turning the pages to find out if Ella gets her happily ever after."

– Jess Riordan.

"Anyone who has ever swiped right will empathise with Ella's plight and the highs, lows and wtf moments in her search for true love. You'll laugh, cry, sigh in understanding and laugh some more at Ella's predicament. A clever illustration of the dating app generation."

– Julieanne Horsman.

1.

The most beautiful woman that ever lived was a redhead.

Think Jessica Chastain crossed with Christina Hendricks crossed with a traffic light crossed with fury.

With her hair curled, wearing scarlet red lipstick, a white dress and white heels, she mirrored Marilyn Monroe in *The Seven Year Itch*.

She exited her posh apartment block and stood on the sidewalk. There were hundreds of men everywhere. They watched her like undercover police waiting to make a bust, with their bikes, newspapers and cigars. One man sat having his shoes polished, even though he wore Reebok Pumps™, another painted a brick wall with a toothbrush, while a third grown man played hopscotch in between the cracks in the pavement. They tried to hide their interest, but they were all so mesmerized by her loveliness, they couldn't. With bated breath they waited for her first move.

And then it came.

She started walking.

Like Cindy Crawford on a catwalk did she walk, melodramatically wiping her brow even though she hadn't perspired. With each step she picked up speed, but so too did her admirers.

This was suddenly a pursuit.

No man could let this opportunity slip, for this was the most beautiful woman that ever lived.

The woman's magnificence side-tracked men running with dogs, so too men running with monkeys. A married man who was having lunch in the park with his wife abandoned her and joined the chase. A gay man having a wine in the park departed his lover. With her potential suitors building in numbers, she began to run. She ran like an elegant gazelle loping across the crystal blue waters of a man-made pond. The chase increased in size. Cars soon followed, a helicopter swooped down from the sky, and guys on segways and cowboys on horseback joined in. A whole lot of firefighters rode on the back of a fire truck, and a tank rolled down a hill and crunched through the brick wall of a corner store. The Prime Minister arrived in the Prime Minister's car – the hot Prime Minister of Canada, not the guy from Australia – and Chris and Liam Hemsworth tangled in their chase and eventually threw fists at one another.

The woman's divine yet effortless running style soon brought her to the front of a toy store. A long line of men stood outside the front entrance. They all gazed at her as she passed them and entered. She studied each one as she moved towards the front counter – there were businessmen in suits, a rough and rugged tradesman, a policeman in uniform, a shaggy-haired surfer, a motorcycle rider and a man with a puppy. The entire ensemble from *Magic Mike* and the animated Prince Eric from *The Little Mermaid* movie also waited. Every gorgeous man in history was there, desperate for a chance at love with this woman.

She leaned over the toy store counter and looked up at he who stood at the head of the line. He was the peanut to her butter, the lolly to her pop, and the small hand on a watch to her big hand.

He was the most beautiful man that ever lived.

He approached and without hesitation took her in his arms and kissed her. It was a delicate, passionate kiss at first, but one that became more heated and intense. A tiny follicle of hair, however, grew from his upper lip. More hair followed until he had a complete moustache. Hair then grew from his chin until he had an Abraham Lincoln-style beard. The momentous growth of hair soon had the lip-locked woman wondering what was going on. She opened her eyes to investigate and discovered...

I was kissing the back-end of a furry toy horse and my fantasy was over.

I was back to being plain old Ella, the twenty-eight-year-old manager of Toy Store E, a toy store in the Parkdale Plaza, which was about forty-five minutes south of the Melbourne CBD.

My devilish Assistant Store Manager, Elliot, had played another prank on me and ruined my daydream.

'This caption will write itself,' he laughed, as he took a photo of the toy horse's bum on my lips.

He saved the photo to his phone and continued to tell me how good it was. 'You've got to check this out, this is koolish.'

Koolish was his go-to word for anything that was good. It was an extension of the word cool, but when spelt out began with a K, to make it even more koolish.

'See? Koolish, right?'

It was one of the worst photos I'd ever seen in my life and it needed to be buried, not posted on his Facebook account, which he had done in the past.

'No silly, it's for your Tinder profile.'

That was definitely not going to happen.

Despite his cheekiness, I couldn't blame him for trying to help my dismal track record when it came to relationships. He was – in that way, and in every way – the kind of best friend every best friend should be.

Elliot was a young man who'd been in a car accident when he was twelve and suffered a brain injury as a result. By definition, he was someone who was intellectually disabled but never described himself as such. He didn't like to talk about his disability, or the accident, and it was something I completely understood.

For eighteen years his name was actually Simon Elliot. Then he met me and – with his mum's permission – changed his name by deed poll to Elliot Elliot.

That's how good-a friends we were – he changed his first name to Elliot so together we would be Ella and Elliot.

He was now twenty-three and had maintained an obsession primarily with two things both starting with T – toys and technology.

'What filter do you think? Retro, vintage or cinematic? I thought seeing as you haven't kissed a man in a long time, a horse's bum was better than nothing.'

Had he have said that the first day he came in looking for a job, I probably wouldn't have hired him. Fortunately, on that very first day, he came in and mumbled, 'Sorry I'm late, I got stuck in traffic.'

This was true, well, the second half anyway. He wasn't late because I wasn't advertising a new position, but he did get stuck in traffic. The day Elliot finished high school, he walked from his house, waited at the traffic lights on Nepean Highway in Parkdale for forty-five minutes because they were broken, and when fixed, walked over to the Plaza.

He and his mum had moved into a house across the road from the store, six months earlier.

He submitted his resume in the hope I'd say yes to his request for a job.

His CV was so impressive I couldn't say no.

PREVIOUS EMPLOYMENT

I took the bins out every Tuesday at 5.30pm on the dot. Which shows I have good time-management skills and I meet deadlines.

I fed my pet fish six times a day, which shows that unlike my Demi – the goldfish – I have a really good memory.

I cleaned the local basketball hoop every three weeks. I had to use a ladder and wear protective clothing. This shows I care about safety. They asked me to clean the basketball court, but I had to go to school.

I was the ramp monitor in Grade Three. I had to make sure my friends didn't run up or down the ramp so they didn't hurt themselves. Only one kid fell over, but he was walking while playing Pokémon™ so that wasn't really my fault.

And I was the bus boy in Year Nine. I cleaned rubbish from the school bus and washed the driver's dishes he left behind so his wife didn't have to. I know this is ironic, because a bus boy normally does these jobs in a restaurant kitchen; I just did them on a bus.

I hired Elliot immediately, and from then the E in Toy Store E stood for Elliot and Ella.

It was also a play-on-words with the film.

Elliot became so good at placing new stock around the store, his customer service skills were so friendly and his knowledge for toys so detailed that I promoted him to Assistant Store Manager within two weeks, and best friend not long after that.

Despite all his successes as a young adult, there were still a few things he hadn't achieved. In that way, perhaps it was our misery that made us get along so well.

'You kissing a horse's bum, it's okay for me to say these things because I've never even kissed a girl before.'

Truth was, he kissed me on the cheek quite often.

'Yeah but that's not a real kiss, and you're not a real girl Ella Bang.'

Unlike Elliot, I hadn't changed my name by deed poll. Elizabeth was my first name, shortened to Ella, and Bang was my surname. Bang was Dutch and pronounced Bong but growing up all the school kids called me Ella Bang, because bang was a synonym for sex and well, sex jokes had always been funny to teenagers.

Mum and Dad sent me to an all-girls school. I accepted quite quickly I would have been teased for my surname no matter what high school I attended, but still hated going there for one standout reason – no boys went there.

Mum told me I was sent there because she went there, and it was important to carry on the family tradition. That was a lie; my two older sisters were allowed to attend co-educational grammar schools on scholarships for sport. That's right – sport, and they weren't even full scholarships; Mum and Dad still had to fork out thousands for my sisters to attend.

Being at an all-girls school, the only time I spent with boys was at the Year Nine social, Year Ten social, and Year Twelve formal. During line dance rehearsal for the socials, I was the girl the boys in the line looked ahead to with dread. I got nervous, sweaty palms and nervous, sweaty armpits and that was before we even started dancing. When the Year Twelve formal came around, my incompetence had seen no boy want to take me, so my cousin took me instead; my twenty-five-year-old, Call Of Duty™-addicted cousin who wouldn't even buy me one bottle of Passion Pop™ for the after party.

Ten years on from that very night and I still possessed the social skills of Mr Bean. Fortunately, the evolution of the Internet and dating sites had helped my cause somewhat.

'Can I save this photo to your phone in case you ever want to use it?' Elliot asked.

'I'll never want to use it, but sure, be my guest.'

In terms of men, I'd never been fussy; short, tall, long hair, no hair, back hair, it never really bothered me, but I did have a thing for nice eyes. Nice eyes were what made me shake on the inside. The only thing I could put it down to was that the only compliment I ever received from strangers was that I had nice eyes myself. I had red hair, a range of small blackheads on my nose and got the sweats big time, but having nice eyes was the one thing that slightly countered all that.

'Hot, Hot Ella Folder? You have a folder called Hot, Hot Ella Folder?' Elliot asked.

I did have a Hot, Hot Ella Folder in my phone, but it was only to separate the good selfies taken from the average ones and the bad ones.

I often felt vulnerable and apprehensive about myself. Around Elliot however, I needn't have.

'I think that folder is koolish. After I save this, I'm going to create my own Hot, Hot Elliot Folder in my phone.'

That's why he was my best friend; he never judged, he always gave me compliments and when he made decisions he always had my best interests at heart.

'There – saved to the folder, saved to your Facebook™ account, and added to your Tinder profile.'

What?!

I snatched my phone back off him, hoping he was kidding, but he wasn't. Me kissing a toy horse's bum was now the first picture on my Tinder™ profile.

'You devil; you could have cost me the man of my dreams.'

'I don't think so; I think with that photo you'll get a match straight away.'

It would have only taken me ten seconds to delete the photo from my profile, but in that short amount of time he was proven right – I got a match.

'You're kidding.'

I'd been a Tinder user for about nine months and initially to-and-fro-ed about it. The old-fashion view singles were better off finding love face-to-face had been implanted in me as a young adult. The older I got, however, the more I subscribed to the argument technology and dating apps were the way the world was heading, and I'd be left behind without them.

Once committed to something, I always gave it my all, including dating apps. At different times I paid for Tinder Gold, Tinder Boost and Tinder Top Picks to increase my chances of finding the right guy. It definitely helped, just not the way I would have liked.

Tinder was something I checked two to three times a day; it was something that had provided me with a hundred or so matches, but only six or seven dates. I could never match with the good men, a lot of the okay men weren't who they said they were, and the bad men used pick-up lines that made me dry reach. I even had to block one guy for telling me he nicknamed his penis Cheney, after former US Vice-President Dick Cheney, because it had a tendency to shoot off uncontrollably and hit people in the face.

Despite those past indiscretions, the hope of matching with a good man kept me going back for more.

'Captain? That's an unusual name,' Elliot observed of my match.

An unusual name it was; that observation of course coming from a boy named Elliot Elliot and a girl named Ella Bang. Some names were unusual, but it was only fair we gave Captain a chance.

Captain had a description underneath his name that read, *Captain of the best team in the world,* and four photos of himself that couldn't have worked harder to convince the doubters his actual name was Captain.

I swiped through them. One photo was of him in a football huddle, one was of him steering a ship with a whole bunch of crew members, one was of him in a military outfit with a bunch of other army guys, and another was of him standing next to a big airplane with a whole lot of other people standing next to the big airplane. They were pretty cool photos but there was one problem – with no less than six people in every picture I had no idea which guy he was.

'So ask him,' Elliot said.

'I'm not going to ask him, you ask him.'

Ella

Which one are you?

I probably should have started by saying 'hello'. He didn't take offence as he messaged straight back. He didn't answer the question though.

> **Hey Ella, I love your photos. I love that photo of you kissing the toy horse's ass.**

Elliot's eyes lit up, 'He liked my photo.'

Captain's reply left the ball in my court; it was my turn to message back, but what was the right thing to say?

Your photos are good also.

I was such an idiot.

'Your photos are good also?' That's the best you could come up with? I thought.

I needed to quickly message again, to distract him from that lamentable first effort, but what to write?

I thought long and hard.

Sorry about my patheticness. God no, don't write that; patheticness isn't even a word.

Thankfully he moved things forward before I could stuff up even more.

> **I love toys, and horses as well. I even have a horse of my own. Keen to catch up and compare whose is better?**

'It's his way of asking you out,' Elliot informed me.

I knew that, sort of.

I messaged back, this time knowing exactly what I wanted to say.

Ella

What time?

Captain

**6.30pm at The Bay Hotel.
I'll have the sugar cubes ready.**

Sugar cubes? Didn't he mean ice cubes, like in a glass, full of vodka?

'Horses eat sugar cubes,' Elliot informed me again.

I knew that, not really.

I responded to Captain's message.

Ella

Sure, see you there.

'Are you sure?' Elliot asked.

He'd been building me up all this time and now he was questioning if going on a date with this guy was the right move?

'No, I mean, are you sure about 6.30? It's almost five o'clock now.'

He was right – the time hadn't dawned on me. Amongst all the stupid horse talk, I'd looked past the fact our date was at 6.30. Me being home, dressed and ready to go, and at The Bay Hotel by 6.30 was like a cat trying to teach itself how to use a knife and fork – it wasn't going to happen.

'Should I reschedule?'

'No, you go, I'll lock up the store.'

'Really?'

He nodded. 'Now go.'

I kissed Elliot on the cheek and sprinted like crazy out the front door. 'Double time for you for locking up.'

'Break a leg.'

2.

I held my leg up in the air and examined it.

It might as well have been broken.

'How long do cuts normally take to heal? Like ten minutes?'

My Uber driver turned to me in the backseat and wondered what the hell I was asking. He was some punk kid that barely looked old enough to hold a driver's licence. He observed my appearance with horror and then spun back around to face the front as we sat at the lights.

I had never been so quick to get ready in all my life but there had been casualties.

Two major casualties.

I had committed to wearing a particular dress – the kind that fell to the knee. Despite the minimal time I had to be ready, I was left with no choice other than to commit to making my legs look like those of Mariah Carey.

I'd read somewhere she had them insured.

Sitting in the backseat of the Uber™, I began to think I should have insured mine, or not taken to them with a razor in the first place. In my haste to shave them, I'd left them covered in cuts. Small cuts I hoped would heal by the time I got out of the car.

From my place to The Bay Hotel was only 1.3 kilometres. It wasn't going to happen.

Fortunately, it was dark enough inside The Bay that I could conceal my wounded legs from Captain's viewing. I was also early, which meant there was no risk of me walking up to a table where he was already sitting, and he seeing my wounds as I approached.

I ordered a vodka and soda, and waited. I was tempted to do the classy thing and order a wine but I only just fitted into the dress and feared anything heavier than vodka might split the seam.

A text came from Elliot an hour-and-twenty minutes into the date.

How's it going?

I texted him straight back.

Good. Captain loves me.

Captain actually hadn't arrived yet and I was beginning to think he wouldn't. I started wondering why he'd be so late.

Guys can take a long time to get ready. Maybe he's shaving his legs too. That would mean we have something in common! I'll give him another five minutes.

A waiter then came over to me. 'Madame, I thought I'd let you know you only have this table reserved for another five minutes. After that, I'll have to ask you to move.'

'Perfect,' I replied with a smile. Five minutes was all I needed.

Unfortunately, Captain didn't show.

Being stood up was new for me. I'd had dating disasters occur as often as the rain but had never been stood up, and was struggling to accept it.

Captain was so nice on Tinder earlier; he couldn't have stood me up. Maybe he went to the wrong part of the bar.

I looked around the room and couldn't see any guys sitting or standing on their lonesome. There was a beer garden around the side however, so maybe he was out there.

Unlike the restaurant, the beer garden possessed a younger crowd, and as a result, more of a party atmosphere.

Knowing I was now approaching Captain with cut up legs, the nerves started to kick in and I started to sweat, so I went to the bar and ordered another drink.

After being served, I turned and scoured the room in search of him again, but he was nowhere to be found.

Truthfully, it didn't go down like that at all.

How it went down was – I turned, walked nine laps of the room in search of my date and then conceded he wasn't there.

Every guy was in a group; there was no one man sitting on his own looking despondently up at the ceiling, and no one man wearing a ship driver's uniform, or an army outfit, or an airplane pilot's hat.

The only person alone was I, and if there was one thing worse than partying alone, then it was leaving alone.

I thought about sculling the rest of my near empty glass and stumbling out like an awesome, drunk chick but was fearful of going home in the back of a police car, so decided upon another plan.

Pretending to talk on my phone with no one on the other end was a strategy I'd become quite good at. Three weeks earlier at Southland shopping centre I'd spent a half hour telling my Aunt Wanda large consumptions of mint sauce wouldn't delay the onset of menopause. Aunt Wanda wasn't on the other end of the phone, I don't even have an Aunt Wanda, but it worked – I escaped Southland alone without embarrassment. Now was the perfect time to fake-call her again.

I thought about pretend calling pretend Aunt Tammy-Jo or Aunt Jeannette but changed my mind. I didn't change my mind to not calling anyone because that would have been the better move but changed my mind to calling pretend Aunt Wanda instead.

I took my phone out, and – as I strode towards the exit – put it up to my ear and spoke. 'No Aunt Wanda, mint sauce won't fix your cellulite either.'

A burst of laughter came from a group of young men who sat in the corner of the beer garden. I thought they might have been laughing at my conversation with Aunt Wanda, but they weren't. They were a group of men from a football team drinking and being rowdy.

They were all wearing the same jacket with the same navy and white club colours, and there was an eagle on the front. I was about to continue my exit strategy when I noticed the guy sitting in the middle of the group had the letter C sewn on the front of his jacket, just below the collar.

C, I thought. *Why is that significant?*

Eventually I realised.

Of course, what else would C stand for?

With a grin from ear to ear, I approached him. 'There you are, do you know how long I've been looking for you?'

He was really attractive with dark locks, dimples and neat facial hair. Despite being covered up by the jacket, I could tell he had a muscular physique underneath. He gave his mate slouched on the lounge beside him a weird look and then turned back to me with an, "I have no idea what you're talking about" tone of voice. 'Here I am, hoping you'd find me.'

'You're Captain, right?' I asked.

He didn't show much interest in me at all, but then again maybe he'd forgotten whom I was. 'I'm Ella, from Tinder.'

With that introduction, his facial expression changed from "you smell, get away from me", to "you smell divine, come and bring your aromas closer to me".

He then said the words I'd been waiting to hear my whole entire life. 'You're the one.'

I began to overthink our relationship.

Golly gosh, he's moving things so fast. Who cares, woman, he's hot.

All of his football boys leaned in closer, as if it was something they'd been waiting for him to say too.

And then he said it again.

'She's the one.'

It made me feel so special; I couldn't hide the smile on my face and neither could he as he rallied his troops to make this even more of a special occasion.

'What are you waiting for?' he said to a friend. 'Let's turn this celebration up a notch and get some more drinks.'

The friend jumped up out of his seat and – with two others – headed for the bar. Captain finished the rest of his glass and then invited me to sit on the chair in front of him, so I did.

I shouldn't have.

'What happened to your legs, gorgeous?'

Oh dear God, the shaving cuts.

I needed to think of an answer quickly. Adlib had never been a strength, but for once I was able to find an excuse that wasn't life-shatteringly humiliating.

'Footy wounds, y'know. Got smashed by some big-arse chicks today.'

He nodded in acceptance, 'you play footy, that's cool.'

Our conversation then ground to a halt. It was like he was waiting for something. Maybe he was thinking of what to say next, as he picked things up again.

'What was your name again?'

'Ella.'

'Ah that's right, I should have remembered... with your... awesome Tinder photos.'

Any doubt this wasn't the Captain I was looking for evaporated with that very comment – he'd mentioned my Tinder photos when we matched and mentioned them again now.

All I needed was for his mates to go away so it could just be he and I.

Instead of the party growing smaller, it grew larger, as his friends returned from the bar with a tray that held a jug of beer. I was surprised to find however only a single glass accompanied it.

His friend put the tray down on the table and Captain reached for the jug at the same time I did.

'It's all right. Allow me to get it for you.'

What chivalry! Keep that coming please.

He stood, took the beer glass as well, moved slowly towards me and stared into my eyes with a great deal of intensity. It felt like he was going to lean in and kiss me before handing me the drink.

Again, my mind went into overdrive.

He is going to kiss me. His lips are going to be on mine. This is going to be amazing. I bet they taste like chocolate with strawberry in the centre.

But they didn't taste like chocolate with strawberry in the centre because he didn't kiss me at all.

Instead he raised the jug of beer and poured it on my head.

I froze, not just because the beer was freezing cold but also because I was stunned by what had happened.

All his friends high-fived one other, jumped on his back in celebration, or rolled around on the floor in fits of laughter.

With beer dripping down my front and my back, I wondered why they'd gone to such lengths of cruelty. Was it a joke? Did the most-desperate girl in the bar always get beer tipped on her? Or was this a football team rule, like a hen's party list, where after a win the captain gave some random girl a beer shower?

'It's revenge,' Captain said. 'Jumbo's girlfriend broke up with him last week. It's nothing personal; you were just the target the boys chose.'

I glanced over to Jumbo. He looked like a blob-fish and wobbled around on the carpet like one too.

I turned back to Captain. 'So you're not the guy I met on Tinder this afternoon?'

Only in asking that question did I realise the answer – of course he wasn't.

'There's no way I'd ever swipe right on a chick like you,' he said.

Captain, Jumbo and the other boys got up, stumbled past me and headed towards the exit, no doubt worried they'd cop the wrath of the bouncers if caught making a mess.

I had no thought of kicking them as they went by, as I wasn't filled with anger or distress, but disappointment.

I just kept thinking, *why?*

Why did so many men look for revenge; to physically or emotionally hurt the woman they'd been rejected by, or any woman, rather than accept not all relationships were going to work out? Why did they have to be like that?

I turned around hoping I'd been teleported from the bar to a twenty-four-hour dry-cleaning service, or anywhere other than where I was, but I hadn't – the whole bar was standing there staring at me.

Could this night get any worse?

I stood from the chair, wiped the beer running down my face and licked my hand. At that very moment, the seam on my dress broke.

Great.

The extra calories in the beer did just what I feared they would.

With it still reasonably early in the night, I needed to find somewhere I could vent, somewhere I could be made to feel better and somewhere all my questions would be answered.

I needed to find my football team.

3.

'I got beer poured on me.'

'Again?'

'This time it was a jug not a glass.'

The tipping of the beer had happened before, and like that previous time, I was shown little sympathy.

'Well don't come in dripping all over my floorboards.'

My thirty-four-year-old sister Hannah came charging out of her kitchen like I'd flooded her entire house. She always did care about her possessions more than her family. Okay, that wasn't true, but she was often critical of my dress sense.

'When you wear a party dress that's two sizes too small, things like this happen. What's wrong with your legs?'

She charged back into the kitchen without waiting for my answer.

That was her – she wasn't your typically supportive, compassionate type eldest sisters generally were, but she wasn't the devil all the same. She was easily stressed, particularly when cooking, and her actions spoke louder than her words. That was to say her words were rarely supportive, but her actions always were. The positive was she lived in a mini-mansion on Nepean Highway, Aspendale. It was on the beach, 1500 metres from The Bay Hotel, which meant I was able to walk there along the sand.

My thirty-one-year-old sister Katie – the middle child whose name was shortened from Katherine – came out from the kitchen and showed the verbal support and compassion I needed. She handed me a tea towel too small to dry a coffee mug let alone a grown woman, but it was the thought that counted. She always did care about her family more than her possessions.

'This is what we call a tea towel; people on your side of the tracks might not have heard of these, no?' she joked.

My "side of the tracks" wasn't a metaphor. Katie, too, lived on the beach on Nepean Highway in Aspendale, albeit in a neat one-bedroom apartment. I lived on the other side of the railway in Aspendale, in a rough little dwelling, in a rough little crescent that ran off Station Street. Katie often reminded me of it.

'I know what a tea towel is,' I replied. 'Have you been cooking with this?'

'Chicken.'

'I'm so grateful for you.'

She hadn't used the tea towel to cook chicken at all, we just used sarcasm a lot; it was our thing. It wasn't Hannah's thing at all, mainly because she never got when somebody else was being sarcastic.

'You better not be using one of my good tea towels,' she barked from the kitchen.

'It's an old tea towel and I'm sure it's had plenty of beer spilt on it before,' Katie barked back.

Hannah came back out and held up a spatula like she was going to hit Katie with it. 'What's that supposed to mean?'

'That you drink heavily, often.'

'I do not.'

She certainly didn't get sarcasm.

There was a stack of alcohol in her house, but she did have good reason for it.

'That's left over from Sunday night's fashion gala,' she defended.

Hannah was an event planner who organised parties for Melbourne's A-List, and was often left with food and drink when catering had over-supplied. Sitting down to dinner it appeared the alcohol wasn't the only thing leftover. The chicken Katie spoke of was leftover too.

Not that Katie or I complained.

Once a week Hannah hosted Katie and I at her Aspendale mini-mansion. It was a tradition she'd begun seven years ago to bring us closer. She called our gatherings *Hannah And Her Sisters*, which she thought was original, and not at all plagiarised from the Woody Allen film of the same name.

Hannah And Her Sisters was a time to talk and listen, but mostly listen, as Hannah fabricated a number of stories.

'Brody told me he loved me the other day.'

Stories Katie called out, and often cursed in doing so. 'Bullshit.'

'He did.'

Hannah had two sons – Justin four and Brody fourteen months – with her husband Brett. He took the two boys to his parents' house in Highett each week to allow us three girls to bond.

Brett was a pretty fancy real estate agent, which was why Hannah lived in such a nice house. Her wealth I didn't despise, but the luck she'd received in love I did. She and Brett were high school sweethearts and there was always a fuss made about any announcement. Family gatherings celebrated the news of an engagement, a new job or a house they'd bought. They also celebrated when they made a decision on where their wedding reception was going to be held, how they were looking for a new car, or what cushions she got for her new lounge. Because of love and all that came with it, Hannah was always the centre of attention, and I ashamedly wanted to be.

Katie didn't share my envy of Hannah, which meant she had no problem openly criticising her. Unlike my single self, Katie was halfway to having what her older sister had. She had been with her boyfriend, Roy, for nine years but the whole marriage and kids' thing had taken them longer to get to. She never envied Hannah's wedded bliss or the happiness her two kids brought, because she knew she wasn't far from it herself. What she did despise were her lies, in this case, her youngest telling her he loved her even though he couldn't yet speak.

'Brody is fourteen months old, he can't even say "Mumma", let alone, "I love you, Mumma".'

She was right, but she should have let Hannah have her lie.

'Well, he did. He said, "I love you, Mumma".'

'All right, fine. When the boys get home I will sit Brody down and repeatedly say the word "fuck" to him, and if he repeats what I say, then I'll believe you.'

'You won't do any such thing.'

'You won't do any such thing? What kind of language is that? Are we in *Downton Abbey* now?'

'My son said, "I love you, Mumma", end of story.'

'I wish someone would say, "I love you", to me.'

My feigned despondence immediately deflated their argument and left them both knowing it was time to talk about me.

'It will happen one day,' Katie told me.

'Just not one day soon,' Hannah added.

Katie gave her the devil eyes, and I fully expected her to swear again, but she didn't.

What Hannah said was mean, but it was also accurate. Typically, she kept talking.

'What? Katie you're an optimist, I'm a realist, I've told you this a thousand times.'

Better than being a pessimist, which was what I was.

Our conversations were like a carousel in that we moved around the house while we had them. From the dinner table we progressed to the kitchen where we washed up.

'He said it was revenge for Jumbo's sake.'

'Jumbo's a man?'

'Yeah, what else would he be?'

'An elephant?'

We then progressed to sitting on the couch in the living room.

'I sometimes wonder if the reason I'm alone is because I'm being punished, or if it's the fat on the inside of my arms.'

'You don't have fat on the inside of your arms,' Katie told me.

'Then how do I make myself more desirable? What do you think, Han?'

Hannah sat there flicking through a magazine. She frustrated me in two ways; first, if we weren't talking about her, Brett or the kids, her attention was elsewhere, and the second was that even though she wasn't listening, she still knew the crux of the conversation.

'A party,' she said.

'What about a party?'

'Let's have one.'

It wasn't what I was expecting her to say. Well, it was, with her being a party planner and all, but I thought she'd come up with something better.

'I see people get together all the time at the events I organize. If it will help, I'll organise a party for you and invite everyone I know.'

She did have a phone book with about five thousand names in it.

I felt more optimistic thanks to her suggestion, but it was quickly quelled by her blunt assessment of my many failures.

'The only people you see in your life are Katie, Elliot, and me. No wonder you're still single; it's all about whom you know in life Ella. I didn't get rich marrying a guy who builds caravans.'

That was a deliberate stab at Katie – she and Roy were caravan builders.

Her phone buzzed with a message from Brett. He'd sent her a photo of the boys having dinner and typically she couldn't help but show us. 'Oh my God, that is cuteness overload. Isn't he the cleverest kid you've ever seen?'

Brody was sitting, doing nothing.

Katie and I smiled as she stood and walked to her bedroom, calling Brett as she did. My smile was forced, and Katie's was through gritted teeth as well, as she cursed in retaliation to Hannah's dig at her and Roy building caravans.

'Our older sister is such a shithead sometimes.'

Like a carousel, Katie and I then moved out onto Hannah's back verandah and looked out over her fancy garden. I sat covered by a doona, while Katie – who never felt the cold, probably because she went to the gym so much – sat eating a bowl of ice cream.

Hannah was still talking to her kids on the phone in her bedroom, even though they were due to arrive home in a half-an-hour. She'd given Katie and I one strict instruction – don't eat her ice cream – which Katie had ignored.

'I don't care if it's expensive ice cream, it's nice. I got three scoops instead of two to annoy her. You want some?'

Hannah would skin me alive if I disobeyed her order, so I didn't. Katie didn't care though; she didn't care because she'd pinched her routine from dad. She pretended to have accidentally consumed something without knowing, apologised profusely, and then promised to buy two tubs of the stuff to make up for it, knowing Hannah would ultimately forget, and she wouldn't have to buy any.

'You're saying no to ice cream? Wow you really are dedicated to finding the right guy. Hell, I'd trade Roy for a lifetime of this stuff.'

'I know.'

What I knew wasn't the Roy thing, but that I was dedicated to finding the right guy. I felt that despite our sisterly chat over the past hour, I hadn't found the answer to my question – how would I find him?

'I think Hannah's party idea is a good start, but I get it, you can't keep all your eggs in one basket,' Katie said.

That was exactly the point I was trying to get across, I didn't know what my other baskets were. Katie told me.

'You're on Tinder, right? That's a good start. I've always wanted to go on it and see what it's like. Maybe I secretly could.'

She was getting side-tracked; I needed to talk about my eggs, and what needed to happen to them.

'They need to be fertilized,' she joked.

Very funny.

Her jocularity normally would have stimulated a response more than that of my eyebrows being raised, but the humour of my meaningless and unfilled love life had worn thin. I was really down on myself and she could tell.

'You all right?'

I wanted to say yes, but couldn't.

'It hurts; I don't want it to be like this anymore; I don't want to be on my own. I know there are plenty of single women in the world, but I know there are not many who are approaching thirty and have never been in love before. It's tragic. I'd take a broken heart just to know what falling in love feels like; to have someone genuinely love me and want to look after me. It doesn't feel like it's ever going to happen, and it hurts.'

I didn't normally express myself in that way as Katie typically responded with tough love. But this time, whilst unable to empathise, she respected how disheartening the single life could be and reacted accordingly.

'Well you have my love, and Hannah's as well, which means you do have someone looking after you. And as someone looking after you, it is my job – when you're feeling down – to build you back up again.'

She put her ice cream down, which I liked because it meant her sole focus was on me, and continued her pitch.

'No single person likes to be told, "you have to put yourself out there more", because it's cliché and shows a lack of creativity, but in your case, I think you need to make some changes. I was going to say before – Tinder's a start but maybe you need to widen your social media usage. You're on Facebook, but maybe you need to get an Instagram™ account going, and maybe Snapchat™ as well. That's how you build your followers, and the more people that follow you, the more chance you have of the right guy following you.'

That was one area in which we differed as sisters – I never took enough photos of myself to need an Instagram account, whereas Katie took five a day. She did have an excuse for taking so many snaps though as she and Roy went on a holiday thrice yearly. They worked and then spent six weeks in Asia, came back and earned more money, and then spent six weeks in Africa.

'And I gained fifteen thousand new followers just from the twenty photos I posted of myself in Morocco. I've now got three hundred and seventy thousand Instagram followers. Do you know how many single guys there could be in three hundred and seventy thousand?'

Most of her followers probably were single guys, as in most of her photos she wore skimpy fitness outfits while doing fitnessy things. Even on her African safari, she took photos of herself in fitness clothing with a lion in the background. Actually, Roy must have taken them because he wasn't in any of them.

'That's because he's not photogenic, and that's beside the point. Forget about what the peeps of yesteryear say; social media can be self-indulgent, but it can also be a brilliant selling tool. Building the right social media profile could see you have a couple of hundred thousand followers in twelve months. The right guy might then walk into your life.'

She made some valid points, but there was always the counter argument. 'He'll then of course keep on walking because of my unrivalled awkwardness and sweaty armpits.'

She paused, before telling me, 'That we might be able to fix as well.'

She went back inside and left me fighting a great desire to ditch her spoon and lick her ice cream bowl clean. I heard her rustling around and then she returned with a newspaper in her hand.

'I saw this the other day by accident, check it out.'

It was a picture of a woman in lingerie, covered in tattoos, with a headline beside it:

'"Nude Nellie will get nude for you",' I read. 'You think Nude Nellie can help me out?'

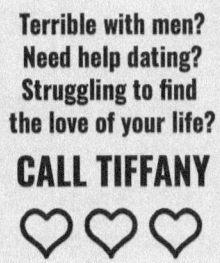

Katie pointed to the advertisement underneath Nude Nellie. 'Dating coach – a dating coach can help you with your awkwardness and sweaty pits.'

Surely, she wasn't being serious; dating coaches were for people who sucked at dating.

'What do they say – knowing you need help is half the battle?'

What did she mean by that?

'You just had a jug of beer poured on your head; you do suck at dating.'

Right, that's what she meant.

She was right, I did suck at dating; I was just looking for a way to convince her a dating coach was the wrong idea.

'Look at her name – Tiffany – she sounds like a massive weirdo.'

'It says she's got a degree in psychology and human behaviour, she sounds like an intellect.'

I hesitated in saying yes, and as a result she took back the newspaper and threw it down on the verandah. 'Forget about it, I was only trying to help.'

She was, and I was being very unappreciative. I knew this was the point where my sister-help session ended, but I didn't want it to end on this note.

'I'm sorry; I was too quick to say no. I do need to be more open to ideas, even though it's not really in my make-up. Let me sleep on it.'

Katie nodded, accepting my apology. 'Sleep, something I'm not far away from myself. I'm going to get another bowl, you want some this time?'

Just as she stood to go back to the kitchen, Hannah arrived at the back door. Having gotten off the phone to Brett and the kids, she should have been in a grossly affectionate mood, but she wasn't.

'You changed the magnetic letters on my fridge,' she barked at Katie. "Just wanted to make sure you have a roof over you ho?' What if my kids saw that?'

Both Katie and I couldn't help but snigger.

'It was supposed to say, "have a roof over your head," but there weren't enough letters,' Katie explained.

Not that Hannah's kids could read anyway.

It didn't exactly ease Hannah's loathing, but Katie wasn't exactly aiming to do so.

'Sis, I'd be more worried about what happened inside your fridge.'

4.

Fifteen hours on from being kicked out of Hannah's house (Katie lied and sold me out about the ice cream), and I still had the same thing on my mind – the dating coach. I knew it was the right thing to do, I was just trying to find a good enough excuse not to do it.

After thinking about the dating coach, the whole social media expansion and Hannah's party idea took over my brain as well. I needed a distraction and knew exactly how to find one.

My favourite part of the toy store were my Ladies Of The World. They were small porcelain dolls rarely bought by anyone because they were boring. But they weren't boring to me; they were the most interesting women in the world and despite not moving or making any sounds, I liked to believe when the store closed at night, they came alive.

My three favourites were Lady France, Lady Italy and Lady Seychelles. With no one around I occasionally went over to check on them, and maybe pretend they came to life when with me as well. I put their voices on, even though I wasn't very good at accents.

'Hello, Lady Ella,' Lady Italy said to me.

Before I could say 'hello' back, Lady France snapped, 'Lady Italy, as you are from Italy, shouldn't you be saying "Ciao, Lady Ella", instead of hello?'

Lady France was very proper, not just her voice, but also the way she dressed.

Lady Italy was dressed quite similarly but it was misleading; she looked like she belonged in the high society of Rome or Venice, but she was actually a waitress in a pizza and pasta restaurant in Palermo, which was run by the mafia. She also didn't take kindly to Lady France's advice.

'You tell me what to do one more time Lady France, and I will get my cousin who works in the restaurant to come down and intimidate you with his slick gelled hair, his slick gelled moustache and his mafia friends that also have slick gelled moustaches.'

'Oh, Lady Italy, you are such a blast! I love hanging out with you!' Lady France replied.

Lady Seychelles never engaged in such talk. She – like the other two – was dressed like she was from the 1940's but was very much up to date with current happenings, particularly when it involved Hollywood.

'Do you think Eva Mendez just pashes Ryan Gosling 24/7, or do you think she lets him do other stuff too?'

I had no idea how people from The Seychelles sounded, so her voice was a mixture of three or four accents.

Rather than bicker like the other two, she only ever worried about what was important.

'The US Government should make a new law that says Zac Efron should never be allowed to wear a shirt.'

There was hardly a time I didn't agree with her, but the other two often did.

'Lady Seychelles you're such a blast, I love hanging out with you,' Lady France said.

'The US Government sucks,' Lady Italy cut in. 'I'm going to get my cousin and his mafia friends to intimidate them all with their slick hair.'

It was time for me to get back to work, which meant saying our farewells. My departure was as tough for them as it was for me, but we said goodbye and wished goodwill on one another.

'I hope you have a blast of a week, I love hanging out with you.'

'I hope Lady France will stop saying the same crap over and over again'.

'I hope you can show me where the Lego is.'

The last voice was supposed to be Lady Seychelles, but it wasn't; I mean, it wasn't even me. It was a customer I hadn't seen walk up behind me. He'd caught me playing with my Ladies and I'd almost dropped Lady Seychelles in trying to cover up what I was doing.

What made it worse was he was a cute male customer; the kind of cute male I wasn't very good with.

'Hey,' I kind of shrieked and whispered at the same time. It was a weird response but the endless seconds of silence that followed were even weirder.

'Lego, can you help me find it?' he asked again.

'Sure.'

The physical act of showing him where the Lego™ was failed to follow my verbal assurance.

'Maybe if you could point in the general direction, that'd be enough.'

I was still dying a million deaths on the inside from having been caught playing with my dolls, but finally my right foot moved in front of my left. I feared it might have been a rather large twitch but thankfully the left leg followed, and I was walking.

I walked him over to the Lego display and felt the sweats starting to come on; I needed to talk as saying anything was better than my ongoing muteness.

Finally, words came out. 'Good for you.'

He looked at me trying to figure out what I meant. 'What's good for me?'

Not even I knew what I meant; they were just the first words that came out of my mouth. 'Um, ah, a grown man still playing with Lego; good for you.'

'It's actually for a child; I don't play with Lego.'

Oh, how I wished I'd stayed awkwardly silent.

I showed him Lego In Space, Lego With Dinosaurs and Lego In The Kitchen, before walking back to the front counter.

I'd been able to wipe the sweat off myself and think of something clever to say by the time he returned to pay for his purchase.

'Our kids are so lucky these days, aren't they? Imagine having someone as kind as you that makes an effort to come into a toy store and buy Lego. And I bet it's not the first time you've bought Lego for them. I bet they've got almost the entire set and this one tops it all off.'

'Actually, it's for my sponsor child. He has nothing; he's never seen Lego in his life. In fact, there's a small probability this won't even get to him. I thought it was important to get him something for his birthday in any case.'

That revelation made me feel even more embarrassed – where was Captain to pour beer on my head now? I definitely deserved it.

I put the purchase through, he paid, and I gave him his receipt. The only way to save this sunken ship was to pay Mr Cute Customer Man a compliment as he left.

'You're hot.'

Yes, that was the compliment I gave him.

He raised a hand as if waving to say goodbye, so I reciprocated, but he wasn't waving goodbye at all. He pointed to his ring finger, which had a gold ring sitting on it. He was married, and I was an idiot.

I slumped on the counter defeated and then the same thought that had consumed me for the previous fifteen hours returned.

Only this time I had a different view on it.

Elliot sat inside a plastic cubby house with his four-year-old friend Evie having morning tea. She was a frequent customer with her mum and once a week stayed for a pretend cup of tea and biscuit.

'What's this?' Elliot asked.

'A biscuit,' Evie said.

It was a Duplo™ block.

'That's koolish. What do you think Play-doh man?'

Play-doh™ man, Cabbage Patch Doll™ and Tickle Me Elmo™ were

all lined up with biscuits in front of them.

Elliot listened to Play-doh man and then repeated his answer, 'He said it's the best biscuit he's ever eaten but he'd love some tea to go with it.'

Unlike me, when Elliot talked to the toys and voiced their replies, it came across as charming.

Evie grabbed four coloured Duplo blocks, 'I've got red tea, blue tea, green tea and another blue tea.'

'Play-doh man says he'd love some red tea.'

The Duplo blocks strangely represented both the tea and the biscuits.

She poured the pretend tea into a plastic cup and handed it to Play-doh man just as I poked my head through the cubby house window. 'I need your help.'

'With tea and biscuits?' Elliot asked.

'With Tiffany – the dating coach.'

'Sure; let me get your phone together.'

He thought I was playing along with the fake tea and the fake biscuits, wanting to put in a fake phone call to a fake dating coach, but I wasn't.

This was real.

'This is real; I need you to help me call the dating coach. I'll even buy you and Play-doh man some real tea and some real biscuits if you do.'

We both understood calling a dating coach was likely to corrupt Evie's young mind and bribery probably corrupted it even more, but my experience with the cute customer man had been the final straw. I wasn't going to find love unless I did what Katie and Hannah told me to do – and that meant getting the ball rolling and booking an appointment with the dating coach.

My first task was to distract Evie.

'Evie, Cabbage Patch Doll has a sick tummy and I don't know

what's wrong with her. If you can find out what's wrong with her, you can have her, for free.'

'Those dolls cost thirty dollars,' Elliot whispered to me.

'Shhh.'

I pulled my mobile from my pocket. With adrenaline rushing through my veins I dialled, but as the phone rang the adrenaline dissipated and I hung up.

'What are you doing?'

'I change my mind.'

'It's stage fright; it's normal. Call again.'

I did, but again I hung up.

'I got spooked, I swear I'll do it this time, third time lucky.'

They were just words; I didn't believe I was going to go through with it third time around, and Elliot didn't believe it either, as he grabbed the phone out of my hand and rung for me. I waited and waited; I could faintly hear the phone ringing on the other end and then it stopped, and Elliot spoke.

'Hi, my name's Elliot and I'm here with my friend Ella. We were hoping we could make an appointment for Ella. She's too afraid to talk.'

Elliot listened and listened some more. The listening went on for a while and I wondered what was going on, but then he told me, 'She's getting her diary.'

Further silence followed and then Elliot said, 'That is perfect; thank-you Tiffany.'

He hung up and smiled at me. 'You're booked in; she sounded nice.'

I was excited but more relieved I was doing something about my situation, or at least Elliot had done something about my situation. Elliot, too, was happy for me, but his demeanour quickly went from one of delight, to one of sensitivity and reflection.

'Visiting a dating coach, that is koolish. Sure beats drinking fake tea and eating fake biscuits.'

I could sense his feeling of envy; it was one I knew all too well whenever I was around Hannah or Katie.

'Maybe one day there'll be dating coaches and dating apps for people like me. Until then I'll have to be content with going on dates with Evie and a sick Cabbage Patch Doll.'

He did his best to try and hide his disappointment.

Not for the first time that morning had I succumbed to a period of silence. This time, however, there were no embarrassing or negative thoughts, just positive ones. An idea for a new assignment had begun swirling around in my brain. I didn't have a full grasp of it, but in time I would.

There was an answer to every problem, as Evie proved seconds later.

'Cabbage Patch Doll has a dog stuck in her tummy. Can I take her home now?'

5.

Out came a dog, alive and well.

After work, I headed over to the Shirley Burke Theatre on Parkers Road, Parkdale. As I reached the entrance, out came a dog, alive and well. It was a Labrador and it stopped and sat a few feet in front of its elderly female owner. She was dressed like Mother Teresa and she stood and stared out into the evening sky.

'Hi,' I said.

'Who's that?' the lady asked.

'Ella.'

'Nice to meet you, Ella. What's wrong with you?'

I was tempted to tell her, 'I can't find a man,' but realised how pathetic that would sound and instead told the truth.

'I'm here because I need some help with a project. Is everybody else inside?'

'They're all watching *The Lion King* movie. Daisy's scared of the lions, so we've come out here to escape.'

'Daisy?'

I was asking if that was her guide dog's name, but she took my question in a different way.

'All right, you got me, I'm scared of the lions.'

'You scared of the lions? How do you even know the lions are... (there)?'

I cleared my throat as if trying to cover; I'd almost put my foot in it.

Good one you bonehead; you almost picked on a blind lady for being blind.

I corrected myself. '*The Lion King* can be scary; I don't blame you. Do you know where I can find the program facilitator?'

She looked down from the sky and in my general direction, 'I'm blind; I don't even know what the course facilitator looks like.'

So much for not picking on the blind lady.

Embarrassed, I slowly crept around her and Daisy and made my way inside.

I walked down the corridor, past the art space, through the foyer area, up a side set of stairs and into the theatre itself. The group wasn't watching *The Lion King* at all; they were sitting on chairs on the stage, in a circle, playing theatre games.

Being at a gathering for the disabled, I didn't really know what to expect, but I didn't expect they'd be doing that. I remained at the back of the theatre and watched from afar.

A guy who was about my age and a girl that was in her early-twenties stood in the middle of the circle and acted out a scene. Neither spoke, but instead used hand gestures.

The whole group laughed. I had no idea what their scene was but was captivated nevertheless.

It was all because of him – the guy in the middle.

He was gorgeous.

He was clean-shaven, had brown, straight, wavy hair that parted from his crown, and piercing eyes that were hypnotic, even from a distance. He was six-foot-tall and slim, and was dressed in neat casual attire.

A voice within the circle yelled the word 'freeze,' and a young, male amputee stood, walked into the centre and replaced the gorgeous guy. The young amputee spoke but the girl continued using hand gestures.

I initially thought the game was one where those in the middle had to communicate without speaking, but the young amputees' words made me realise it wasn't. It was a simple theatre game where those in the middle acted out a scene in whatever way they liked. I'd simply entered at a time when the two performers were both deaf, and therefore communicated with sign language.

At least that's the way it looked.

The game concluded with a short applause a couple of minutes later and everyone took a break.

The purpose of my visit was to have a chat to the facilitator, and after observing the group, it became apparent it was the gorgeous, deaf guy with the mesmerizing eyes and the wavy hair.

I didn't know sign language and worried how we would communicate with each other.

In the foyer, I uncomfortably made myself a cup of tea at the condiments table and waited for him. It wasn't long before he came over, but the deaf girl from the game joined him. I tried to figure out whether they were boyfriend and girlfriend or brother and sister but was interrupted by my phone ringing – it was Katie.

'Ella, where are you?'

'I'm doing some work.'

'What, at the store, this late?'

'No other stuff; hey, have you ever thought a deaf guy was really hot?'

It was arguably the strangest question I'd ever asked anyone, let alone my sister, and she took it that way.

'What?'

'A deaf guy; have you ever looked at a deaf guy and thought, *Wow he's really hot*?"

'No. Where are you?'

I vaguely explained what I was doing without giving away the secret reason why, and then asked her again.

The guy – and the girl who may or may not have been his girlfriend – still stood about three metres away at the other end of the table. A life of embarrassing tales had me triple-checking he was definitely deaf and unable to hear me. With a sneaky look over my shoulder, I saw him again using sign language, and knew I had nothing to worry about.

'So do you think I should ask him out?' I asked Katie.

'How do you even ask a deaf guy out?'

'Hand signals I guess.'

'What kind of hand signal are you going to use?'

'I have no idea.'

'Maybe point to your boobs.'

She was being crass, but I should have expected nothing less.

'Point to your heart I mean; how hot is he?'

'Hot-hot, like one of the hottest guys I've ever seen, let alone one of the hottest deaf guys I've ever seen.'

'Well I think you've got your answer; hurry up, I need you to get over to Hannah's ASAP.'

Without explaining why, she hung up. I put my mobile phone back in my pocket and swung around to find hot deaf guy still at the table beside me. He now stood on his own.

This was it, this was my moment, but what flipping signals was I going to come up with? I slowly took three steps towards him, raised my arm and then... pointed at my boob.

I hoped like anything he understood I was pointing at my heart, and he'd point to his in return, but he didn't.

He instead did something completely different.

'Hey, I'm Max.'

He spoke.

I stood there in total fear and shock.

He spoke, Oh my God, he spoke. He's not deaf at all.

I had stuffed up with men but could not have been any more offensive than what I had been over the previous five minutes. I had gate-crashed their gathering, drunk their tea, and disrespectfully rambled on about how hot the deaf facilitator was, without introducing myself to anyone.

'What's your name?' he asked.

Whether he had heard me or not, he was still really sweet. 'I'm Ella, and I am here for a reason.'

'We're not due to resume for another five minutes, come and tell me about it.'

We sat down on a couple of lounge chairs in the foyer. He told me the theatre games were a warm-up exercise for a proper rehearsal – the group was performing a stage play of *Noah's Ark* in a few months and it was going to be held at the theatre.

'It's our bi-annual fundraiser, so we can keep helping the disabled community for many years to come. So, what can I help you with?'

I told Max of my plans – I had a best friend named Elliot who had a brain injury. His only wish was to fall in love and I wanted to help him find love by creating a dating app for the disabled. The truth was I was at the gathering in the hope of meeting someone from the disabled community who might be able to put me in touch with a computer wizard.

'An app developer,' he corrected.

That was it – an app developer.

I knew it may not have been the best place to start but I also knew maybe someone could put me in touch with someone, who could put me in touch with someone else, who made apps.

'I think I might know someone,' Max said. 'I can give them a call if you like and see if they're free over the next week or so.'

Max was too good to be true; not only did he have an overflow of aesthetic appeal, he also made looking for a needle in a haystack like looking for a really large hippopotamus in a really small backyard.

I was desperate for reassurance he hadn't heard my phone conversation with Katie but was more eager to know what his current situation with the ladies was; or just one lady in particular.

'The deaf girl in the game, she was great.'

I wished I'd have broached that topic with a little more subtlety, not that it offended him.

'That's Chloe, she's kind of like my little sister; we're always messing around and playing games together.'

"Messing around" could have meant girlfriend, but surely "kind of like my little sister" meant not. I would have analysed those words for another five minutes, had he not asked me another question.

'So have you got some way I can contact you?'

'Contact me?'

It had been so long since a guy had asked for my number that I wanted to confirm he was indeed asking for my number. Of course, I'd forgotten the very reason he was asking for it.

'So I can put you in touch with the app developer.'

Right.

I handed him my business card. He chuckled upon looking at it; it had rainbows, robots and balloons drawn on it.

I owned a toy store and had to have a toy store-like business card.

'Ella Bang,' he read off the card.

It's Ella Bong; oh never mind, you're cute; you can say it however you want.

'It's been very nice to meet you Ella Bang, I'm Max Hatheway.'

He held out his hand and I shook it.

Max Hatheway. That rolls off the tongue nicely. Max and Ella – that sounds like the perfect couple. Ella Hatheway – that's a married name I suppose I could take.

He then let go, and I let go of such splendid thoughts.

The gathering finished eating and drinking and made their way back inside the theatre. Max stood, too, which meant our meet-cute was over.

'We should get back. It was really nice to meet... actually, did you want to play?'

Theatre games weren't really my thing but I was so desperate to impress him, I said yes.

I sat in the circle on the stage at the front of the theatre and listened to Max as he recommenced the gameplay. 'Okay team we have a new addition; she's going to play our final warm-up game and maybe stick around and watch some of our rehearsal,' he said, using sign language. 'Everyone say hi to Ella.'

The group said 'hi' and Chloe leant forward and smiled at me.

'Okay Chloe, you and I will kick things off again,' he said. 'Owen, you're in charge of yelling out "freeze" this time. The scene is you're stuck in an elevator and you can't get out.'

Chloe joined him in the middle and the game got going again. The group laughed at their shenanigans and I laughed along as well.

The call then came to freeze.

The game went around the circle and being seated next to Chloe, only then did I realise I was next up.

Me? This soon? I can't do this, no way; not with a brick wall let alone Max and all of his attractiveness.

But I didn't have a choice, Chloe jumped out of the scene and back onto her chair and I had to jump in.

I slowly walked over to Max and tried to figure out what I was going to say.

Just say the first thing that comes to mind. Yes, because that always works. What other option have you got?

I put my hand on the back of Max's leg and kick-started the new scene with the first thing that came to mind.

'No Aunt Wanda, mint sauce won't fix your cellulite either.'

6.

I ignored Katie's "ASAP" call and chose to casually walk back to Hannah's from the theatre along the beach at sunset. I needed to examine and digest all the feelings I'd felt over the past hour and try and understand what they all meant.

I'm in love.

Don't be silly, you just met him for crying out loud.

Yeah, you're probably right.

Oh My God, you've just written "Max 4 Ella" in the sand with a stick.

I got to Hannah's and found Katie sitting on the floor and Justin and Brody sitting in front of her. They weren't saying anything; they were just staring back and forth at one another.

'Everything okay?'

She wasn't mad at me for taking so long because she was distracted by something else.

'I knew Hannah was wrong; it's been forty-five minutes and Brody hasn't made a sound, let alone said, "I love you, Mumma".'

'The boys have been sitting there for forty-five minutes like that? What's going on? Where's Hannah?'

She was out on a date night with Brett and had left Katie in charge. Katie often babysat but not often at such short notice.

'I got her and I tickets to the moonlight cinema but when I got here she was going to dinner with Brett and the kids.'

It was a typical Hannah thing to do – organise something with Katie or I, but forget about it and go out with Brett instead. I understood exactly why Katie wanted me to get there so fast – she'd had the boys dumped on her, she was bored out of her brain and she wanted some company.

'No, I wanted you here fast because the spare ticket is yours, the movie starts in forty-five minutes, and I don't want to be late.'

'But what about the boys?'

Katie didn't see a problem with taking a four-year-old and a fourteen-month-old to the moonlight cinema in the Royal Botanic Gardens without their mother's permission, but she did see a problem with wasting movie tickets, especially when they were to *Grease*.

I stood by the two kids in the pram inside the front entrance while she bought a couple of choc top ice creams. Despite being summer, it wasn't the warmest of nights. I had concerns about Brody being warm enough so put six extra layers of clothing and blankets on him to make sure he'd be okay. Justin was asleep, which was good because he was likely to be the more menacing of the two. He could sleep through a war that kid, which was something he definitely got from his mother. While I was often kept awake by anxiety or bouts of insomnia, Hannah could put her head on the pillow and be out like a light.

Katie and I were forced to sit towards the back due to the pram blocking other people's view, which meant we were quite a way away from the screen.

With our legs crossed like school children, we sat on a picnic rug. She handed me a choc top while the ads played before the film.

'So then what happened?'

I'd been telling her about Max, in the car on the way over, and had gotten to the point where I had to step into the theatre game.

'I touched him on the leg.'

'Did he get all creeped out?'

'No, it was a good touch, and the tension shook the room.'

That was a lie of course; the tension and the room shaking didn't happen at all, but I couldn't tell her what really happened. I needed her to think there were possibilities with this guy, not that I'd blown it on the very first night.

'That's unlike you; normally you blow it on the very first night. So when are you seeing him next?'

I had no idea, maybe never, but I couldn't tell her that either. 'Soon.'

My phone, which sat on the picnic rug between us, vibrated.

'Maybe that's him texting you now.'

It wasn't; it wasn't even a text message, but a Tinder message.

'From who?'

'Who cares, I've got Max now; I don't need to worry about Tinder.'

That was never going to suppress her curiosity.

'Remember the part about you not leaving all of your eggs in one basket? Come on show me; I was supposed to help you with this stuff anyway.'

I put down the choc top, picked up my phone and opened my profile. She took it from me and began fiddling around with it. This was her first experience with Tinder and her initial reaction to my profile was positive.

'This is amazing; this is fantastic; this is the greatest thing I've ever seen.'

It soon became clear however she was talking about the app itself and not my individual page.

'But your profile is crap; what the hell is that?'

She held up the phone and showed me what she was talking about. It was the photo of me kissing the back-end of a toy horse, and that wasn't the worst of it, as she observed.

'There's a photo of you looking like you've eaten a lemon, and the rest of your photos are just white pages with black writing that idiots put on Instagram when they're trying to be righteous and inspirational.'

As usual she was being quite harsh, and she didn't stop there, as she read those quotes I had stolen from Instagram.

'Create your own Sunshine? I need Vitamin Sea? Go where you feel most alive?'

In my defence, I was trying to be righteous and inspirational.

'They don't tell me anything about you and neither does this profile description – "Dear whoever is reading this, I hope you have a reason to smile today".'

I'd stolen that from the Internet as well.

'No wonder this thing hasn't worked out for you; if I was a guy and that profile came up I wouldn't swipe right; I'd break my phone in half and eat it.'

She could be quite cruel this sister of mine; she wasn't trying to hurt me but it hurt nonetheless. Thankfully she changed her tune, well sort of.

'I suppose there are some good aspects of this Tinder page of yours, like your background.'

The background was something generic the designers at Tinder had chosen and had nothing to do with me.

'Well then let's fix the foreground, put some gorgeous pictures of you in there and give the men in this world the best impression of the girl they're chasing. Now, how do you add photos?'

I took the phone from her and opened the page where I could upload photos from my Facebook and my photo gallery. I had changed the name of my folder from Hot, Hot Ella Folder to Ella Folder 1.

By that stage, the movie had started and despite loving *Grease*, I was too engaged in what we were doing, or more accurately, too desperate to get things right, to watch.

Katie moved in closer and together we started flicking through all my photos. To begin with she decided whether a photo was worthy or not.

'Nay, nay, nay, nay, nay, nay.'

Was she going to say nay to all of them?

'That last one you had your finger in your nose.'

There was a photo of me on a hilltop that showed I was well travelled, even though I wasn't.

'You're in Lycra™ shorts, nay.'

A photo of me playing lawn bowls with old people that showed I had hobbies.

'You're in Lycra shorts again, nay.'

A photo of me at our cousins wedding and I was smiling.

'And you're not wearing Lycra shorts, yay.'

A photo of me at Brody's first birthday party dressed as a fairy – 'Yay.'

Me and Katie at the beach coming out of the water like swimsuit models – 'Yay.'

Things were definitely looking up…

Me beside my oven holding a book titled *100 Ways To Pork In The Kitchen*, dressed in Lycra shorts again – 'Definitely nay.'

… But were quickly looking down again.

We chose four photos and I was happy to settle with that. With my name and age entered and my partner settings adjusted from 155 kilometres away to twenty-five kilometres away, all that was left was for me to come up with a tagline.

'My name is Ella, and I am twenty-eight.'

She looked at me like that was the worst tagline ever. 'Your name and age underneath your photos say that; think of something else.'

I did; I thought really hard; as hard as I could…

I'm ready to leap into the unknown, like a frog.

I want love more than the band Queen wanted to break free.

I wish my name was Lucinda, so everyone could call me Lucinda from Tinder.

… But I still couldn't come up with anything good.

However, Betty Rizzo from Grease provided what Katie thought was the perfect one liner – Peachy Keen Jelly Bean.

'It tells me you like movies, it tells me you've got a sense of dare in you, and it tells me you're there to find the right guy, not waste time like some other people.'

Whether it was good or bad, one thing was for sure – it helped me complete my Tinder profile and I was excited to start swiping through my next few potential partners.

Katie watched as I did so and unashamedly had some input on whether I should swipe left or swipe right. I swiped right on Sloan, Bobo, Daniel and Chad. Katie's renovation of my profile worked wonders as within seconds I matched with Chad. He had sandy hair, was unshaven and had blue eyes. And he was quick to say hello.

I tapped on the speech box icon at the top and opened it.

It read –

Chad

> Hey, I want to have sex with strangers who are skilled and very intimate in bed. If you are of the same interest like mine meet me at http://seeXX99sexed45 and we will have intimate and unforgettable bed experience.

Like I hadn't seen that a hundred times before.

'Okay delete that guy,' Katie warned. 'Delete him and delete him now.'

It took me a moment to remember Katie had never used dating apps before, and thus had no idea Chad was a scammer.

She'd held the power since Tinder had first buzzed on my phone, but now I did, and it was time to have some fun with it.

'You're right, definitely deleting disgusting Chad. Vulgar, repugnant, rotten, yucky Chad, who doesn't even speak English properly, is getting delet... wait.'

She looked at me unsure what "wait" meant.

'I bet everyone deletes Chad, and I bet no one ever fights back; I bet no one ever calls Chad out for his repulsive behaviour, so I'm going to.'

Her reaction was priceless – this unbreakable warrior-woman was now engulfed with the fear I was inciting a potential sex predator. 'You're going to what? Talk to him? Are you serious? What are you doing?'

I was typing back.

Ella

**Mine are the same interests as yours Chad.
Tell me, what sex positions do you like?**

'Are you serious? You're asking him that? What if he's a serial killer?'

She was petrified my stupidity was going to get us both killed. I was tempted to tell her Chad wasn't a serial killer but wanted to mess with her some more, so feigned trepidation myself.

'What? Serial killer? I didn't even think of that; I thought he was just horny. What if he's a serial killer? Do you think we should go to the police?'

I tried to think how I could get Chad to write back the words, "I'm a serial killer", but there was simply no way of that happening, so I told the truth.

Actually, I laughed in Katie's face and then told the truth. 'You should see your face; Chad's not a serial killer; he's a fake, a scammer, someone who's trying to get money out of me.

She hated being made to look like a fool and her dagger eyes sure made me know it. 'You're a dirty, lying mole and I'm going to smash your face in later. I should have known; as if Chad ever wanted to have sex with you.'

That I couldn't deny. Still for ninety seconds, someone did want to sleep with me, which was better than no one, which was normally the case.

'Except he wasn't real; now go and find a real guy.'

I touched the icon to take me back to my potential partners and continued swiping. I immediately started scoring matches all over the place.

Rory, Omar and Tom.

Eddie, Freddie and Phil.

Martin, Kieran and Anthony.

I tried my best to hide my smile but the more I fought it the more it stretched across my face. I was yet another small step closer to finding the man of my dreams, and it was all thanks to Katie.

She brought me in for a hug; a loving, "I'm here for you day and night", sisterly hug, which made me feel special.

'I'm still going to kick your butt for lying to me about Chad.'

I could have sat there and held on to the hug way longer but felt the sweats coming on around my groin area. Strangely enough I didn't feel the anxiety I felt when I normally sweated up. What the hell was this sweat then? Was my own sister turning me on?

I broke from our hug to investigate and found it wasn't sweat at all –my choc-top had melted all over my leg.

7.

I mismanaged my time.

I always told myself if ever I had somewhere to be I'd give myself double the amount of time to get there in case something bad happened along the way, like a car accident or a train being delayed. Neither of those things happened of course, which meant I reached the city for my appointment with the app developer an hour earlier than when I needed. I decided to stop into a music store and listen to some tunes to kill the time of day. The music was a nice reminder of how awesome the 1990s were.

No sooner had I stopped dancing and put my headphones down, did Katie text me.

> If Hannah calls, don't answer.
> She found out I took the boys to the movies last night. I accidentally told her you were half to blame.
> She wants us both dead now. Hi!

'Accidentally?' As if.

I knew it was her way of getting back at me for Chad. Still, I appreciated the heads up; the next half-an-hour was going to be really important and I didn't need any interruptions.

The east end of Collins Street was where I needed to be. High-rise buildings made me nervous for several reasons – you finally found the right floor for your appointment, only to discover the floor had thirty different glass doors along three different corridors all with different business names on them. And they were all written in the smallest font, so you had to stop and read each one to know if it was yours or not.

Thankfully the third glass door had the number of the office I was looking for, although the name on the door didn't exactly match – Dentist & Co.

I popped my head in, fearful I might have seen some kid getting his teeth yanked out of his head and blood going everywhere, but there was a receptionist. A sign behind her read Dapper App-ers and the coffee table had computer magazines all over it, so I knew I was in the right place.

Max had texted me the address for the app developer and organized a time for the appointment. I was pleased to now have his mobile number saved in my phone but was nervous I hadn't yet been in contact with the guy he was putting me on to.

I entered and stood in front of the reception desk. The female receptionist was on the phone, but it sounded like she was talking to a friend more so than a client. I waited but she wasn't in any hurry to hang up, so I interrupted.

'I'll be just a minute,' she said.

Just a minute, she was never going to be. She continued talking, gossiping to her friend about a dress she wanted, only to have had a mutual friend of theirs go and buy the exact dress behind her back.

I looked at the clock behind her. Precious seconds were ticking away. I was paying for this appointment and felt I might miss it entirely if I didn't do something.

Pretending to examine the paintwork on the walls I slowly moved towards the door separating reception and what was likely the main office. I got to it without giving away my intentions but found the door was locked and security coded.

I should have accepted defeat, but of course, I didn't.

Codes are always 0000, just type it in, she'll never notice.

Except the code wasn't 0000, and because I'd guessed the wrong code, the security system went off.

'What the hell are you doing?' she yelled.

I'd stuffed up, but at least it got her off the phone.

She hurried over in an attempt to turn the alarm off but was beaten to it by a hand from the other side of the door. It was a really attractive man's hand that was connected to a really attractive man's forearm that belonged to a really attractive man. He had brown, wavy hair, gorgeous eyes, was really well dressed in a collared shirt, trousers and was...

'Max, what are you doing here?'

'I'm your app developer; sorry, I thought I'd be a smarty-pants.'

It was certainly something I didn't see coming but was a welcome surprise nonetheless.

'Come through, my office is at the end of the hallway on the left; I'll get us some coffee.'

The wider office looked like a really fun place to work. There was so much colour, so many cool pieces of artwork on the walls and several unique sculptures.

His personal office followed a similar theme; abstract artwork, a desk that looked like a milk carton, a number of odd statue men that looked like they'd been bought while on vacation in Asia, and these round blow-up seat things that looked like fitness balls.

'They are fitness balls; please take a seat.'

I did so and so did he.

While he found his balance straight away, I wriggled around trying to find mine, wriggled some more, and then wriggled some more, before finding the right spot. Only then did I realise how embarrassing I must have looked rolling around on a fitness ball that long.

'So this project of yours, tell me more about it.'

Despite us having spoken at the theatre, talking to Max still meant having to converse with a cute man and typically I felt an uncomfortable feeling rise in my stomach. It was the anxiety kicking in and with it getting worse, I knew the sweats were only seconds away. I feared things going belly up at any second so tried to answer the question.

'My tummy hurts.'

'My tummy hurts?' That's what you said? You idiot.

'It's okay; that's from the ball, it engages your core; you're probably using some muscles you don't often use and that's why it's hurting. You can stand if you like.'

I should have known that, being an occasional gym goer with Katie, but she was all about the weights, not the balls. It hurt so much I desperately wanted to stand, but damn it, this guy was hot and no matter how much it hurt I was going to show him how much core ability I had.

'Can I ask a question first?' I said.

'Sure.'

I truthfully did have a proper question in mind but the devil in my head disturbingly kept saying the same thing.

Would you make-out with me? We can turn the lights down, light a few candles and make-out amongst the fitness balls?

I shook my head like one does after they sneeze to eradicate such thoughts and got things back on track.

'I was curious about the name on your front door; why "Dentist & Co"?'

He smiled, with his nice smile that I wanted to turn the lights down and make-out with.

No; just nice smile; no lights down and make-out. Just nice smile.

I was desperate for many reasons; a devious mind was just one of them.

'The last guy who was in these offices before retiring was a dentist; we just never got around to taking the sign off. We thought it might be clever to leave it there, but we've been getting visitors and people phoning in about toothaches and fillings. I think that's why my receptionist only answers the phone to her friends nowadays.'

He was so funny and so casually content with himself and his sign, even though others might have seen it as stupid.

'So, this project,' he pressed again.

'Yes, the project.'

I had given him a basic outline of my idea at the theatre but went into more detail – it needed to be safe and easy to use, free of scammers, pure and honest in its motivations, have a catchy name and be full of colour, like his office.

'I love it, I love everything about it.'

I couldn't help but think of the subtext to those eight words. He was saying "it", but did he really mean "me"?

My phone then rang. It was Hannah. Katie had warned me not to answer but for seven years my rule was if my phone rang I should answer it, in case it was an emergency. Plus, my tummy was throbbing in pain from the stupid fitness ball and I badly needed to stand.

'I have to take this sorry; I'll be one minute.'

I ducked out of his office, raised my arms and stretched my stomach with a great deal of relief and answered the phone with a great deal of dread.

'Hey Han, I want you to know straight off the top I'm sorry, I'm really sorry.'

'Sorry for what?'

Was she not ringing to grill me about taking her kids to the moonlight cinema?

'For... taking so long to answer the phone.'

'No worries; I thought I'd let you know straight away – we're all set for next week.'

I had no idea what she was talking about; what was next week?

'Your party... To find the right guy... Is next week.'

My party? Oh yeah, right.

It wasn't so much I'd forgotten, it was I thought she would have. She always floated these ideas and never went through with them. When it came to parties however it was clearly a different story.

'It's going to be a night you won't forget,' she added.

That I didn't doubt, only, it was a night I didn't need anymore. I had Max right in front of me and things were going well; I didn't want to jeopardise that by going to a party full of other guys I may not have even liked. I thought about saying thanks and then not turning up to whatever night it was on, and saying I'd forgotten. But that was the kind of stunt she pulled all the time and I hated it. So I told the truth.

'I don't think I need a party anymore.'

'What, why?'

'I think I've found a guy that likes me.'

'Oh.'

She sounded disappointed at first that she'd gone to such trouble for nothing, but then came around and was happy for me.

Sort of.

'I'll talk to you later then, bye.'

She hung up.

I hated upsetting my sisters more than anything in the world, and in any other situation would have dwelled on my stuff-up for hours, maybe days, but there was something more important at hand and I had to put all my energy into that.

I walked back into the office and found Max standing in front of a giant whiteboard on wheels. I felt better about that, too, as I didn't have to sit on the fitness ball anymore. I was, however, slightly confused by all the words he'd written on the whiteboard – Wireframe, Interface, Data, Visuals, Image and Colour.

Was this process really that complicated?

I apologised again for taking the call. 'Was my sister; wouldn't have answered if it was anyone else.'

'All good. So, like I was saying, I love this idea. First thing we've got to do though is a brief, which means outlining exactly what your project is and how much it's going to cost.'

Wait, what? Cost?

I hadn't thought of that word, primarily because I didn't think it was going to cost me, or the people using it, anything. I wanted my project to be free, a free app people could download... for free.

'It's okay, we'll make it so they can download it for free, and don't worry, you'll make back whatever you spend through advertising, in-app purchases, subscriptions to added content, that kind of thing.'

But I didn't want to use any of those; I didn't want people to be messed around by ads or have to pay for added content. My project was there to help the disabled find love, not to sell advertising to them, or encourage them to spend money.

I realised I hadn't really thought the whole project through. I imagined it being much simpler, like setting up an email or importing a CD onto iTunes™. As a result, I felt really uncomfortable knowing I'd wasted Max's time and overreacted accordingly.

'I need some time to think; I thought making these things was different. I stuffed up, I can see myself out, I'm sorry.'

I hurried out of his office all flustered. I felt like I'd been hit with two giant water balloons – one filled with guilt for being a disrespectful customer, and the other filled with disappointment because this was an idea I thought could really work.

I was also hating on the world – I had always been my own kiss of death and had been yet again; things were going amazingly well, then I told Hannah on the phone things were going amazingly well, and then everything unravelled.

I passed the receptionist who was still on the phone and walked back out into the corridor towards the elevator. At least getting out of the high-rise building wouldn't be as hard as it was getting in. I stepped inside the elevator and frustratingly pushed the bottom floor button with my thumb a few times. Finally, the lift doors began to close, but then a hand stopped them from shutting completely.

It was Max.

He got caught between the doors but managed to squeeze his way in.

'You make a quick getaway; what floor?'

For a second, I thought he was chasing after me.

'I am. I like you, you're cool, and you said something about helping a friend, which I respect. Most people come in with an idea because they want to get rich.'

He was right, but it didn't stop me feeling like I was bothering him with something I shouldn't have been. It was a silly idea; I needed to let it go.

'The Snuggie™ was a silly idea too, but look how that turned out. You should know something...'

He was about to tell me what it was I should know when the elevator doors opened on a different floor, and two women entered.

I found it strange he wouldn't tell me with the other two women standing there. I also found it completely ironic we were standing in a real elevator after playing a theatre game where we stood in an imaginary elevator. I looked down at his leg and thought about repeating what I said about cellulite that night, as a joke, but thought better of it. He caught me looking at his leg, wondered what I was doing and then hit the button for level six, which was the level we were approaching. The elevator stopped, the doors opened, and he excused himself between the two ladies before ushering me out.

He guided me into the corridor, which, like the level his office was on, was like a maze. 'Sorry, call me paranoid but people steal ideas and I didn't want to continue talking about your project with those two women standing there.'

'That's weird.'

'I know.'

'No, *that*, is weird.'

I wasn't talking about him being weird but a sign on an office door behind his head. He turned to the door himself and looked at the sign on it. It read – Tantric Sex Therapists. It wasn't the greatest place to stop in front of.

'Maybe it's a dentist that didn't get around to changing the name,' he joked. 'What I was going to say was you should know I've been looking for a side project for a while now and I think your idea is perfect. I get it and I agree, the opportunity to find love in this world is everything, and some people are missing out. That needs to be fixed; you want to fix it, and I want to help. No cost, no advertising, no subscriptions to added content, just you and I out of our own goodwill. Will you let me help?'

Again, I couldn't help but think of the subtext.

I've been looking for a side project for a while now = I really want to spend more time with you.

The opportunity to find love is everything = I'm in love with you.

Will you let me help? = I'm in love with you.

Regardless of whether there was subtext present or not, he continued to make me feel good and therefore of course I was going to let him help. I really wanted to hug him, even to say thanks, but I didn't. Because some fat guy exited the Tantric Sex Office and walked between us, shirtless with nipple clamps on.

'Maybe we should keep talking about this somewhere else.'

We sat on the steps of the Old Treasury Building and drank juice. Hanging out and drinking juice was new for me; I was more of a coffee girl.

Max was like one of those people you knew for ten minutes but felt like you'd known for ten years; he was so easy to talk to. I thought we'd get straight into the nuts and bolts of my dating app, but he had other ideas.

'So what do you look for in a guy?'

What did that matter?

'I'm going to need to get to know you if we're going to be working on this project together.'

Get to know me? He'd have been better off asking how many

empty shampoo and conditioner bottles still sat on the floor of my shower.

'Nice eyes; I like nice eyes.'

'You do have gorgeous eyes yourself so that makes sense. What else?'

Admittedly, I had thought about that question a hundred times in my life and come to several answers rather quickly. Being asked out aloud however, I couldn't think of a single response.

'It doesn't have to be looks,' he pressed. 'Or even the way a person acts; just something you look for.'

I sat there thinking but still couldn't come up with anything, so I asked him to give me an example.

He thought about it for a few seconds. After a sip from his juice he told me about that "something" he looked for.

'When I was younger my mum and I played this game called "Ellen and the Moon". It normally came about when we were trapped in a boring extended family dinner. You know the one's where the rest of the family are complaining about their health issues, all while giving you a headache.'

I chuckled.

He continued. 'Anyway, how the game works is you say you're going to the moon and you're taking something or someone with you, and whoever takes the most random thing wins. You get three seconds to answer and you get a point for each win. If the second person's answer is too like the first person's, the first person automatically gets the point. First person to six points wins overall.'

It was slightly confusing, but I eventually wrapped my head around it – we had to take a random thing to the moon, and the most random thing won.

'And there's one person who automatically guarantees a win,' he added. 'Ellen DeGeneres – if you take Ellen DeGeneres to the moon you automatically get the point. Hence why it's called "Ellen and the

Moon". But you can only use her once.'

I liked that part; it was cute, as was the fact he played the game with his mum.

'So that's something I look for in a woman,' he concluded.

'Someone who's like your mum?' I teased.

'What? No, someone who can engage in a silly exercise like that.'

I now had more to work with in coming up with my own answer, but before I could give it, he asked me another question.

'Want to play?'

Not really... Wait, yes you do; he said he looks for that in a woman and if you say no, he'll reject you for sure.

'Okay, let's do it.'

He decided to go first to allow me time to think of what I was going to take, which was good considering my record of blurting stuff out.

'I'm going to the moon and I'm taking a Leonardo Di Vinci original painting,' he said.

I took some time with my response before coming up with what I thought was the cleverest thing I'd ever said in my life.

'I'm going to the moon and I'm taking a finger painting I did in kindergarten, where my dad's head is bigger than my house.'

I was pretty confident I got the point; my moon item was far more random than his was. But I was wrong.

'I took a painting and then you took a painting, so your item's too similar to mine,' he said.

Crap, I forgot about that.

'And you did take longer than three seconds to think of it. But for a first go it was pretty good.'

We'd gone to the steps of the Old Treasury Building to discuss my dating app project yet hadn't spoken a word of it. Somehow though I preferred it that way; he'd learnt more about me and I'd learnt more and more about him. The more I learnt, the more I liked, and the more we played, the more I realised he liked me too.

To no surprise he won the first five games and took a five-nil lead. He only needed one more to win and hadn't used his Ellen DeGeneres card, so I was doomed.

But he didn't use it.

'I'm going to the moon and I'm going to take you.'

'U? Like the letter U?'

'No, not the letter U, *you*... I'm going to take you, Ella Bang.'

'Me? Why would you want to take me? Because I'm random?'

'No, I'm taking you because I want to take you. Now what are you going to take?'

I took a miniature porcelain doll that dressed like Italian royalty but spoke like the mafia.

'And that point goes to you because your answer was far more random than mine.'

I was pleased with myself.

'You thought you were going to win six-nil didn't you?'

He paused for a second and then answered. 'It's funny, I kinda feel like I have.'

Max sipped from his juice, as did I. Despite the juice being ice-cold, I felt this warm feeling inside.

Was Max just as smitten as me?

8.

I caught the bus to Tiffany's house.

After what had occurred with Max days before, I was certain I didn't need her help anymore; I'd fixed my nervous, sweaty self and no longer required the assistance of a dating coach.

Still, I would have felt bad cancelling at such late notice.

After being so early to my appointment with Max in the city, I decided I didn't need to give myself an extra hour to get to Tiffany's house, which was in East Bentleigh, just behind the hospital.

I should have given myself the extra hour.

I sat up the back of the bus. I got my phone out and nervously tracked my journey on Google Maps. I was worried I'd go past my stop so pushed the bell and got off four streets early.

Four streets earlier than what I should have.

I began walking. I thought I was only a couple of hundred metres from her house but realised I'd misjudged the distance – I had 1.4km to walk and only six-and-a-half minutes to do so.

I started running.

When sitting on a train, I often watched as people ran to try and make it before the doors closed and thought, *I wonder if they realise how silly they look.*

Running down Centre Road to Tiffany's, all I could think about was how all the passing traffic must have thought the exact same thing.

My running style was like that of a Lar gibbon monkey. It was like I'd gotten out of the shower, forgotten to put a towel on the rack, and run into the bedroom trying to put the least amount of water on the floor as possible.

Despite my urgency, it was clear after two blocks of running I wasn't going to make it on time; I was out of breath and sweating like a pig.

At least for good reason this time.

Someone clearly wanted me to make my appointment on time, however, as a kid came out of his driveway on a bike that had a pair of old-school 90s pegs sticking out from the back wheel.

'I'll give you ten bucks if you give me a lift to a house two streets away.'

He agreed.

The ride itself wasn't without its nervous moments either. Without a helmet on I dreaded a police car driving past and stopping and fining me. Or worse, me being too heavy for the pegs, the pegs breaking and me face-planting so hard I'd no longer have a face.

Thankfully neither happened.

I arrived at my destination and handed over my ten bucks. There was a woman in her forties standing in the front yard of the house beside Tiffany's, and by the look on her face I think she thought I was selling drugs to a minor. I felt the need to say something to the kid to make her think I wasn't.

'It was really nice riding you.'

If she looked worried before that comment, she looked full on disturbed now.

'No, I mean... thank-you... for letting me ride on your bike.'

The kid took my money and rode off, fixated on the money and a possible new business venture.

Tiffany's house was the most enchanting cottage I'd ever seen in my life. It looked like something straight out of a Tim Burton movie – white weatherboards with silver railings and an immaculately groomed front yard with a garden feature were surrounded by a white picket fence and a letterbox. It was a far cry from the crabby shack her neighbour lived in; a neighbour who continued to stare at me with what now appeared a heightened level of intrigue.

'You must be Ella.'

I was, but how did weird neighbour lady know this? Had Tiffany told her?

'I am Tiffany.'

What?! No-o.

Any remaining enthusiasm I had for this appointment dissolved.

Tiffany's residence wasn't the divine cottage but the raggedy old eyesore next door that barely resembled a house? That's where we were going to have our appointments?

'Judgmental much? Now I can see why you're single,' she grinned, and then continued. 'This place was sold recently; I'm removing any unwanted mail before the demolition starts tomorrow. I'm in that one.'

She pointed to the house next door; the gorgeous cottage I initially thought was hers. 'Come inside; I'll put some coffee on.'

The interior of the cottage was just as exquisite as the exterior. Vintage furniture, bouquet art, a shabby red table, a miniature farmer's bench and a floral rug were all complemented by pastel green paint that covered the walls, and a strong scent that flowed from several candles. The sofa was almost too good to sit on, but she insisted, and then insisted I take a baked cookie from the plate to go with my coffee. I didn't know what the cookie was made from but it was yum.

'You know how some women make sourdough from their own vaginal yeast?'

I stopped chewing and felt my throat dry up at the very fear the cookie in my mouth had been made from her…

'I'm messing with you,' she laughed. 'Nothing but flour and water in those things; trying to see if I can make you more nervous than you already are.'

Mission accomplished.

I was relieved it was a prank but curious as to what kind of special creature this Tiffany lady was. She was very pure looking with fading blonde hair, a pair of specs and a demure but stunning fashion sense. Her image spelt out the word innocence but the words that came out of her mouth spoke anything but.

'I can be a rascal. I like to make life entertaining; it's all about perspective, as you'll soon learn. Now sign this.'

I put my coffee and my cookie down and accepted a clipboard from her. I expected it to be a contract, but it was a page ripped from a male bodybuilding magazine where the muscular man in the photo was dressed in nothing but a pair of tiny latex shorts.

'You want me to sign this?' I asked, without a clue why.

She nodded.

'At the top or the bottom or where?'

'On the chest; write your name on his chest.'

I did but still didn't get why. Was it some kind of sick sexual joke? Like the vagina yeast?

'Now write your phone number underneath it.'

What on Earth?

'It's an exercise. You'll have to write your name and number down for man at some point; might as well start getting used to it now.'

With that, things became a lot clearer, but why on a picture of a near-naked bodybuilder I still didn't get.

'I don't have any white printing paper at the moment. It was the first thing I saw when I walked into my office. My son's trying to put on muscle mass, or so he tells me. Follow me.'

Follow her I did, towards that aforementioned office. The first steps into her home were very much the first steps to her gaining my trust, and me gaining hers. She opened the door and ushered me into her office, which had a car parked in the middle of it.

Her garage and her office doubled as one.

'We're going for a drive, get in.'

Trusting her wasn't as easy as I thought it was going to be; she was taking me somewhere in her car five minutes after meeting me. I thought the first session would have been the two of us sitting down and talking about my past and then her handing me a folder that outlined her past and how she was going to fix me.

'Take this,' she said, as we drove out of her driveway.

I'd jumped too soon – it was a folder that outlined her past and how she was going to fix me.

I was nervous about where she was driving us and what she had planned so I read the opening page to distract myself.

Her profile gave little away; she enjoyed investing in property, liked to bake, was a qualified relationship coach, and – as mentioned – had a son. I flicked through a few more pages which began to outline the structure of the program; she really had run out of white rag as the last few pages were regular loose-leaf.

'Don't go any further,' she said. 'The info' about me is all you need to know at this point. We're here anyway.'

We'd arrived out the front of a DVD rental store.

A DVD store? I didn't even know those still existed.

'It won't in about six months, which is why we have to use it now.'

Use it? Use it for what?

'Think of it as match simulation. Soccer players don't prepare for the big game by sitting around a living room talking, so why should we?'

What?

The nerves started to kick in and sweat started to seep through my pores; I thought we were there to rent an educational love DVD.

She walked through the front door and I followed. The girl behind the counter said hello to her by name; she must have rented from this place a lot. The girl then looked at me as if to say, "Good Luck".

Did Tiffany bring all her desperate and dateless clients here on their very first day?

'Not all but some,' she grinned again, with a grin that was becoming all-too devilish.

She leaned forward, took a DVD from the shelf and held it up so I could read it – Fascist Fundamentalism.

I didn't really know what a fascist was.

'What's fundamentalism?' she asked.

'I don't know what that is either.'

'We won't find a man in this section anyway; let's try drama.'

I looked around the store at the headings that sat on the DVD shelves and eventually found the drama section. How very unsurprising was it that a man with his back to us stood in that very section.

Seriously? She'd seriously brought me to a DVD store, so I could walk over to a man and chat him up?

'It's a baptism of fire, I know, but I need to get a gauge of where you are at. Go over and say hello, find out what movie he's keen to see and then ask if he'd like to come back to your aunt's place to watch it.'

Come back to my aunt's place to watch it? What was I, like fourteen years old?

'This is not to trick you or make you look stupid, it's simply to find out where your strengths and weaknesses lie.'

She was so sincere and reassuring I couldn't back out. With all the courage I could muster I slowly walked towards the man in the drama section. He was in his early twenties at best. I had no idea what I was going to say to him, but five feet away remembered what Tiffany said about finding out what movie he was keen to see, and took that as my introduction.

I turned my head sideways to check the cover of the DVD he was holding and then asked him about it.

'You like Jesus huh?'

Oh crap, what kind of a question was that?

He looked at me as if certain I was talking to someone other than himself.

'*The Passion Of The Christ*, it's in your hand,' I added.

He smiled with relief, having realised what I meant about the Jesus comment. I could have shut up and let him answer my question but like an idiot, I didn't.

'You know, for the so many times I've started watching that film, I don't know how it ends.'

The same way this chat was going to end, with me being crucified.

The quickest way to get out of this awful situation was to introduce myself, ask if he wanted to watch it with me, be rejected by him and then leave. Except by some divine work of God or Mel Gibson that didn't happen.

'Sure, I'd love to watch it with you.'

He was coming back to my "aunt's" house to watch *The Passion Of The Christ* with me.

'Great,' I uttered, happy but in shock all the same. 'I'll get the popcorn.'

We sat in Tiffany's living room and watched *The Passion Of The Christ*. He was so into it whereas I thought it was the most boring thing I'd ever watched in my life.

And Mel Gibson wasn't even in it.

He paused it halfway through so he could get up and go to the bathroom. Three seconds after he'd left the room Tiffany walked in and challenged me again.

She was literally spying on me.

'When he gets back you've got to ask him out to dinner.'

She then walked out again.

He came back in from the bathroom and pushed the play button. I'd never asked a guy out while watching another man get nailed to a cross but that was about to change.

'Would you go out with me? We could share some bread somewhere, or some wine.'

He looked at me like I'd offended him, primarily because I had. 'Are you making fun of Jesus?'

What? Oh God, the bread and the wine thing; I didn't mean it like that.

I was keen to rectify my mistake. 'No, it doesn't have to be bread and wine, we can abstain from that.'

He looked at me even more aghast, 'Are you making fun of abstinence now?'

What? Oh God.

I suddenly had two mistakes to rectify but wasn't given the chance.

He stood, took the DVD from the DVD player and made haste towards the front door. I followed and apologised but it was too late – the door slammed shut.

It was a new experience for me; men had slammed doors in my face because they found me ugly, awkward or annoying, but they'd never slammed a door in my face because I'd insulted their religion.

Tiffany came back in and put her arm around me. I honestly thought I had made some ground with Max outside the Old Treasury Building, but the previous hour with her reaffirmed I still had a lot of work to do, and it hurt.

'It'll be all right, hun'.'

At that moment, nothing was going to convince me of that. 'How? I'm never going to find the right guy; I'm going to die alone.'

'Well if there's one thing we've learnt tonight, it's that even if you die alone, there's still a chance you'll rise again.'

For the first time all night I was certain she was being a smart alec, but before I could call her out on it, the front door swung open again.

It was the guy from the DVD store, who happened to be more than just the guy from the DVD store.

'Dead-set Mum, that's the last time I do that; I hate making your girls cry.'

Mum? Oh no she didn't.

Oh yes she did; he was her son and she his mother.

I cursed myself on the inside – how had I not seen the signs?

Tiffany mentioned she had a son when I signed the bodybuilder's chest, she used the word "baptism" at the DVD store and he was holding *The Passion Of The Christ*, and he said yes to watching the movie with me at "my aunt's house" even though I'd embarrassed myself during our introduction.

'And I knew where the bathroom was without having to ask,' he added. 'I really am sorry; she didn't give me a choice.'

Apology accepted.

One thing that wasn't put on was his desire to leave in a hurry. 'Can I go now? I have a girl of my own to date you know?'

She nodded, and he left.

I still couldn't believe how naïve I'd been, but there were more important things to discuss.

'There are more important things to discuss,' she told me. 'You did a lot right today so be proud, but there are still some things to work on, like the fact that at no point did you ask the man his name.'

Oh my Lord, I didn't either.

I felt myself go red in the face and realised my mind was starting to say a lot of religious words like "God" and "Lord".

'His name is Liam, and yours is Ella, which he knows, not because you told him, but because I did before you arrived.'

Yes, I forgot to tell him my name too.

'As for the "more important things", there are some notes in your folder; please read them at home so you're ready for our next appointment. And remember to be kind to yourself; lose the doubt and negativity. You will find your prince charming by the time we're finished.'

She sounded like a clairvoyant the way she said that.

Her confidence should have given me confidence but having failed session one so badly all I could think about was how quickly things had changed. Before meeting Tiffany, I was convinced I no longer needed relationship help from a dating coach, my sisters or any form of social media.

By day's end, I was convinced I did.

9.

Doubt and negativity consumed my mind in the days following my appointment with Tiffany.

There was the possibility I may one day find my prince charming but what was more possible was he'd slam the door in my face just like Liam had.

My thoughts only got worse from there.

You have weird eyebrows.

You have a weird sounding voice.

You should buy some shapewear lingerie, so your bum doesn't hang so low.

There was only one solution to turning my frown upside down and that was to go back to the guy who made me feel better about myself in the beginning – Max.

After putting up with my thoughts at the toy store for a couple of days, I worked up the courage to call him on my day off. I used our dating app project as an excuse to catch-up but also suggested we do something fun at the same time.

'Sure, I can meet you at Chelsea library,' he told me on the phone, clearly thinking by "fun" I meant tobogganing or water-skiing.

You should have organised water-skiing, woman. You don't even know how to water-ski though.

My thoughts sure were in overdrive.

I arrived at Chelsea library five minutes early and – contemplating how to kill time – decided to use Tiffany's trick on Max. I was going to pick out a book as awkward as *The Passion Of The Christ* DVD and see if Max embarrassed himself in front of me, like I had in front of Liam.

I started in the Religion section but couldn't find anything so moved to Environment, then History, before settling on How To, where I found the book I was looking for.

'Hey, there you are, what are you reading?'

I didn't answer, but smiled, and let Max creep closer and find out for himself.

'*Big Dresses And Other Ways To Hide Your Baby When You've Cheated On Your Partner,*' he read, off the cover.

Again, I didn't answer, but let him wallow in his own awkwardness.

Awkwardness – it turned out – he never really wallowed in.

Instead he looked worried. Really worried.

'That's an odd choice of book; you're not a cheater, are you?'

I panicked immediately. *My oh my what have I done?*

The plan backfired completely; I didn't embarrass Max at all; the only person I embarrassed was myself, and not only that, the guy I liked now feared I was a cheater.

'No, I swear I've never cheated in my life, I was just curious what other ways there were to hide a baby.'

From looking like a cheater, to sounding like I was pregnant, yet again I made a bad situation worse. 'Not that I'm pregnant, I'm...' I scrunched up my face with self-hatred. Much like I did at the DVD store, I felt like one giant, pathetic loser. This time, such feelings were accompanied by guilt, as I'd tried to make Max feel the same way I had. Deservedly, I'd set a trap for Max and fallen into it myself.

If there were any positives, his confident, mature response again showed me I was still a long way off where I wanted to be when it came to my behaviour around men.

In this instance, there was only one thing left to do. 'I'm sorry; I hope you'll forgive that attempt at humour and join me at a free table by the computers.'

Max's laptop was like this endless world of computer programs, private folders and other stuff. I didn't know what any of it meant or how any of it worked but he opened it up and showed me a few things he'd been working on for our app. He'd created a shortlist for the heading font, written up a page of personal details one might wish to convey in their profile and even drawn with his fancy graphic tools five animal mascots to make the app more user friendly.

'Who's that?' I asked, pointing to a cartoon kitten that held a stick.

'It's a magic wand, actually; she's holding a magic wand that will hopefully help everybody find love.'

The words "help everybody find love" saw me fall into a trance – boy how I wanted to find love with him.

He continued showing me the other potential cartoon animals we could use as a mascot, but I wasn't listening; I sat there and stared at him, wanting and wanting and wanting.

My enjoyment at staring was broken by my vibrating mobile phone. I pulled it out from beside my hip and looked at it – it was Katie. I had my emergency policy when it came to answering phones but chose not to answer because I was sick of my sisters interrupting me when I was getting somewhere with Max. If she rang a second time I'd answer.

'And that's the five mascots I've got,' he said, as he observed me putting my phone away. 'You need to get out of here?'

I thought about that question a moment and then thought about how much more fun we'd have somewhere else. 'I think you and I should both get out of here.'

He was keen to return to the steps of the Old Treasury Building and continue brainstorming ideas, but being so far away, we instead went for coffee at Hendriks Café on White Street, Mordialloc.

Correction – he brainstormed ideas and I found them all amazing.

'I'm thinking we follow the trend of swiping left or right but rather than it being known as a dating app, it's called a friendship square. There's one other thing too – these apps can be littered with fake accounts so to try and combat that, every user must record and upload a fifteen second video introducing themselves. So it's clear they are who they say they are.'

That was an idea I really liked, as safety for the users was important.

I was about to suggest a break from brainstorming and instead spend more time getting to know one another, when my phone rang again.

This time it wasn't Katie, but my landlady. I apologised and stepped away to answer it. I was glad I did as she told me she'd received a call from one of my neighbours saying someone had broken into my apartment. She rambled on and on and only stopped when I told her, 'I'm leaving now; I'll be there in ten minutes.'

I hung up and turned back to Max but was stunned to find he was talking to another woman. She was tall, blonde and leggy, wore a white polo with short green shorts and a pair of white low tops. He spoke to her with quite a level of excitement.

Who was this girl? And what was she doing with my guy?

'Oh, hey Ella,' he said like we hadn't been hanging out for the last hour. 'This is Shelly, she's an old friend of mine.'

Shelly held out her hand and I shook it; she was friendly and attractive, and well-spoken and attractive.

'She's an assistant greens keeper at Woodlands golf course next door; she's just popped in for her lunch break.'

With her freshly conditioned hair, feminine shoulders and sparklingly tanned legs, she didn't look like an assistant greens keeper. Where were her gloves?

The two of them made a couple of in-jokes that made no sense to me. They seemed really close, and then... she touched his arm.

And he laughed and let her touch it.

Max's eyes didn't waver from hers and nor did hers from his. It was evident this was fate, and both were thrilled it had occurred.

I was less thrilled; I felt really tired. I was overcome with disappointment and wanted to escape.

How had I not seen this from the beginning?

Max wasn't interested in me, he only saw me as a friend, or even a client he was helping out with a computer project. The girls he went for were the Shelly types – the athletic types who looked as hot in boy's clothes as they did in girl's. Not the me types, whose idea of fun was hanging out in a library and reading books on how to hide your pregnancy.

His voice snapped me back to reality, '...isn't that great?'

I hadn't heard anything before that but assumed he was telling me all the great things about Shelly that were already going through my head.

'Sure. Hey, I've got an emergency I have to attend to.'

'No worries,' he replied, no doubt thrilled I was leaving he and Shelly alone. 'If you have any ideas give me a call.'

He meant for the project but the only idea I had for him was to dig a hole, climb into it and never get out.

There was no hug or kiss on the cheek, he simply allowed me to walk off, which then allowed my mind to lash me with insults, one after the other.

Why couldn't you have gone back to the Old Treasury Building steps? Shelly would never have been there you idiot.

Surely they would have run into one another at some point.

Having exited the café, I stopped and looked back, as if to accept the realness of what had happened.

Max and I were never going to be together. I needed to find somebody else.

10.

How was it the radio knew how I was feeling and played just the song to make me feel worse?

Sitting in the back seat on an Uber, the classic hits station the middle-aged female driver had the dial on played *It Must Have Been Love* by Roxette. It really did rub salt into the wounds of a dreadful last twenty-five minutes.

My bitterness and disappointment lasted the whole car trip home – all five minutes of it. It wasn't until the driver pulled up outside my unit that I remembered what I was actually doing. If my flat had been broken into, shouldn't I have called the police?

It had been almost fifteen minutes between the break-in and me getting there, so surely whomever he or she was, was long gone by now.

But they weren't.

'What the hell are you doing here?'

The fly-wire and front door were wide open, and in the living room were four clothes draws lying on the floor and my sister peering over them.

'Trying to find that top you borrowed from me six months ago,' Katie said.

'So you break into my apartment to find a top?'

'I've lost my key somewhere at home, plus, I called you and you didn't answer.'

And she didn't think to leave a message?

'What, you've never forgotten to do something because you weren't thinking straight?'

She did have a point, and a fine way of getting inside the apartment without doing any damage at all.

'I build caravans; I know how to break into a house. Now where is that top?'

She was talking about a blouse I hadn't borrowed, but rather she'd left at my place having drunkenly spilt wine on it the last time she came over.

'And I'll probably spill wine on it again tonight.'

That's what the urgency was – she needed the top because she had plans; something that was no doubt another run of the mill party.

'Not just any party, your party; its tonight.'

Hannah had failed to inform her my party had been cancelled due to me having found a man myself. The party's cancellation was something we both now detested, as that very man I'd found, I'd since lost.

'She did tell me you cancelled on her, but she also told me she'd already organised it, so was going through with it anyway.'

'What?' Hannah's still going through with it? My party's still happening?'

'Yes, hence my urgency.'

'Urgency for what time?'

'6pm.'

It was four o'clock; how the hell was I going to be ready in time?

'Thank God your sister broke into your apartment and is standing here ready to help right now.'

Help I'd only get once she found her blouse.

Spotting something in one of the draws, she leant down and pulled it out from the stash of clothing. 'My top! It's party time baby.'

Party time it was.

11.

That radio thing again.

The clean version of *She Hates Me* by Puddle Of Mudd played on Katie's car radio.

She drove with a hateful look on her face – we were running late to the party and she wasn't happy about it. Hannah got festivities underway early because she wanted everyone out by midnight, so it wasn't entirely my fault.

'You were in the bathroom shaving your legs for over an hour,' Katie exclaimed.

Okay, it was entirely my fault. 'I had to go slow; the last time I did it in ten minutes and I had cuts all up and down my legs.'

'You didn't need to shave your legs at all; you're wearing an ankle length cocktail dress.'

I could have argued I shaved them because I was going to get some action, but we both knew I wasn't that kind of girl.

It was a six-hundred metre walk over the railway from my place to Hannah's, but the afternoon sea breeze had picked up and would have messed up our hair. We drove, but being late, we ended up parking on Nepean Highway about six hundred metres from Hannah's house anyway. I expected further scorn from Katie at us having to walk so far but her mood softened the closer we got to the party.

'Thank God Roy likes looking at men as much as I do.'

After a long week of work, Roy had stayed home to watch sport on TV. Like Brett, he wasn't the biggest party animal.

'Hannah tells me there are going to be so many hot guys at this party.'

My lack of response was due to me being scared witless at having to approach the "so many hot guys at this party", but Katie thought

I was sneering because of her insinuation she was going to cheat on Roy.

'I'm kidding; there's nothing wrong with a quick perve when the boys aren't around. I'll never act on it. You and I will be the taken girls for the night.'

'Um...'

There was no reason to hide the truth – I wasn't a "taken" girl anymore. In fact, I had never been a "taken" girl.

Katie wanted details but I wasn't eager to relive them, so I told her the basics of what had happened – Max only saw me as a friend.

'And he's keen on someone else,' she guessed.

'Yes, he's keen on someone else,' I confirmed.

'I bet she's a tramp.'

I could always rely on Katie to have my back.

'Who needs him? There'll be plenty of guys at this party who don't see you as just a friend. Remember, Han and I are doing all this to help you find someone, and that's what's going to happen.'

After walking down the front drive, she opened the front door and allowed me to enter ahead of her. As evidenced by all the cars parked on the property, Hannah's place was packed; there were people everywhere – it was like a scene out of *The Great Gatsby*. She had giant lights installed, a champagne tower, a red carpet with a backdrop where people could have their photo taken, and a DJ on a stage with what looked like designated dancing girls either side of him.

I could hardly believe it; Hannah flew off the handle at one of her good towels being used yet she'd invited this many people into her home and risked it being turned into a rubbish tip.

Moving further inside I spotted a number of signs taped to the walls. Each one of them had a viral image and a stern message on it.

That's more like Hannah.

There was a poster of a shirtless Vladimir Putin that read – If you break it, you pay for it.

A poster of Kim Kardashian with champagne that read – if you spill something on it, you pay for it.

A poster of John Travolta's awkward kiss on Scarlet Johansson's cheek that read – If you leave any kind of weird mark on it, you pay for it.

And a poster of a pregnant Beyoncé that read – If you make a baby on it, you pay for it.

There was also one last sign; it was much bigger and was roped from one side of the main party room to the other. It read – Tinderella Wants A Fella.

'I came up with that,' Katie bragged. 'Get It? Cinderella, Tinder-Ella?'

I got it; it was quite clever.

'We better go and tell Hannah we're here,' she said.

She walked over to the stand the DJ was playing at. He helped pull her up, cut the music and handed her a microphone. It was evident she had no intention of telling Hannah we'd arrived – she was intent on letting the entire party know she had.

The crowd paused as she introduced herself. 'Ladies and gentlemen, my name is Katie and thank-you for attending my party.'

A few hostile looks from the partygoers made her realise her introduction and shameless self-promotion wasn't welcome, so she changed her tune.

'I'd like to let you know that – Tinderella is here.'

She pointed directly at me, which prompted every single partygoer to turn towards me and give me the same stare.

They didn't clap or cheer but stared, in silence. Maybe they were just annoyed she'd interrupted them having a good time.

I raised my hand and softly said, 'Hi.'

'She is here to find a man, so let's make sure that happens okay?'

I expected Katie's inspiring welcome to actually be Hannah's inspiring welcome, with it being her party, but also expected if Katie got up there, she'd raucously fire up the crowd in a similar manner to Leonardo DiCaprio in *The Wolf Of Wall Street*.

She concluded with something of a genteel-like tone of voice...

'Now you may all go back to your conversations. And have a fizzing good night.' ... Handed back the microphone and allowed the DJ to turn the music back up.

It didn't take long for Hannah to arrive on the scene and let her feelings known. "Fizzing good night'? Who says that? And why were you stealing my moment?'

The party was wild. I chatted up countless men, danced, had loads of drinks and was wildly popular.

By the early hours of the morning however, after six hours of full on partying, I was exhausted, so retreated to Hannah's room for a rest. I'd only been in there ten minutes when the door flung open and slammed shut.

'What the hell are you doing in here?'

It was Hannah.

Sitting on her bed, I lifted the book I was reading. 'This is actually a really good read.'

It was *Charlotte's Web* and it was Justin's, but it was still a good read.

'I don't care; you've been at this party fifteen minutes and you're already hiding away from everyone?'

Okay – the stuff about chatting up countless men, being wildly popular and retreating after six hours wasn't one hundred per cent true. I'd retreated shortly after arriving, unable to deal with the nerves that stemmed from having to introduce myself to men I didn't know.

Men full stop really.

'Well you're not sitting in here all night if that's what you were thinking.'

That's exactly what I was thinking. 'I need to warm into it. Or have somebody help me,' I explained, but also pleaded.

That "somebody", of course, was her.

'You want me to hold your hand as you walk around the room and say hello to people?'

I saw it more as her introducing me to people, but yes, that was exactly what I wanted her to do. 'It's the approach I need you to help me with, then you can leave me and the hot guy alone; whoever he is.'

She drank the rest of her glass as if to sedate herself from the impending pain. 'All right, but we need to stop by the champagne tower on the way.'

There were so many faces in the crowd I knew but couldn't quite put a name to. There were actors, models, footballers, comedians, fashion designers and a handful of reality stars and starlets who looked sloppy and drunk already.

'Is that Jimmy who came runner-up in that singing contest show?' I asked.

'Yes and no; yes it is, and no I don't want you going up and talking to him; there are better guys here.'

I looked at Jimmy and found that hard to believe. Han turned and looked over to the other side of the room. 'Ah, I know which guy I want you to meet.'

Before meeting him, we made our way across to the champagne tower. Instead of taking a glass, she lifted a huge bottle off the top and handed it to me. It was open and smelt really good.

'That's because it's eight-hundred dollars-worth of champagne; drink a glass now and then re-fill so you've got a glass to approach with.'

I hesitated; it wasn't that I didn't want to drink it; it was that I didn't think it was the best move to scull a glass of champagne right before meeting a guy.

'You always look at things the wrong way. Who's the most confident woman in the world?' she asked.

'Hillary Clinton?'

She looked at me like that was the wrong answer, probably because it was. 'All right, well, with this champagne in your system, you'll be like Hillary Clinton to every man in this room.'

Okay, it was definitely the wrong answer. She must have meant like Cindy Crawford or J-Lo.

She took me by the arm and led me over to two gentlemen dressed like they belonged at the polo, not a party. One was older and worn while the other was younger, cute and smelt like he used aftershave that was as expensive as the champagne I was holding.

'Ella this is Brad, he's a record label executive. Brad, this is my little sister Ella, she designs toys all over the world and she's also Tinderella.'

That was a blatant lie; I worked with toys but didn't design them. Still, Brad didn't see through the lie and was instead extremely impressed by it. I didn't feel right lying but at least Hannah's lie had put me in an area I had plenty of expertise in. So I went with it and then lied about other things.

'You design toys? That's impressive.'

'And I'm only twenty-seven.'

When required to speak truthfully and articulately I was a gibbering idiot, but when it came to the art of dishonesty, I was a champion. Maybe Hannah was right – maybe it was the champagne.

Brad and I didn't speak very long. Ten minutes later Hannah yanked me by the arm, still holding the gigantic champagne bottle, and led me over to another guy who was in advertising.

'You design toys? That's impressive.'

'And I'm only twenty-six.'

A wandering photographer walked past and took our photo. He'd been taking snaps of me all night.

After that she led me to another guy who was the son of a big supplement exporter, then another guy who had won millions playing poker around the world, and then another guy who had a multi-million dollar property portfolio and was often in the social pages of the newspaper, spruiking his latest purchase with a gorgeous woman by his side.

'I'll call you next time I buy and am about to have my photo taken.'

I certainly enjoyed meeting all these men; Hannah had done well. They were all handsome and successful, but they were also surprisingly grounded and polite.

I was conversing confidently with one of them when Katie took the DJ's microphone and again interrupted the party.

'Sup all you peeps. Is this party cray-cray or what?!'

She was drunk, and unlike her first address, was now in full Leonardo DiCaprio *Wolf Of Wall Street* mode.

'This is going to be the greatest party ever, are you with me?'

The partygoers raised their arms and cheered. With alcohol in their system, they too had let their hair down. Katie raised her arms but lost her balance and leant on the DJ.

She then spotted me in the crowd next to Hannah and pointed at me.

'There's my girl Tinderella. This is her party. Are we gonna help her get some man-love tonight or what?'

Hannah briskly walked over to the DJ stand and pulled her away from the microphone, but not before she could solicit one last cheer from the partygoers.

The DJ then turned the music back on.

I made my way over to them. Before I even reached them I could hear Hannah reprimanding her.

'What are you doing?'

'Talking to my fans.'

'This party is two hours old and you're already drunk?'

Hannah was really unimpressed and wasn't about to be embarrassed any further – Katie's Tinderella party experience had started late but was finishing early.

'In my room now; I don't want to see you out here for the rest of the night.'

I expected Katie to put up a fight, but she didn't; she trudged off in the direction of Hannah's room.

I thought it was fair enough; these were Hannah's loyal friends and contacts, and she didn't want anything jeopardising that.

Hannah introduced me to several other eligible bachelors in the hours following. She topped up my glass before each one however, which meant I was quickly heading in the same direction as Katie – back to Hannah's bedroom.

Feeling exhausted and rather tipsy I instead headed for the backyard and a bench seat, in search of some fresh air.

I wasn't alone for long.

'Tinderella, I was hoping we'd cross paths.'

This time it wasn't a handsome and successful male, but a woman, casually dressed in a sweatshirt and jeans.

'I'm a friend of your sisters; we've known each other for years.'

She sat down next to me and placed her phone, screen down, in between us. 'Having a good night?'

Having drunk six glasses of eight-hundred-dollar champagne it was a fair assumption. She continued with her questions.

'Good to hear; so what's this party all about?'

'Hannah didn't tell you?'

'She's been so held up.'

Through tipsy eyes she looked trustworthy enough, so I told her. She was very inquisitive and then simply shook my hand, wished me a good night, said something to the guy taking all the photos and left.

Must have another party to get to, I didn't even get her name.

Not that that was the first time that had happened.

Katie stumbled over. I realised why she didn't put up a fight when Hannah sent her to her room for the night – because she never intended on going, and never actually went.

She was just as drunk as before and as a result struggled getting her phone out of her pocket. 'I phoned my photo phone.'

'What?'

'I mean, I took a photo with my phone. Phones can do that did you know? Let me show you the photo I took.'

She did so; it was hard to make out what it was.

'It's grass; I took a photo of the grass. Cool.'

'That is cool.'

She sat down next to me and found the composure to ask me how my night was going.

'Good; I even organised a month's supply of protein powder from that supplements guy for you.'

She sat back, pointed at me with glee and then hugged me. 'I love you.'

'I love you too.'

'No, but I love you. I'm going to take you the best photo ever. Even better than the grass.'

Why she wanted to take photos for me I didn't know.

She lowered her head on my shoulder. It was definitely time she called it a night. I encouraged her to take her phone and have a lie down on Hannah's bed. I thought she'd take some convincing, but she propped up from her doze as if she'd just discovered electricity.

'I could take a photo of the linen!'

She moved off in the direction of Hannah's bedroom, but this time did walk into it.

Katie calling it a night was a relief; if Hannah had seen her back out amongst the party, she would have lost the plot.

Not long after Katie was out of sight, did Hannah come across. 'There you are.'

I could have sworn she had consumed as much champagne as I had, yet she was well and truly more sober. She did attend parties on a far more regular basis than me though, so perhaps her body and brain had acclimatised.

Instead of taking me inside the house again, she led me to the other side of the yard, but stopped. 'Desmond must have moved; don't go anywhere, I'll go and find him and be right back.'

I did as she said although didn't care much for Desmond because with a name like Desmond he was probably a nerd with three nipples.

'Hey,' came a voice from behind me.

It was a voice I recognised, and a face I loved, when I turned around and saw who it was.

'It's Tinderella, isn't it?'

'Hey Jimmy, I'm Ella.'

Bizarrely – which I could only put down to my alcohol consumption – I was playing it cool, even though Jimmy was really hot and really single.

'You're hot. Do you have a Hot, Hot Jimmy Folder in your phone? Because you should have one?'

Okay, I wasn't playing it that cool, but still, he was into me.

'You're hot too. I reckon we should be hot together; you ready?'

By 'hot together,' I fully thought he meant go down to the back of the backyard and make-out, but he meant pose together for a photograph. The pesky photographer again bobbed up and took a snap of us. Hannah then returned.

'What a surprise to see you down here; get lost Jimmy.' She gave him a kiss on the cheek – which demonstrated she was only playing with him – and he left.

She handed me another glass of champagne and drank from the other she held.

'He's probably been waiting for a girl to come down to the back of the yard for the last half hour. You don't want him; he'll be on the scrapheap in twelve months.'

'And Desmond won't be?'

'Desmond's a lung surgeon, and I couldn't find him because he took the girl who's on this month's Bras And Things™ ad home to inspect her airways.'

That was too much information.

She finished the rest of her drink, encouraged me to, and held out her hand to take me back inside. 'Come on, I found someone else for you to meet instead. We have swing by the champagne tower first though.'

I could feel the pillow marks on my face when I woke and lifted my head the next morning. I was still fully clothed but only had one heel on, presumably because I'd lost the other during the party. I would have found the Cinderella/Tinderella lost shoe coincidence funny, if not for a throbbing headache, and a couple of sore ribs.

Had I been cage-fighting the night before?

No.

Despite having the boys' rooms and two other spare rooms in the house, Hannah, Katie and I all slept in Hannah's bed. As I slept in the middle, the sore ribs were the result of Hannah and Katie's elbows digging into me, as they fought for more space on the bed.

That Cinderella coincidence again, I thought. My two evil stepsisters, who were actually my blood sisters, had deprived me of sleep and caused pain to my body.

I raised that body gingerly off the bed, took my other heel off and opened Han's bedroom door to find the rest of her house absolutely spotless.

After the carnage of the night prior, how was it not a pigsty?

From the kitchen came a man with a vacuum-pack on his back and a vacuum hose in his hand. He was overweight with a beard, wore cargo shorts five sizes too big and an I'm A Gleek™ t-shirt. He was one of the cleaners and one of the reasons why Hannah's house was immaculately clean. They'd been at the house since sunrise fixing it up before Brett and the kids arrived home from his parents' place.

For a second, I wondered how Hannah, Katie and I had slept

through all the noise but remembered soundproof walls surrounded Hannah and Brett's bedroom.

'Oh My God, it's you,' the overweight Gleek-man cleaner said, having spotted me. 'I have to get a selfie.'

He grabbed his phone from the pocket of his cargo shorts and hurried over with his vac-pack. There in all my ugliness I stood as he opened his camera, stuck the phone in our faces and took the picture. Only, he hadn't turned the flash off, and when the blinding light came shooting out, I was reminded of the raging headache and hangover I had. He then walked out the front door and I headed to the kitchen for some coffee.

The fridge door was hard to miss. Someone – clearly Katie – had rearranged the magnetic letters to read 'Jimmy is babes' – with the second m actually an upside-down w – and there was a piece of scrap paper under a magnet with a whole lot of phone numbers on it. Brad the record label executive's number was on it, as was every other guy's I'd met the night before. At the top of the list read the heading – Phone Numbers For Tinderella.

I couldn't even recall the list-making part of the night happening.

I finished making coffee but as I went to grasp the mug, a hand beat me to it.

'Good morning.'

It was Hannah and I figured it was only fair I let her have it, considering what she'd done for me the night before.

If she weren't my sister, I would have found it impossible to interpret her feelings towards me. She never listened, was self-absorbed and rarely gave verbal support, but her actions had again spoken loudly as she'd thrown the best party ever, and it was all for me.

She also had magic powers – she'd drunk a spa bath's worth of alcohol the night before yet bounced around the morning after like she'd enjoyed the pleasures of a relaxing... spa bath.

'Do I get a coffee as well?' Katie asked, slowly creeping in like the

Hunchback Of Notre Dame.

'Not until you've checked out the back,' Hannah said.

'Out the back for what?'

Hannah didn't trust her cleaners; she wanted us to each inspect a part of the house to ensure the place was clean, and nothing had been stolen, for when Brett and the kids got home.

'Which is in twenty-five minutes, so move it.'

She headed out the front, the Hunchback Of Notre Katie took herself out the back and I carried my beaten-up body and throbbing head around to every room in the house.

The house was sparkling clean. Inspecting a windowsill in the second living room that hadn't been used the night before, the only risk of something unhygienic arising was me being sick all over the floor; a circumstance that was becoming more and more likely due to the sunlight shining through the window.

Through the window I observed Katie in the backyard; she wasn't even bothering to look around but was instead on her phone. She giggled, and giggled some more, and then went all serious-face and charged back towards the house.

I went to meet her to find out what she was reacting to.

'Okay something's not right,' she said, as she re-entered through the back door.

She held up her phone in front of my face and showed me what she was looking at. It was an Instagram account with my name on it, approximately fifteen photos underneath and 150,000 followers.

I didn't even know I had an Instagram account.

'I set it up for you; I told you I was going to. I did it the other day and I checked it yesterday and you had one follower – and it was me. I took some photos for you last night and uploaded them straight away, but they weren't very good. I mean – I don't even know what that is.'

She showed me a picture – it was the photo of the grass she'd taken. The photo of the grass, and her saying she wanted to take photos for me, suddenly made sense – it was for my Instagram.

She checked the account again as if to try and figure out what had caused the change. I didn't really get why that was so wrong, but she explained.

'It took me eighteen months to get one hundred and fifty thousand Instagram followers; it's taken you twelve hours; we have to have been hacked.'

'You haven't been hacked.'

Hannah came back through the front door reading the newspaper she'd collected from the front yard. She walked over to us and revealed why the account hadn't been hacked – the social pages of the newspaper had an unmistakable photo of Jimmy and I in Hannah's backyard, and above it read the heading – *Tinderella Wants A Fella*.

'She stole my line,' Katie said.

'Worse, she quoted Ella. We could take legal action against her for writing things you didn't say.'

I read the quotes –

This party is to help me find a man.

I can't seem to find "the one" and I really want to.

I've never been in love and I just want to fall in love once.

For some reason the quotes rang a bell, and then I remembered why – that was what I'd told the girl in the sweatshirt and jeans when she questioned me the night before. She'd put her phone down in between us to record me and then wrote an article on me, and the party of the year.

'She didn't tell you she was recording you; we can still take action.'

There was no need. Thankfully – despite my drunkenness – she hadn't been horrible in writing about me. If anything, she'd promoted me as Australia's Tinderella – the most single, single gal, in all of Singletown. And someone the whole country should be barracking for to fall in love.

But I still didn't understand why I suddenly had so many

Instagram followers.

'You really are dumb, aren't you?' Katie said.

'No just really hung-over.'

'One hundred and fifty thousand people have read this newspaper article and decided to follow you on Instagram.'

Okay, maybe I was dumb, but what were we to do now, delete my Instagram? Hide in Hannah's house like it was a bomb shelter in case any more newspapers rang?

Hannah's mobile rang, and she answered it. She listened to whoever it was and whatever they were offering and then said, 'I'll have to call you back.'

It sounded like another newspaper.

'Magazine actually.'

'What do they want?' I asked.

'I need time to think.'

'We... need time to think, you mean.'

As part-party planner, Katie took offence to Hannah's use of the word "I".

Hannah in turn took offence to Katie taking offence. 'What expertise do you have here?'

'I helped start this crusade to help end Ella's single life; I came up with the party name, I set up the Instagram account, I have a hand at this table.'

'All right, fine. Help me think of what we should do next.'

Katie had a point and Hannah knew it, but both ladies knew thinking time came a distant second to something else.

'I think I need a coffee first.'

'I think I need another one too.'

12.

Hannah and Katie sat at an outside table at Main Street Café in Mordialloc, drinking coffee and scribbling on a napkin. I needed more than just coffee; returning with food from the other side of the road, they stared at me like I was eating ice cubes on a freezing winter's day.

It was only a Rod and Reel Combo from Tommy Ruff™.

'Fish, scallops and squid after a night of drinking, how?' Hannah asked.

Katie reached in, picked up the piece of fish and took a bite out of it. 'This is how.'

I appreciated her sticking up for me, but did she really have to eat my food?

I sat down and changed the topic. I now had 180,000 Instagram followers and counting. I was keen to let my fifteen minutes of fame play out, if only to see how high my following would get, but also saw the negative side to it – people would get bored of me quickly and become unmannerly.

I assumed that's what Hannah would be thinking so made my decision accordingly. 'I think it's a bad idea.'

'I think it's a good idea,' Katie replied.

Her enthusiasm didn't surprise me; she'd always been happy to try new things. But Hannah had more expertise when it came to fame and publicity, and I fully expected her to agree with me.

'Come on, Han, I'm not sure we should—'

'I think it's a good idea too.'

What?

She also thought logic first, and for that reason I couldn't figure out why she thought it was a good idea.

'Because you'll get what you want.'

I felt like playing stupid and telling her I didn't want to be famous, but I knew what she meant – love.

'Hannah's right,' Katie said. 'We were semi-serious about this before, but now that it's happened, let's be serious. You said you don't want to be alone anymore; you want someone who'll genuinely love you and look after you, well this might help you find him. He might even find you. Be your honest, kind-hearted, loveable self and then when you've found him thank everyone for their interest and support, and drift back into the wilderness with the love of your life.'

Half-an-hour earlier Katie had been too hung-over to speak; now she had produced a soliloquy Cate Blanchett would have been proud of.

'Coffee saves lives,' she joked.

I still wasn't one hundred per cent convinced, and it was because of one overriding feeling.

'It's okay to fear,' Hannah said, having read me like a book. 'But it's also okay to believe in yourself and it's okay to make changes to your life. And that's what you'll be doing. If you do it for the fame then people will react badly, but if you say and do nice things for others, wear your heart on your sleeve and be true to whom you are, people will like you.'

Another soliloquy, the second just as convincing as the first.

'Okay,' I told them.

The decision had been made; I was going to give Tinderella a shot and I was going to find my guy, but not before one last piece of advice from Hannah.

'And remember to always be honest. Especially when you're scanning my house after the cleaners have left.'

'What did I miss?'

'The words 'Jimmy is babes' written on my refrigerator.'

Her glare turned to Katie as she said it.

If I was being honest then I had failed to remove the stupid message Katie left on Hannah's fridge. But if I was being honest full stop, then I wasn't going to find Mr Right with just the occasional newspaper article and a legion of Instagram followers.

I needed extra help.

13.

The things you don't notice when you're hooked on social media.

Katie had helped me link my Instagram account with my Facebook account, and helped me upload my first Snapchat video. She'd made me say the words, 'He's out there somewhere, I just need to find him', and used an effects app that saw stars and a few planets circle around my head. I actually thought it made me look like a space cadet.

Instagram needed updating as well. In addition to the photos from the party, Katie and I put up a few photos of me with Justin and Brody, her and I having a drink at a bar and the two of us shopping. In the four days following the party, I'd managed to rack up 232,467 Instagram followers, and that number grew every five minutes. Yep – that's how often I was checking this thing.

I was hooked; sometimes I checked it every two minutes and despite no change to the followers count or the comments, I checked it two minutes later and then two minutes after that. The comments made me feel good, well liked and warm and fuzzy on the inside. Except for one of the photos Katie happened to be in with me. It had received the most comments, but mainly by men who wrote, "Ur Sis is Sizz", "Ur Sis is bangin" and "I be bangin' your Sizz Sis". In fact that was the same guy, and I think "sizz" meant sizzling.

I rewarded myself by getting an Uber to Tiffany's and refreshed the page every two minutes to see what changes had occurred. So fixated was I, I barely noticed a great change that had occurred beside Tiffany's house. The crabby shack was gone from next door and all that was left was an empty block of land.

She had said something about a demolition.

It was kind of symbolic – her neighbouring house, like my love life, was getting rebuilt.

Rudely, I kept checking my phone during the appointment as well. Tiffany called me out on it, and I apologised. We spent the first half-an-hour doing what I thought we were going to do during session one – going through the folder. The first few pages related to self-analysis; there were two islands with a bridge in between; I was on the "avoiders" island, not the "seekers" island, even though I thought my real position was probably half-way across the bridge. Tiffany told me by the end of our sessions together I'd be on the "seekers" island.

We also talked about my voice and how it was important to be articulate; say "going to", instead of "gonna", not to use the word "like" so often, and not finish every sentence with the word "y'know". We talked about how to deal with anxiety, exhibiting the right body language and asking questions and being truthful if I didn't know much about the topic of conversation. Of course, we were just scratching the surface; we'd delve into all topics in greater detail as the sessions rolled along.

'Okay time for a game.'

Liam was back, well not back, because it was his home too, but he was there again, sitting in the kitchen in nothing but a pair of football shorts and a singlet, and eating cereal from the box.

Breakfast at Tiffany's. That's cute.

'Any chance you could get some food, woman,' he said cheekily, as Tiffany and I entered the kitchen.

It was no wonder he bought bodybuilding magazines; he was quite muscular for a young guy.

Tiffany ignored him and instead spoke to me, 'Ella, there's a plate on the kitchen bench; take two items from the refrigerator, any two items, place them on the plate and bring them over here to the kitchen table.'

I opened the fridge and understood what Liam meant by, "get some food, woman"; there was only a carton of eggs and a punnet of strawberries in there. I put one of each on the plate and then put the plate down on the table.

'Ella, I want you to use one of those two items as a way of breaking the ice with Liam. Remember, it's banter, it doesn't have to be perfect, it's just a game.'

I looked at the strawberry and nothing came to me, so I switched my focus to the egg and thought of something brilliant straight away. 'Hi Liam, I'm Ella, do you like eggs?'

Liam looked at me, looked at his mother and then looked back at me, 'Sure.'

Okay, so it wasn't that brilliant. In fact, I'd stuffed my introduction up completely, but I wasn't exactly sure what Tiffany meant. She ordered Liam to go next, to give me an idea of what I should be saying.

He picked up the egg and with manufactured sadness, said, 'Only one of us has been laid in the last six weeks, see if you can guess which one.'

He came up with that on the spot? I was impressed by his wit but also half-tempted to tell him six weeks wasn't that long; I hadn't been "laid" in... okay, yeah, I didn't need to go there.

'Your go, Ella,' Tiffany told me, nodding to the lone strawberry on the plate.

I picked it up, stared at it a few moments and then said the first thing that came to mind, 'Strawberry cream in my pants.'

It was bad; I knew it was bad, and the way Tiffany looked at me, told me she knew it was bad.

'Try again, love,' she said simply, trying to keep any confidence I had left at a reasonable level.

I glared at the strawberry and thought. Not about what to say, but about what technique I could use to prevent another vulgar response. For some reason my childhood came into my mind.

Growing up, I could never smile in photos. Then one of my aunts told me the secret to getting it right – I should look off to the side right until the very moment the flash was about to go off, and then turn towards the camera. That way I'd have no time to think about smiling, but just turn and smile. I thought I'd try it with the strawberry.

I turned to the right and stared at the kitchen wall, and then turned back to the strawberry and spoke. But it didn't work, and I said something stupid again.

'Strawberry jam in my pants.'

First cream and now jam? What was it with me and my own pants?

Following a second failure, I felt completely gutted. It was only a game, but I was desperate to get it right. If I couldn't excel with a strawberry, how could I excel with a real man?

With my head in my hands I felt Tiffany's hand touch the back of mine.

'It's all right, Ella, it's okay. Remove the expectation, be aware of your surroundings, and be aware of how you feel. And then tell Liam something about the strawberry.'

She'd managed to settle me, which I appreciated. I was also much more in touch with my feelings and ready to make things right. There was no wall-staring this time, no thought of pants, just my heart on my sleeve and an expression of what I wanted most in life.

'Strawberry fields are forever and I'm hoping you and I can be the same.'

'Good,' Tiffany said.

But I kept staring at Liam and went again. 'Strawberries grow on trees, but guys like you... not so much.'

I wasn't even sure if strawberries did grow on trees.

'That was good too,' he replied.

I kept going again, but began talking about strawberries rather than delivering one-liners about them.

'Have you ever had a strawberry milkshake where the bits of strawberry get stuck in the straw? And you're like, "they are called strawberries, so they probably belong in the straw", but then you make it your mission to suck the bits up, and when you finally do it's like you've conquered all the villains in the world?'

Liam looked at me like we'd been panning for gold and I'd found a gold rock the size of a meteoroid.

'That has happened to me before. That was a very good conversation starter.'

'Except you said the word "like" twice,' Tiffany added with a smile.

Liam put the cereal box down on the table and stood to head off, 'I've got to get some things from the hardware store. Good to see you smiling instead of crying today, Ella Bang.'

Tiffany also rose and left the room, as if Liam's farewell had reminded her of something. When she returned, she handed me two envelopes, one white and one yellow – it was another exercise.

'I want you to keep the contents of the white envelope beside your bed, while I want you to leave the contents of the yellow one at the bus stop. You made good progress today, it's all positive from here.'

The white envelope had a piece of paper in it with the word "belief" written on it, while the yellow envelope had a piece of paper with the word "doubt" written on it. I got it – she wanted me to leave my doubts at the bus stop.

'Think you can do that, Tinderella?'

From the envelopes I looked straight up at her, surprised. *She knew about Tinderella? We'd gone through the whole session and she'd known the entire time?*

'You think I don't read the newspapers, lovey? Don't worry, I think it's charming, but I think it could easily come unstuck if you don't make the right moves.'

With my newfound fame I wasn't overly keen on getting the bus home, but with yellow envelope in hand, she'd left me no choice. I ripped some tape off an advertising poster and stuck the piece of paper on the glass of the bus shelter. Through the glass I noticed a photographer take numerous snaps from a nearby bush.

How weird will that look in tomorrow's paper? Kylie Minogue stuns in red dress, Nicole Kidman with adorable daughter, Tinderella sticks the word "doubt" on a bus stop.

Seated on the bus, I was getting looks left, right and centre, but tried to convince myself it was because I was being squashed by two overweight men sitting either side of me with their man-spread. For some reason, only then did I realise I'd foregone my Instagram obsession for an hour-and-a-half and I could use it again to save me from this uncomfortable situation.

My follower count had grown again and there were a few extra comments, but for the first time, there was a comment underneath one of the photos that wasn't so nice.

Geoffrey_awesome_dog142 @Tinderella Your body looks like a stack of pancakes with a turkey head on top of it #gobblegobble.

His name was stupid, and his description of my body made no sense, but his comment still hurt my feelings. I was tempted to write something back but chose to ignore him. I instead studied my photos to see if my body did look like a stack of pancakes. One of them did; I didn't look like a whole stack, maybe just two or three pancakes, but I wasn't happy with how I looked.

Maybe I needed a gym session with Katie, maybe that would fix it. But I didn't have time. I needed to get back to the toy store.

As I studied my photos further, I got the feeling the two overweight men beside me were rudely sticky-beaking in on my business, so I closed my phone down. To avoid making accidental eye contact with them, I looked out the opposite window and saw we were getting close to Southland shopping centre.

Interesting.

I stood and pushed the button to get off. An idea had come to me as a way of enhancing my social media profile and fixing my "pancake" image, and this time I didn't need Katie or Hannah's help.

14.

I really should have asked for Katie or Hannah's help.

What I'd done had seen me feature in the newspaper and online again, but not in a good way.

In my eyes, it was a silly mistake.

'This is the stupidest thing anyone in the world has ever done,' Katie said. 'We go to all this trouble to make you an innocent, genuine, lost in love little poppet and you go and ruin it in one fell swoop. I can't believe it.'

I had a perfectly reasonable explanation that would help Katie understand everything. 'Geoffrey_awesome_dog's comment hurt.'

'Who the hell is Geoffrey Awesome Dog?'

Okay, it didn't help her understand, but it was still a perfectly reasonable explanation. Geoff dog's comment hurt because it was true. I looked ugly in my photos, so I'd decided to do something about them. I got off the bus I was on, went into an electronics store at Southland and bought Photoshop™. I then spent the rest of that day at the toy store trying to make my stomach more toned, my legs skinnier and my boobs look bigger in a particular photo, and then posted it on Instagram. Twenty-four hours on and that photo had been put in the newspaper, had been talked about on radio and had Katie blowing up like it was the end of the world.

'Hannah's going to kill you, you know that, don't you?'

She dropped the newspaper on the coffee table between us.

'You know how she gets when you use her good towels or when I eat her ice cream; times that by ten – that's what she's going to be like.'

She was right; she – Katie – rarely lost her cool, so if she lost her cool over something, Hannah was definitely going to be angry.

'Relax it's not that bad,' Hannah said, as she joined us in her living room.

'What?!' we both responded rather loudly. Me with surprised relief, Katie with just surprise.

'Shhh, it's taken me twenty-five minutes to put Brody down. If you wake him, I won't just kill Ella, I'll kill you both.'

Hannah had the ears of a fox, and she came across and sat next to Katie.

'You haven't seen this have you?' Katie asked, and pointed to the newspaper.

'I've read it three times, I've seen the *Daily Mail* article, plus others, and I first heard about it on the radio this morning.'

'And you think it's not that bad?'

Hannah shook her head.

Katie persisted somewhat graphically, 'She's photoshopped the photo that badly her left leg is coming out of her vagina.'

I couldn't help but snigger.

'You think this is funny?'

She was getting wound up over nothing; well not nothing but wound up that Hannah wasn't as aggrieved as what she was.

'Katie, it's all right, trust me. For this one and only time, go and eat some of my ice cream out of the fridge and chill.'

Katie took a deep breath, 'Fine, you're right, I'll take a step back. And yes, I would like some ice cream.'

She headed into the kitchen. For a second, I thought the last minute-and-a-half was all an act from Hannah, and now with Katie out of the room, she was going to drop the curtains and really let me have it.

'It's drop the mask not drop the curtains hun', and no I'm not going to let you have it; this is actually a piece of genius from you.'

Genius? What? How? How was it genius?

'But that was just step one.'

Step one? What was step two? Photoshop all the photos?

Hannah told me how one manipulated photo could be publicity gold but also how I could make so much more of it if I played my cards right over the next few days. Through a contact, she was going to organise a radio interview over the phone for the following morning and have me explain everything that had happened. The best part about it was I was going to tell the truth – I, like many women, had found it hard to accept the way I looked, and when a bully wrote a mean comment on my Instagram, I went to extreme yet foolish levels to paint myself in a better light. The bullying, the expectation so many men had, and the pressures to conform had become so much I'd looked past what really mattered – what was on the inside. I was to apologise to young girls for being a poor role model and encourage everyone to be the best version of themselves they could be.

'I heard Katie call you an "innocent, genuine, lost in love little poppet",' Hannah added. 'Be that girl, admit to your error, learn your lesson and then let me move things forward so your admirers have something new to talk about.'

I liked and agreed with everything she said but found myself doing a double take and questioning the very last part. 'What do you mean "move things forward"?'

'I've organised a date for you,' she revealed.

Having improved my conversation skills with Tiffany, I was keen to hear more details, but Katie beat me to it.

'Which guy is it?' she asked, as she re-entered with the biggest bowl of ice cream she'd ever made.

'How the hell did you get that out?' Hannah asked. 'I put a padlock on the freezer door and deliberately invited you to help yourself to the ice cream so for once you'd be disappointed you couldn't have any.'

'I got a screwdriver from out the back and took the whole freezer door off its hinges. When will you two learn? I build caravans for a living; I can break into anything. So, who is he?'

Having had her ice cream stolen Hannah didn't really feel like telling but changed her mind when Katie handed her a spoon and gestured she join.

'He's a friend of a friend; a guy who is going to knock your socks off. So this friend says.'

That sounded promising but was this guy actually into me?

'My friend didn't say. She said he's absolutely your type though, and she's normally a pretty good judge.'

'What *do* you know about him then?' I asked.

Katie and I waited for Hannah to spill, but after thinking for a second, she spilt nothing.

'Not much. Look, I think it's best you go in there with a blank canvas. And anyway, you should worry less about what he's like and worry more about what you're going to be like.'

What I was going to be like? Why did I need to worry about that? I wasn't going to be nervous, anxious, uneasy or apprehensive.

'All those four words mean exactly the same thing,' Katie said with a mouthful of ice cream.

I was going to be my relaxed, calm, composed, stress-free self.

'All those four words mean exactly the same thing too,' Hannah said, also with a mouthful of ice cream.

Pick on me all they might, I was going to own this date.

This was going to be the best date ever.

15.

I leant up against a *No Standing* sign outside the casino.

In other words, I was standing next to a sign that said *No Standing*.

It had been that kind of day. My digestive system had given me a hard time prior to so many dates in the past, and it did so again. I was determined not to let it happen with Wesley.

I got up early and drank a green tea. That was followed by a peppermint tea, which was followed by a lemongrass and ginger tea. They were consumed to speed up my metabolism and they worked; I went to the toilet at work so many times throughout the day it was impossible for me to still have any food running through my body. I then went for a ninety-minute walk after work. The tea and the exercise had done the trick; so starved was I, my nervous system had nothing feed off.

Standing next to the *No Standing* sign though, I felt an uneasiness of a different kind – fatigue. I wasn't leaning up against the sign to try and act chilled; I was leaning on it because I was too tired to stand up straight.

Outside the casino, I waited for Wesley to come and re-energise me. Yes – outside the casino.

We were having dinner at a place named Artistic Fare. That was the name of the restaurant and a TV chef owned it. I'd never watched cooking shows, but that was less of a concern than what dinner at Artistic Fare was going to cost. I feared the meal would be well beyond what I could afford.

I stood, leant and watched as men walked towards me and then past me.

And then this voice came from behind, 'Hi, how are you going? Did you get lost?'

For a second, I thought he was kidding but he was being serious. I waited exactly where he texted me to wait, having changed the location twice in the half-an-hour prior to our date. Typically, I had gone to great lengths to get ready; I'd bought a new dress, bought new heels and had my hair done for the occasion.

He rocked up from work.

I knew this because he had his work suit on, with his tie loosened, a button undone and a coffee stain on his white shirt. He looked well older than me – like forty, his fair hair was receding from the front and his hand was like that of a mechanic, all rough and grubby.

I shuddered – on the inside anyway – at where it had been, as I reached my hand out and shook it.

'Hi Ella, I'm Wesley.'

'Hi Wesley, it's nice to—'

'No, not Wesley with a "Z", Wesley as in with a double "S".'

In a thick tone he certainly made sure I knew how to pronounce his name. *Precious much?*

I was tempted to correct him and tell him it was Elizabeth not Ella, but feared he may call me "E-liss-abeth" all night long.

I was relieved when he finally let go of my hand, as he held on way too long and way too tight.

'Shall we? I'm starved.'

The restaurant was spectacular but heightened my fears I'd have to sell my television to pay for dinner.

Everyone around us was in good spirits, talking, drinking and laughing away. I sat in silence as Wesley gave his full attention to the wine list for ten minutes.

'So tell me about yourself,' I said, reluctantly.

I'd never been huge on gender roles but at that moment I couldn't help but support them. I was on a date and the man was supposed to ask the woman that question, not the other way around. Plus, I'd worked so hard with Tiffany to improve my social skills, I was really looking forward to telling him about myself and seeing how much I'd improved. But he was never going to ask, so I did. And I really shouldn't have.

He told me about his family, his job (he was a stockbroker), his hobbies (which were really buying and selling stocks on the stock exchange) and a recent holiday (which he went on, on a whim, after making a lot of money on the stock market). Telling me about himself, he didn't even notice a male photographer creep nearby and take our photo.

Wesley's life story wasn't exactly exhilarating but knowing the picture would find its way online or into the newspaper, I pretended to be particularly engaged. He told me he had a sister, which prompted me to mention I, too, had sisters, but that's where talk of Hannah and Katie ended, as he never asked about them.

Finally, a question came my way. 'You said in one of your texts you live in Aspendale; what's that like?'

I could hardly believe that was the first question he asked me; I mean, it was Aspendale, it wasn't Barcelona or Prague or Phuket. Plus, he lived in Brighton, which was twenty-five kilometres from Aspendale. Surely he had driven down and seen what it was like for himself.

'Don't feel the need; there's nothing down there that interests me,' he said.

Oh snap.

It was his way of telling me he had no interest in me. Not that that surprised me; I got that feeling the moment he'd introduced himself. Truth was, I wasn't keen on him either. All I kept thinking was:

How could Hannah, someone who knows me better than anyone, get me so wrong as to think I would be interested in a man like this?

And...

How can I make the best of this bad situation?

I'd never walked out on a date as I saw it as simply too rude, and I wasn't about to do it then and there. Having ordered dinner without consulting me, and then having finally decided what wine he wanted, he turned to me and asked me another question.

'So what's Aspendale like?'

I bit my bottom lip in frustration.

It's a haven for crackheads, you numbskull. You've already asked me that.

It was at this point I wished like crazy I'd packed headache tablets into my handbag.

Without a moment's hesitation he picked up his phone, made a phone call, stood and walked to the toilets.

Our food was served five minutes after he left and was going seriously cold five minutes later. It would have been rude to start eating without him but the thought of eating a cold dinner gave me more anxiety. A full ten minutes after the food was served he returned with his phone to his ear, still in conversation.

'Okay, I'll see you soon. Bye.' He hung up. 'Great, food is here.'

He didn't apologise or explain but instead dived into the food and ate with no table etiquette. And while he barely said a word pre-meal, he happily spoke with his mouth full.

'So tell me, what's it like living in Aspendale?'

Again, that question ignited a battle in my mind; part of me wanted to walk out, part of me was thinking about payback and the other part thought it best to remain polite.

'Aspendale is...'

He didn't wait for me to answer, nor even to finish his mouthful but simply stood with his phone and walked away again. Walking off once I could forgive but a second time? That was really cruel. He was figuratively driving a utility truck and I was being towed with the rope around my waist at the back of it.

The night had reached a critical point and I decided if he came back and asked me about Aspendale again I was going to thank him for the night and graciously leave. He didn't, but instead returned on the phone again, said the words 'five minutes', hung up and then ignored me.

I'd been on some horrible dates where the guys had smelt terribly, laughed like an orang-utan or been disrespectful, but never had someone been so emotionally neglecting. It made me sad. It was far easier to accept the choices of someone who was openly bad mannered, but for Wesley to play with someone's heart like it was some kind of stock exchange thing was crossing the line. Fortunately, thoughts of my mother turned my frown upside down. She often said to me growing up, 'You don't have to be good at anything, you just have to be good.'

That quote never left me and off the back of Wesley's antics it re-entered my mind again, and reminded me being the bigger person was always the best thing to do. Not that Wesley saw it that way.

He ate about ten mouthfuls of food in about sixty seconds, wiped his face with his dirty hand and turned to me and said, 'My friend's in a cab out the front. I'm gonna go and have a drink with her.'

Her? Well this night is full of surprises.

Not that it made any difference, but he said "gonna" rather than "going to", which meant Tiffany wouldn't have approved.

He whistled for the waitress to come over, shovelled more food into his mouth, slugged his glass of wine and then took the bill from her and paid for it.

'We have to split the bill,' I insisted, as I reached for my credit card in my handbag. I'd drunk water and barely touched the food but always felt it was right to share the costs.

'They won't let us split the bill.'

I looked over at the final payment. *$350? Is that for real?*

I knew it would be expensive but for what we ordered, that was ridiculous. I really couldn't afford it, but I was a woman who stuck to her morals and again insisted I pay my share.

'I'll find an ATM and get some cash out.'

But he wouldn't let me.

I couldn't help but think he knew how awful he'd been over the past forty-five minutes and to soothe his conscience he'd decided to pay for dinner. It was also obvious, however, he didn't want to wait for me to find an ATM, get cash out and cover half the bill – he wanted to pay and get out of there.

He knocked back the offer of a receipt, grabbed his jacket, gave me something of a hug – it was more of a lean in – and left.

'I'll see you soon,' he said.

It was a figure of speech but still a poor choice of words; we were never going to see one another for the rest of our lives, I'd make sure of that.

I sat and waited for five minutes after he left so I wouldn't bump into him getting into a cab with his friend, and my thoughts went into overdrive. They were the same thoughts that consumed me the night Captain poured beer on my head.

Why are guys so nasty? How can a guy be so nasty to someone who's never done anything wrong by him? Was it Wesley's plan to make me feel worthless before he even met me?

I didn't have a broken heart because I had no feelings for him but why did it still hurt? It wasn't rejection because that had happened heaps of times before. So what was is it?

I thought back to the two envelopes Tiffany had given to me. *Maybe that's what it was.*

One-hour with Wesley had seen me lose belief. It had been replaced by doubt – doubt true love could ever happen for me.

Despite the date being over, the knife continued to twist. I waited out the five minutes and then trudged out of the casino and back towards the train station. As I exited the premises however, there was Wesley, hanging out of a taxi with some cabaret dancer-looking woman hanging out of it with him. I lowered my head in embarrassment at having bumped into him again. He and his friend sure weren't embarrassed; he'd clearly started re-telling the night as the two of them stared at me and laughed as I walked by.

Sitting at Southern Cross train station, the doubt intensified due to the fact my own sister had set this up. Another thought that crossed my mind earlier in the night returned and set up camp.

How could someone who knew me so well, make plans with a friend, and set me up with a man who was so unsuitable?

Hannah was, of course, only trying to help.

My phone buzzing was the final straw. It was Wesley again, this time providing an account and BSB number via text and requesting I transfer $175 into his account to cover my side of the dinner.

Seriously?

I did so, thinking it would lessen the risk of seeing him again.

Ironically, as I went to step onto the train, I noticed part of the yellow line in front of me – the line pedestrians should never stand in front of – had been painted with silver spray paint.

Silver lining? I thought.

That's exactly what it was; it had been a horror night, but it had helped me gain perspective. Hannah and Katie had been fantastic in helping me with my quest, but staring at that line, I realised it was time for me to help myself.

And order an Uber… as the train doors closed and the train left before I could actually get on it.

16.

Aaron

Sure let's get a coffee. Do you have a Tim Horton nearby?

Ella

Sorry don't know; never met anyone with that name.

Hannah was apologetic.

As she'd said – a friend of hers had rung her up and decided to play matchmaker, insisting she knew the perfect guy for me. Hannah had never met Wesley but trusted her friend and also her judgement; she didn't think this woman was only after the fame that came from matching Tinderella with her prince charming.

I'd asked Han why she didn't set me up with Brad or one of the other guys from the party and she told me she also liked the idea of her and her close friend setting Wesley and I up together.

The newspaper published a photo taken of the two of us on the date and wrote a spiel to go with it. It meant the full stop I was eager to put on the night had become more of a comma.

'Has Tinderella found what she's been so desperately craving all of her life?' Katie read from the entertainment pages, as she walked around Hannah's living room. 'She and the mystery man looked completely in love as they had dinner at one of Melbourne's most exclusive restaurants. "She's never been more in love, she's head over heels, and they're going to get married", a source told *Celebrity Scoop*.'

Source? What source?

I sat with Justin in front of a broken-down puzzle. It symbolised the current status of my quest for love – I had all the pieces in front of me, I just had to put them together. The box said the puzzle was recommended for eight-to-ten-year-olds, which meant Justin – being four – had no hope of figuring it out.

Boy how I hoped that didn't mean the same for me.

'You know that puzzle is way too hard for him,' Katie said to Hannah.

'That's the point; if it were easy I'd only get twenty minutes respite. This way I get four hours.'

'Can we get back to what's important here,' I pleaded.

'Relax; a lot of source quotes are made up,' Hannah said. 'They're there to add more spice.'

'You're actually in the celebrity pages twice,' Katie said. 'Spotted – Tinderella staring at a cat in Aspendale.'

'What?'

I jumped up and had a look at the accompanying photo. Staring at a cat was exactly what I was doing but there was way more to it. 'Spotted? Are they serious? I'm outside my unit, and the woman in the unit beside me has three cats that come and go throughout the day.'

What took me longer to realise was the more pressing issue – photographers were now waiting for me outside my unit. But why?

'It's in case any men ever come or go,' Hannah explained. 'And it's not just your apartment; they'll probably bob up when you're at the grocery store, or hairdresser, or in the shower.'

She was joking about that last part. Nevertheless, the thought of being followed was scary; I was after all some normal lass who lived in the suburbs all by herself.

'Not any more you're not,' Hannah continued. 'Everyone wants to know what you're doing; you're clickbait, which means more articles, which means more photos.'

She was right; in the last twenty-four hours, the followers on my social media pages had almost tripled. I had over 650,000 followers on Instagram, half-a-million likes on Facebook and over 200,000 followers on Snapchat. With my growing popularity, I needed to continue giving my followers what they wanted – more to talk about. And the only way to do that was to go on more dates.

'So who should I call?'

'No one,' Hannah replied.

What, why?

I didn't have any of their phone numbers to call anyway but why was Hannah standing in the way of progress?

'Standing in the way of progress'? What are you, a politician?' Katie asked.

It was kind of a weird thing to say but what was just as weird was Hannah telling me to 'cool my jets'.

'For a few days, maybe a week, then I'll put you in touch with one of the guys from the party.'

A week? Was she insane? I wasn't going to wait a week; the men were in front of me now and I wanted to date them. It was like putting a tub of ice cream in front of Katie and telling her not to eat it for a week – she couldn't do it.

Brody woke up and began to cry so Hannah attended to him.

I turned to Katie hoping her opinion would differ. 'You think I should wait a week too?'

'I think you should do whatever you want.'

Yes! That's what I wanted to hear, even if Katie was still ingrained in the celebrity pages of the newspaper.

I looked over at Justin who, in less than five minutes, had completed half the puzzle.

Freak of nature was the first thing that popped into my head but then followed something else. According to the box Justin was way too young to complete the puzzle, yet he had proven the manufacturers recommendations were not always accurate. In my eyes neither was Hannah's recommendation. I may have had the mishap with Wesley, but it had helped me see clearer.

I knew what I was doing.

I stayed up late that night and swiped through Tinder. After about two hours I matched with someone who was cute, adventurous and funny.

His profile tagline read –

Looking for love just like all those fishes were looking for Nemo.

His name was Aaron and he sent me a message asking if I knew of a Tim Horton in the area. I didn't, thinking Tim Horton was a man. He explained Tim Horton™ was a café. I'd never heard of that either.

I rang Elliot the next morning and told him I was taking the morning off work. I'd missed a fair bit of work in the days prior and hadn't seen much of him. Appointments with Tiffany had been one reason while photos with Katie had been another.

After my Photoshop mishap and before my date with Wesley, she had decided to take the reins and teach me a thing or two about Instagram. Over two days she took me to different locations around the city and took no less than one-hundred-and-fifty photos. And made me change my clothes about twenty times as well. We went to the zoo where I fed a eucalyptus leaf to a Koala, we did yoga at Fitzroy Gardens, drank coffee in trendy laneways in the city, browsed the city markets, and re-enacted Mariah Carey's *Fantasy* music video by going on the rollercoaster at Luna Park.

Initially, I didn't get why we had to do so many things in such a short space of time, but that was because I was an Instagram novice.

'You have to post a photo every day, end of story,' she told me. 'That's not the easiest thing to do, so to make it easier, you take a hundred photos in two days and then slowly filter through one a day for the next hundred days. People will think you're doing something different every day. Trust me, everyone does it.'

It was a good plan, but it came at the expense of work.

Phone calls with Elliot normally lasted an hour but that morning – despite having so many stories to tell him – the conversation lasted two minutes.

'I'm sorry, Ella, I wish I could talk, I've got a lot to do this morning, and Evie's coming around.'

It sounded more like an excuse than the truth.

I really wanted him to know what was going on with me, but he did his best to make it sound like he didn't have the time to talk, and then hung up.

The hour the phone call would have taken up left me with way too much time for my brain to play tricks on itself. I didn't eat breakfast but strangely enough only used the bathroom three times before I left because I didn't feel my normal levels of anxiety. My brain was okay and so too was my stomach, at least compared to what they had been like. I thought the nightmare date with Wesley would have induced more fear but perhaps my pre-date anxieties lessened as my mind knew things would never be that bad again.

Aaron and I agreed to meet at Beach Café in Seaford and – me being me – I was early and got there before he did.

The sun was out, and it was warm, which I saw as a good sign; if the weather outlook was positive then hopefully the relationship outlook would be too. It also saw Aaron rock up in loose fitting clothing, which really suited his athletic body. He had a singlet on, jeans rolled up above his ankles, and a backpack on his back. It seemed as if he liked what he saw too, although his introduction wasn't overly detailed.

'You look really nice.'

He was taller than me, had short, shaped brown hair, a soft nose but sharp jawline, and kissed me on both cheeks, which I never knew the Americans did.

'I'm from Canada actually. Is it okay if we sit outside in the sun?'

He was confident, and confident men normally rattled me, but right from the moment I met him, I felt okay. He made me feel relaxed, like I was hanging out with a really good friend and not a potential love interest.

'I'm so glad you picked this place, they do a really good Blue Heaven spider.'

I hadn't picked this place at all; as he was living in Frankston, he'd picked it.

'Well I'm glad I picked this place. They do a really good Blue Heaven milkshake.'

He smiled a cheeky smile before apologising, 'Sorry, I can be a bit silly sometimes. "Dag" is it? Is that the word you Australians use?'

It was. My mum often told me I was a dag.

Aaron was a newly qualified accountant who had transferred from Montreal to Melbourne to gain experience. He'd always wanted to see Australia and a work transfer was the perfect way to do it.

'Perth was amazing, as was Adelaide. Darwin and the top part of Perth?'

'The Kimberley?'

'The Kimberley, that's it, Darwin and The Kimberley were hot but still really nice, and Sydney was great too. But I still feel like Melbourne suits me the best; it feels like Montreal in so many ways.'

I was happy to hear that; you're always happy to hear someone tell you how much he or she loves your city.

I was intrigued to hear he was a newly qualified accountant. Due to his age, that being close to mine, I expected he'd been doing it for years.

'I was in fitness first...'

Of course he was; look at those arms.

'... But it was too hard, starting at 6am, working through until midday, going home to sleep and then being back at 4pm and working through until 8pm, and on weekends too. I needed a change.'

Again, I was sceptical; you didn't often hear of someone in fitness moving into accountancy. One pushed the body while the other pushed the brain.

'I get it a lot; sports and mathematics was all I was good at while at school. I know most people are defined by one area of life, they love their sports teams, or music and dance is their thing, or they're into cars and anything with an engine. For better or for worse I love sports and I love numbers; I have interests in a lot of areas.'

I didn't mind that.

Lunch was nice; we both ate salmon bagels, we had numerous things in common and he had nice arms.

After lunch, he suggested a stroll on the beach.

'Bit soon,' I joked. 'We've only just met.'

'Not a romantic stroll,' he laughed. 'Just a stroll.'

At that point I realised I'd conversed without error (or sweat) for the previous hour and made him laugh. Maybe Tiffany's classes were working.

We split the fifty-seven-dollar bill and headed for the sand.

With my last session with Tiffany – and truthfully a little bit of Max – ringing in my ears, I suggested to Aaron we play a game.

'I call it nineteen questions. It's like twenty questions, but instead of twenty questions, it's nineteen.'

Admittedly, I was keen to find out what else we had in common, and he happily obliged.

'Question One – what's your favourite thing about Montreal?'

'Ice hockey; the Canadians are my team.'

The national team was his team? That was no surprise.

'No, the Canadians aren't the national team, that's what Montreal's team are called – The Montreal Canadians.'

Really? I found that rather unusual. Imagine if there was a football team called the Melbourne Australians.

'Question Two – what's your cheat meal; what's the one junk food you can't resist?'

'I've been known to eat a whole packet of peanut M&Ms in one sitting.'

Wow – another thing we had in common. Truth be told, I'd actually eaten two packets in one sitting.

That truth wasn't going to be told.

We reached question three, which had always been a fork in the road for me. I had a rule when getting to know a guy that if he didn't ask me a question after I'd asked him three questions, then it was a sign he wasn't as keen on me as I was on him. And thus, the chances of a relationship were slim.

'Question Three – what's the most feminine thing you do?'

He thought about it for a couple of seconds and then answered. 'I feel like this is going to haunt me later but… when I was younger I knew every word from the movie *Mean Girls*.'

That was classic and would definitely haunt him later. 'When you say "younger", how young were you?' I asked.

He hesitated again and then conceded, 'I can still do it now.'

I loved that movie growing up, and didn't at all think less of him for possessing that skill. 'What part did you replicate the most?'

'The part at the end, where Karen puts her hands on her boobs and predicts the weather,' he said embarrassingly.

'Okay you have to do that for me.'

'No way.'

'Yes way, right now, put those hands on that chest and tell me what the weather's doing, now.'

He wasn't keen to but yielded for the purposes of my entertainment. He raised his hands and placed them on his chest muscles.

Those glorious chest muscles.

Blushing fiercely, he reported – 'the sun is out and it's a beautiful warm day. There's a fifty-eight per cent chance of cloud cover later this afternoon, but depending on who you're with, you might not even notice it.'

It was one of the sexiest things I'd seen in my life, and boy did it strengthen my crush on him, as did what followed.

'What kind of flowers do you like?' he asked.

My initial thought was – *Flowers? I'm a woman; I love all flowers.* But then I realised he'd asked me a question back, and thus was as keen on me as I was on him.

I thought about it, as I really didn't want to get my answer wrong in case he bought me a bunch one day. 'Faint pink tulips; I like faint pink tulips.'

'Good choice; can I take my hands off my chest now?'

'No... yes of course you can.'

We stopped walking and sat on the soft sand, but kept playing and discovered we had more in common. Katie and Hannah would have seen our commonalities as nothing out of the ordinary but Question Nineteen was a sure sign there was more to Aaron and I than salmon bagels and occasionally inhaling a bag of M&Ms™.

'What star sign are you?' I asked.

'Capricorn.'

'December or January?'

'December.'

'What date?'

'The 31st.'

That had to sting. If Christmas Day was the worst day to have a birthday then New Year's Eve was a close second. When everyone should have been celebrating you, they were instead celebrating the start of a new year.

'It's not great,' he agreed.

'As tough as that is, only the very, very best are born in December,' I said, trying to soften the blow.

'You're born in December too?'

I was. In fact, my family often joked my misfortune in life was due to being been born on a Friday the 13th.

I expected Aaron to ask if I were unlucky, having learnt the date of my birth, but he didn't. He instead identified something that proved there was more to he and I than gorging on chocolate.

'So I'm December 31 and your December 13. Can't get much closer than that; I mean, 31 is 13 backwards after all.'

We had commonalities, but it was his want for us to be more alike that gave me a rush of delight I'd rarely experienced. It wasn't just the words he said, but the way he said them, and the way he looked at me as well. It was like he too saw this huge force swirling between us that with each moment pulled us closer together. I tried to tighten my mouth muscles so not to smile too much, but the more I fought it, the more my smile expanded.

Silence then positioned itself between us. It wasn't the usual nervous silence I was accustomed to, or typically initiated, but a powerful all-conquering silence that – had we been in a romantic comedy film – could have seen us jump one another in that very moment.

God, how I wanted to.

His eyes stared into mine unashamedly and he used them in such a way that made my heart beat faster. Stupidly, I broke first, and looked down at the sand.

'I guess I should probably get going.'

I never wanted to ever leave that moment but remembered something Katie said to me once. I never followed rules, but she told me to always get out early, and leave them wanting more.

We walked back to the cafe and I told him how much I'd loved spending the last two hours with him, but following that declaration, things turned for the worse.

He didn't reciprocate but kept walking in silence. As every second passed I felt my heart start to break and break some more. And then my mind sped up.

After the great time we've had together, is he really going to tell me he doesn't want to see me again?

But it wasn't that.

'I've had fun too, there's just something you should know,' he said.

Here we go. Married? Divorced? Done jail time for armed robbery? There's always something.

It wasn't as bad as those things but it still wasn't something I wanted to hear.

He stopped walking, and so too did I.

'My stay in Australia finishes up soon; I head back home in six weeks.'

I suddenly understood the real reason behind his compliments, the playing along with the games and the flirting, and it made me kind of angry.

'Oh, I get it,' I told him, my disgust deepening with every word. 'You're only here to sleep with the girl. How honourable of you.'

'Well you did meet me on Tinder.'

That was a defence I couldn't argue with; I hated it, but I couldn't argue it. I turned and walked off, 'Well then enjoy the rest of your stay... loser.'

He called out after me as I strode away, and then ran up and asked me to stop and listen. 'For thirty seconds, that's it.'

I did so, and he continued.

'I'm sorry, I shouldn't have said that; you were getting angry with me and I didn't know how else to respond. I am not that guy, I promise; I can count my sexual partners on one hand. I swear I didn't come here today to score a one-night stand. The truth is I came here to meet somebody new and find somebody cool to hang out with for the next six weeks. I wouldn't have cared if we didn't kiss in six weeks let alone sleep together, because that's not me. I just thought you should know.'

I had got him wrong; I should have judged him on his kindness over the past two hours, rather than one throwaway line said out of fear. It had taken a lot of courage for him to reveal what he had, and I had to respect that. But I also had to respect who I was, and what I wanted, and I had to find the courage to tell him.

'I'm sorry I called you a loser, you're not a loser, but you're not what I'm looking for either. I'm looking for a soul mate, not a six-week friend, and I need to put all my effort into that.'

He accepted what I told him, kissed me on each cheek and let me walk on. The heartache started to kick in as I walked up the beach, but it stopped momentarily as he chased after me one more time.

'This is the last time I'll stop you I promise.'

He took a piece of paper and a pen from his bag, wrote something on the paper and handed it to me. 'My email, if by chance you happen to make it to Canada or even The States, you can always get in touch. I might even buy you a bunch of faint pink tulips.'

It was he who then walked off, but not without one final display of genuineness, which left a large part of me wishing he'd never gone.

'I hope you find what you're looking for Ella.'

17.

I sat on Hannah's couch and watched *Notting Hill* on Netflix™.

I chose it intentionally – the famous girl got her guy in the end, and I hoped that conclusion would reignite the spark within me.

But it didn't.

By the end I was still wallowing in disappointment. Twenty-four hours had passed and what had happened with Aaron still stung. It was the Max-kind-of-hurt I was experiencing. Guys like that were hard to find, yet when I found them, there was always a reason I couldn't be with them.

Why? Why did he have to be from Canada and be going back there in six weeks? Why couldn't he have been from the next suburb across and be staying there for the rest of his life?

Looking back, I would have almost preferred not to have met him.

The Max situation only made me feel worse. He'd called three days earlier and then again that morning wondering if we could talk about our dating app project. It wasn't that I didn't want to talk to him; the time away had made me feel better about us, it was that it wasn't a good time. I didn't feel like talking to him after what happened with Wesley and I definitely didn't feel like talking after what happened with Aaron. I felt like talking about it of course, just not with Max.

My thoughts were overwhelming me...

What if I die never having fallen in love?

What if the man I'm meant to fall in love with was born a hundred years ago and has already passed?

What if I'm simply unlovable?

... So I called Katie. She didn't answer, so I called Hannah.

I told her my all-too-familiar feelings were back and causing me despair – I once again felt like I was destined to be miserable and alone for the rest of my life. She told me to use the spare key and wait at her house until she got home from work and she'd make me feel better when she got there.

Something changed considerably in the two hours in between however, as from the moment she came through the front door, she made me feel worse.

'Are you freaking kidding me? I mean seriously, are you out of your mind?'

I had no idea what she was talking about, at least until she threw the day's newspaper in my face.

The headline read – *Tinderella Cheating On Boyfriend Already?* And there was a photo of Aaron and I flirting on Seaford beach.

I hadn't seen a cameraman anywhere during our walk on the sand; where could this photo have come from?

'Ella those camera guys have really long lenses; he could have taken it from Sorrento.'

Sorrento was sixty kilometres south of Seaford.

'Really?'

'No; he was probably hiding in the bushes right in front of you.'

Gullible me.

'Sweetheart, this is a really bad mistake...'

For a second, I thought her use of the word "sweetheart" might have meant she was going to go easier on me, but I was wrong '... And now you're a cheater; a dirty, rotten, cheater.'

Cheater? That wasn't the truth; I wasn't cheating; it wasn't like that at all. Aaron was some guy I was never going to see again.

She threw her bag down on the couch and took her frustration to another level. 'It doesn't matter! You're with another guy days after being with Wesley. People believe what they see and read, and if they don't think you're a cheater they sure as hell think you get around fast. Damn it, Ella, I specifically told you not to see anyone else for at least a week, and you still went against what I said.'

That's why she didn't want me seeing anyone else? Why didn't she say so? I suppose she didn't need to. I should have known there was a reason she didn't want me going on any other dates so soon; I just thought she was punishing me for the sake of it.

She was mad, and I was worried, but she was the expert when it came to this publicity stuff so surely there was a way to fix it.

'Maybe another radio interview?' I suggested.

'You only get one radio interview; all another radio interview is going to do is paint you as a fame-seeking cheater. Trust me, you won't mean it that way, but they'll spin it that way. I need a second to think.'

She didn't get one as Katie walked through the front door, 'So what's this big world-ending mistake she's made?'

World-ending mistake? That's how Hannah had described this to Katie?

I couldn't feel much worse after hearing that.

Hannah snatched the newspaper out of my hands and flung it over to Katie.

'Ha, yeah I saw that this morning. Geez they can make up some shit these so-called journalists, can't they? He's hot though, are you going to see him again?'

I looked at Katie as if to say, *now is not a good time.*

She took my look for something else and continued to see the humour in it. 'Funny how I cracked it big time over the Photoshop incident and Han didn't think it was so bad, and now she's cracked it at this and I don't think it's so bad.'

Hannah began to sniff like she was looking for a clue. She turned to Katie and realised what she could smell and thus why Katie was in such a good mood.

'You just finished another caravan, didn't you?'

Katie didn't answer, but grinned.

She and Roy had this thing – whenever they completely finished building a caravan inside and out, they christened it by having sex inside of it. They then cleaned it before selling it.

In the world of TV and movies, a woman could have sex in the bathroom at work and then attend an office meeting without anybody suspecting a thing. But in the real world, it was impossible. Katie might have been able to hide her *I'm on top of the world because I've just had sex* face, but not even the strongest perfume nor deodorant would be able to remove the lingering sex smell she carried into Hannah's house.

'Get out the back and put yourself under the hose now,' Hannah ordered.

She headed for the back door. Han sat down on the couch and I went over and sat down next to her. I initially thought she was talking to me when she spoke, but she was voicing her thoughts out loud in the hope she'd come up with an idea that would rectify the situation.

'Put a ring on her finger to distract the media from her cheating and have them concentrate on her impending marriage.'

That idea would paint me as a woman desperate to marry the first guy that came along, rather than the patient type who was willing to give the process time.

'Get in touch with the mystery man and see if he'll say anything.'

There was no way I was contacting Aaron again after what happened the day before. In Hannah's mind, he could also potentially say negative things about me and make a bad situation worse.

'Reveal the pain of your past through one of your sisters,' she said, grinding out the last part of the word "sisters", as she realised that was a terrible idea as well.

The extremely personal things that had happened to Hannah, Katie and I needed to stay out of the newspapers, end of story.

She turned to me and shrugged apologetically; I knew what she was going to say before she even said it.

'I don't think there's any way out of this one, Ella. I know it's early days, but I think we cut our losses and fade back into oblivion before the whole nation turns on you.'

She was right – I'd read about nice guys in the public eye who dated Australia's sweetheart. Everybody loved the guy, but when he broke the darling girl's heart, he went from nice guy to love rat and from Australia's most loved to Australia's most hated.

I was disappointed, but never wanted to be someone everybody hated.

'Probably should shut down my social media accounts first then?' I said.

She was about to say yes when Katie charged through the back door. 'Not yet; I think I might have an idea that can turn this around.'

She held her phone in front of Hannah's face. I couldn't see what she was showing her but could see she had my Instagram account open.

Hannah looked up at her and then across to me as if to say, *that might actually work.*

Her look quickly changed however as her sense of smell kicked in.

From me, she turned back to Katie. 'You haven't used the hose yet have you?'

'Not yet.'

18.

'You look handsome.'

There he was, in his tuxedo and his bow tie, sitting in his wheelchair at the top of his driveway with his parents.

His name was Kye and he was the next guy I was going on a date with.

His mum wheeled him down to the edge of the street and allowed the driver of the disabled van to push him up onto a platform and electronically raise him into it. I went to get in with him but stopped when she touched me on the arm and said, 'Thank-you.'

Kye was seventeen years old and in his final year of high school. He was a quadriplegic who'd had an accident eighteen months earlier. He was very little for seventeen – he looked more like fifteen – but both of his parents were petite also.

Kye had reached out to me on Instagram and asked if I'd go with him to his school formal. Both Hannah and Katie thought it would be a good publicity move to go, as it would turn around my previous "cheating" indiscretion. I thought that was crap; I couldn't have cared less about publicity. I told them I thought it would be a kind gesture for a boy who was quite obviously facing a day-to-day battle.

On second thought, "quite obviously" wasn't the most accurate description – Kye spoke like a kid who had the world at his feet. Not two spinning wheels.

'How good is life right now? A school formal, fancy clothes and I'm going with a celebrity. This is awesome.'

Kye's attitude said a lot; I'd have been bummed out we were en route to the formal via some weird shaped van and not a limousine, but he was unfazed.

'Hey driver, can we get some "doof doof" music in here?'

I had replied to Kye's message on Instagram and then followed it up with a phone call to his mum. She was happy for me to go with him. She also told me about what had happened to him. In his company, however, I pretended she hadn't.

'So Kye, what's your story?'

'Had an accident and now I'm a cripple.'

'No, not that story, your other story.'

He had no idea what I meant so I clarified, 'Who are you? What's your favourite subject at school? Which girl are you most keen on?'

Without missing a beat, he replied, 'I'm Franklin D. Roosevelt's secret love child, I'll be dux of my physics class and it's not so much who I'm keen on but who's keen on me. Emily Travers is always passing me notes in English and every one of them says the same thing.'

'What's that?'

'"Let's have sex".'

That seemed drastically inappropriate for a seventeen-year-old girl. Although truthfully if a seventeen-year-old boy had done that to me in high school, I would have kept all his notes as souvenirs in a washed-out Vegemite jar.

Kye certainly didn't lack confidence, and while it made me a little uneasy, I wasn't going to mother him and ruin the biggest night of his year.

'If you happen to disappear throughout the night, I won't come looking for you,' I joked. 'What other hobbies do you have?'

'Apart from sex?'

I nodded, really hoping he wouldn't say foreplay, and we'd finally get the conversation off sex.

'I'm learning how to call horse races; my voice is still squeaky, even though it dropped years ago, but it's the only thing that still works, so I figured I'd start putting it to good use.'

His mum had told me that.

Having grown up around horses, Kye wanted to become a jockey. His mum told me on the phone of her and her husband's reservations but agreed to his career decision on the proviso he completed his final years of school. Six days a week he got up at 4am and rode track work before heading into school for roll call at 8.30am. At sixteen, just nine months after starting out as a rider, a horse he was on was spooked, and flipped over backwards onto him, crushing his cervical four and five in his neck. It was nothing more than an accident, as his mum had told me – the horse he was on was a seven-year-old and was the most placid horse in the stable. Not being able to ride anymore, he'd turned his attention to race commentating.

'Don't really care for anything else; only want to be around horses. And girls.'

Girls, of course.

His school formal was being held at Leonda By The Yarra in Hawthorn, and he was ecstatic to find a photographer from the newspaper waiting at the entrance when we arrived.

I felt guilty at knowing it was – in part – a publicity stunt, but the guilt eased when I saw how much joy he got from his new notoriety.

'I don't know how this works; do we pose for him or do we move on by like he's annoying us? That's what celebrities do right?'

I didn't know, but he answered the question himself.

'Maybe I'll give him the finger like a brash, young rock star.'

'I don't know if that's the best idea.'

'It was a joke. I'm a quadriplegic; I can't raise my arm let alone give someone the finger.'

I really should have known that.

I wheeled him inside and we had our official couples' photo. I then wheeled him into the main dining area. We'd only been in there three seconds when every kid in his year level turned and stared at us.

The silence of the star struck crowd held my attention until he made what was a pretty funny joke.

'Is this the part where I stand up out of my chair and they applaud? Because it ain't going to happen.'

The only reason thirty-odd female students left the surroundings of our table was because dinner was being served. I thought being desperate and dateless would see me disliked by the large majority of the teenage girls in attendance, but being in the newspapers and magazines for it saw them entranced by me.

'You're so pretty; who did your make-up?'

'I love your dress, where did you get it?'

'Did you ever wear Ugg Boots to school, and get coffee on the way, and look super cool while you were doing it?'

The last girl asked me that question with a thermometer hanging out the side of her mouth.

'Is that a thing now?' I asked Kye.

'Yeah, whenever anyone asks them how they are, they take the thermometer out of their mouth, look at it, and say in a sultry tone of voice, "I'm hot".'

What was going on with today's kids?

Dinnertime was certainly a new experience for me, but one I had to undertake as maturely as I could. Kye couldn't feed himself so I had to feed him. As it turned out, we had many things in common. Apart from the fact we both hated overcooked meat – which we traded for the chicken when others at our table were in the bathroom – we were also avid movie watchers.

'I'm disturbed by the fact we're seated at table nine,' he said.

That observation rang a bell, but I couldn't pinpoint it.

'*The Wedding Singer*; surely you know *The Wedding Singer*.'

I did, and had seen it many times, but couldn't recall that bit.

'You know, "the mutants at table nine". That makes us the ugliest people at this thing,' he laughed before muttering, 'they wish; we're the most attractive.'

I fed him another forkful of chicken and vegies and he continued talking with his mouth full. 'This is so degrading when Mum does it, but so damn sexy when Tinderella does.'

There was the "sex" word again; teenage male hormones were certainly something new to me, never having had a brother.

I put the fork down, grabbed his glass from the table and let him drink from the straw. He didn't drink for long.

'What's this water? Where's the hard liquor?'

For a second, I thought he was serious, but he wasn't. 'I'm kidding; I don't need the booze, I'm already legless, kind of.'

His eyes moved to a nearby napkin. I picked it up and wiped his mouth with it. He continued yapping. 'Seriously though, you better have a hidden flask somewhere – tucked in your pantyhose or something – or you're the worst date ever.'

Part of me wanted to call him out for being inappropriate, but I did envy his quick wit. As if reading my mind, he made a suggestion and then wheeled himself off.

'I'd love to stay and feed you, that'd be kinky, but with dinner in my belly and my hot body again full of energy, it's time to hit the dance floor. Emily Travers here I come.'

I turned to my plate and began feeding my own mouth. My chicken however was cold, and I only discovered this once it was in my mouth. I thought about spitting it out but with teachers around and eyes all over me, I had no choice but to swallow it.

As it rolled down the back of my throat, I found myself cursing I didn't have a secret flask in my pantyhose.

The next hour was strange; I lost sight of Kye and hoped nothing bad had happened. I tried not to think he and Emily Travers were getting it on somewhere but also couldn't help but think something might have been wrong. He'd been so psyched to be going to his school formal with me earlier in the night, it seemed strange he'd leave me alone for so long. Not that I was really alone.

A dozen teenage girls came back for round two and their questions were even more intrusive than the first time around. When they left, two female teachers in their late twenties sat down next to me and asked for the latest gossip, and when they left, another female teacher in her mid-fifties sat down and – like a therapy session – went into excruciating detail about how going through menopause and being single with it was, 'the greatest difficulty of my life... apart from the six months I tried to make it as a pole dancer.'

I should have joked about Aunt Wanda and mint sauce, but she wouldn't have got it.

She was sweet and vulnerable but totally self-absorbed. As were the popular students who attended the school – well, sweet and totally self-absorbed, not vulnerable. These girls had the self-esteem of Kanye West.

I found this out in line for the bathroom, which never shortened because none of them actually needed the toilets; they just wanted to use the mirror. I'd always made it a rule never to use the disabled toilets, as it was bad karma. Using it while being on a date with a quadriplegic would have made it the worst karma. I was busting, but fortunately, just before the night's fluids began to trickle down my leg, the menopause lady came over and informed me there was a staff bathroom I could step right into.

It was a bathroom break, but a time-out as well. I felt like a sportsperson who'd been running up and down the field all night and had finally been given a rest by the coach. I checked my phone; there were no messages from Hannah or Katie, but I had been tagged by a number of the schoolgirls on Instagram.

After catching my breath, I thought it was time to go and find Kye. I was, after all, his carer for the night.

I flushed the toilet and in exiting the cubicle noticed the door had been graffitied with the words –

Feetlicker Timmy. He does Specialist
Maths, but also enjoys feet licking.
Call 0343 343 3932 234 2 234 234 324234.

My first thought couldn't have been more odd – *had Katie done this?*

She did write messages on Hannah's fridge with the magnetic letters, but no, this wasn't her. It was clear Feetlicker Timmy's phone number had been disclosed by one of the truant kids, intent on leaving a message for one of his or her teachers.

I walked a lap of the dining room, but couldn't find Kye anywhere, so decided to check the side balcony. Sure enough, he was out there, taking a break of his own.

'Hey, what are you doing out here?'

He looked over at me; he was embarrassed he'd been caught out alone but was quick to try and hide it. 'All danced out; giving my legs a rest.'

He was peering out at the night sky, so I walked over and stood next to him. 'Pretty cool isn't it? I sometimes wonder if there's another planet out there and another Ella living on it. Do you ever think that?'

He took a moment to respond; I could sense a level of despondency but had been warned by his mum he may get tired as the night progressed.

'I wonder if the Kye on the other planet is able to walk.'

I knew exactly what was going on.

The hand I'd been dealt in life had been far less harsh than Kye, but I, too, had suffered through some tough times. Time healed all the wounds, but each day still brought with it a short period of negativity. I could be enthusiastic about life for twenty-three hours and fifty-five minutes of every day, but for the other five minutes, all that consumed my mind was how shitty life was and how shitty the thing that happened to me was.

I was no psychologist, but I figured the best thing to do was try and distract Kye as a way of making him feel better, rather than ask if he wanted to talk about it and let him fall deeper into a whirlpool of sorrow.

'How'd you go with Emily Travers? Didn't see you for a while there; figured you two must have snuck off into a corner somewhere.'

He didn't answer and instead kept gazing out at the sky.

I talked a lot; I was a serial chatterbox, but I was aware in circumstances like this, continued talking only made things worse. I let the silence take hold, and after a while it worked, as he spoke to me again.

'You know how I've been working on my race calling?'

'Yeah.'

'Could I show you some of it now?'

'Absolutely; I'd love to hear it.'

He cleared his throat and began; he spoke in a way that was completely different to the way he had all night. He was very good too, but slowly I realised he wasn't calling a horse race but providing the commentary on something else. As the race continued and finally finished, the exuberance in his voice faded until there was nothing left but discontent.

'They're off, and the starter caught them in a good line, too. Kye Brewer is showing good early speed and this well-bred youngster is going to lead them in the early stages from the inside gate. They go past the eight hundred metre mark and things look good for Kye although he's over-racing, in fact now he's pulling quite badly, resenting the rider, and as he approaches the home turn, he's completely lost his advantage. His dream of becoming a jockey is gone, his school mates have deserted him and two days after his accident, his girlfriend Emily has broken up with him; she doesn't even want to be seen hanging out with the cripple. His independence has vanished, he can't feed himself and he'll never be able to walk again. The only short-lived happiness he experiences in life is when he puts a photo up on Instagram and gets a hundred likes. And unlike Franklin Roosevelt, he doesn't have the brains to counter such a hurdle; he's not a physics student at all, in fact, he's only capable of doing two of five subjects in his final year and they're English and Drama. Only doing two subjects means he'll fail, but it doesn't matter because he's not there to pass anyway, he only goes to school to distract himself from the burning pain in his head, that tells him he'll be in this stupid chair until the day he dies.'

Tears welled in my eyes; his extended hardship had been incredibly difficult to listen to. I'd been naïve at the start of the night to think he was Mr Positive, not thinking it was mostly a façade and that deep down, severe pain still gnawed away at him. Then and there it became obvious the sex talk was a way of using humour to blanket his aching heart and mind, and then and there it became obvious I needed to step up to the mark and tell him something he needed to hear.

'Fuck Emily Travers.'

I never said the 'F' word, and while there was a tinge of humour attached to it, there was also a large amount of gravity.

He laughed, and I kept going.

'She walked away from a great guy because he's in a wheelchair and she has to live with that. And trust me, deep down, part of her still feels awful, and when she reaches my age, it's still going to be with her.'

A tear ran down his cheek.

I wasn't finished. 'And as for the other stuff; I'm not going to tell you everything will be fine, you'll be all right, it's just a wheelchair, because it must suck. But you do have a lot going for you. Who cares if you're in English and Drama, that's awesome. Physics is a load of shit anyway. Loads of successful people didn't finish high school, and heaps of those that were dux work in stupid jobs like event planning.'

Yes, that was a dig at Hannah.

'What matters most is you're a good guy; you're a nice person. Most of your body doesn't work anymore but your soul still does, and you can have way more of an impact with that. And tonight, you have.'

Tears rolled down his face.

Still I wasn't finished. 'I have had the best night in a long time and that's solely because of you. Your kind heart has taught me a lot in three short hours. It's normal to think of what you don't have now, when you're my age, or when you're an old, old man...'

He chuckled through another tear.

'But kid, you've got what most don't – you've got selflessness, you've got courage and you've got a lot of love for other people, and that will take you a long, long way.'

He swallowed his sadness and his tears dried up, as did mine.

He softly tapped a finger. I initially thought the gesture was an invitation to sit on his lap but realised he wanted me to put my hand on his, so I did.

'Thanks, Tinderella. I'm glad I asked you to the formal.'

I would have hugged him if possible, but I thought of something else we could do together that was a better way of ending the night.

'What do you say we get out of here? I know this awesome ice cream parlour. Would be unfair to have dinner and not let me spoon-feed you dessert as well.'

The night ended on a good note. The look in Kye's mum's eyes when he returned home was one of gratefulness. All she wanted was her son to enjoy life again, and for one night with me, he had.

She hugged me.

'You are one of a kind, Ella.'

I left their family home in an Uber.

Sitting in the passenger seat, I got my phone out. Katie had sent me a text message that simply read –

> Looks like it worked.
> I'm a genius.
> You owe me presents.
> Going to bed now.

Her message wasn't the reason I went looking for my phone though. Kye's desire for love got me thinking about my dating app project for the disabled, which in turn got me thinking about Max. His rejection still stung a bit, but it was time to put what happened between us to the side, for the betterment of the project.

I scrolled through my contacts list until I reached his name. My finger hovered over the *call* button.

But I couldn't do it; I couldn't call.

On a night when courage had been a theme, I couldn't muster enough of it to ring him, and I knew exactly why.

I still liked the guy and it was going to be too hard.

I put the phone in my bag, placed the bag at my feet, and closed my eyes to rest.

Closed my eyes to fight off the growing negativity in my head.

19.

I went to sleep that night feeling apprehensive, and consequently woke up feeling like crap.

I considered going down to the chemist and buying some sleeping tablets, intent on sleeping through the first part of the day because I simply couldn't face it. I chose instead to bury my head in a Sudoku book and eat an entire packet of Tim Tams™ for breakfast. I finished the Tim Tams but gave up on the Sudoku. I couldn't concentrate; all I kept thinking about was how unfair life was, which was in stark contrast to what I'd said to Kye the night before.

Good things happened to others all the time and yet I had to battle my way through everything.

Mum always said I had a chip on my shoulder.

I went into my bedroom, stood on a chair and pulled a collection of old VCR tapes from the back of my wardrobe. The writing had faded but twenty years on, the labels hadn't peeled off.

Still in my pyjamas, I put the first of the tapes into an old VCR player I'd bought and had restored, and watched vision of myself as a child. There was a common theme throughout the video. Actually, there were two common themes.

The first was that my knack of embarrassing myself began at a young age – I dressed in Dad's clothes at five, went into Mum's beauty bag and tried to do my own make-up at six, and rode around on a bike with one of those giant, fluorescent green Stackhats™ on when I was fifteen.

The other theme was that I was a happy child and I loved being around my parents and my sisters. There wasn't a second of the recording where I was grumpy or sad.

Unfortunately, I couldn't say the same of myself as an adult.

A knock at the front door interrupted my viewing and I snapped, 'Not now.'

Whoever it was seemed to get the message as the knocking stopped and dead air followed. But as I pushed play on the videotape again, the knocking continued, and continued, and continued some more. I got up ready to smash whoever's rude face it was on the other side of the door but couldn't, because it was Katie's boyfriend Roy.

He, like her, was a gym-addict, and he was that bulky I wouldn't have been able to push him over with a snow plow, let alone smash his face in.

'What do you want Roy?'

'You okay?'

'I think the terminology is, "having a shit day".'

For someone who didn't swear much, I'd sworn a lot over the previous twenty-four hours.

'Get dressed, I'm taking you to Hannah's house.'

'I don't really feel like it.'

He raised his eyebrows as if to tell me I didn't have a choice.

A voice belonging to that of someone I couldn't see came from outside the door.

'That's what I said too, but he's still making me go to Hannah's house.'

I ducked my head around the corner and spotted Katie, dressed nicely, but sitting down on the pavement beside the rail.

Roy too turned to her, 'You actually said, "Leave me alone, you prick".'

'Yeah, and you didn't listen,' she argued.

Roy turned back to me. I wasn't going to call him a "prick", but I was going to do what he said. I wanted to be alone but knew as sisters, the three of us were better off being together.

I walked in the front door of Hannah's house with three bunches of flowers. I'd bought three because Katie hadn't bought any and I figured Hannah wouldn't have either. I was right.

Brett was sitting on the couch with Justin and Brody, watching the television. Roy sat down next to them, 'Score?'

'Eight points,' Brett replied.

Katie walked over, still in her mood, 'This is a game from 1998; you know who wins. Stupid football.'

She then slouched down on the couch opposite them and watched that "stupid football" game.

I placed the flowers down on the table and asked Brett where Hannah was.

'On her bed.'

On her bed she was, lying in a pretty dress, looking up at the ceiling.

I lay down next to her. 'You all right?'

She didn't answer straight away, but when she did, it was with the same ignorance to her own emotions that Katie and I had shown to ours throughout the day.

'What possessed my husband to paint our ceiling red?'

She was the one who demanded he paint it that colour. I knew this because on a drunken night out months after her marriage she revealed the reason to me. Painting the ceiling red would heighten the intensity of their adult time. She said she'd be on the bottom most of the time so wanted a "passion-inducing colour" to look at while she was.

I wasn't going to remind her.

'Yeah, shit colour,' I responded.

We lay a few moments longer in silence. Without my urging, I knew Hannah could quite easily lie there all day, but it wasn't the right thing to do.

'We're going to be late.'

She turned to me and accepted we needed to get going, but again conceded how difficult it was going to be.

'How do you find the strength?'

I shrugged. *I don't know.*

It might have looked that way to her, but the reality was I couldn't find the strength. I never had the strength. I knew this day was an important day and being where we needed to be at 4.08pm was an important time.

'I get it from you,' I told her.

She pushed herself up off the mattress, sat on the end of the bed and took a deep breath. 'Let's go.'

Springvale Botanical Cemetery was a beautiful place. The trees were full of character, the water features were beautiful and the open spaces reassurance to the living that those who lay in peace had plenty of room to have a cup of tea under the sun, or kick the footy around with a mate. Tea of course, was one of Mum's favourite past times, while football was Dad's.

Arms locked together, Hannah, Katie and I held our flowers and walked across to where their bodies were laid to rest. It was never easy; that day seven years ago, at 4.08pm, they had been involved in a car accident on the Hume Freeway and been killed instantly. A pure accident caused by another driver had seen us lose our parents, just like that. I was twenty-one, Katie twenty-four, and Hannah twenty-seven.

'Hey Mum, hey Dad,' Katie said solemnly, as she lay her flowers over their graves.

Once at the cemetery, Katie was always the brave one. It took much longer for her to break; if Hannah or I spoke, we burst into tears, which we eventually did anyway.

It had come as a major shock – three young sisters, embarking on the early stages of adulthood, suddenly found themselves without the guidance they'd had their whole lives. In time, life had gotten easier, but it had still been really hard. The only way we had got through seven years was by sticking together.

'Roy's good, Mum,' Katie said. 'Still building caravans, being a spunk,' she laughed through a tear. 'Hannah and Brett are working hard, Dad; best parents you've ever seen. And the boys are growing up so fast; Brody spoke his first words the other day.'

That comment made all three of us laugh a little, as we thought back to the night Hannah and Katie had that disagreement.

'And Ella's good, too. She's running the toy store as well as you used to. She misses you both. We all do.'

Hannah and I lay our flowers down, kissed the tips of our fingers and then touched Mum and Dad's plaques – Jacob and Linda.

We then sobbed, all three of us.

Katie pulled both Hannah and I in for a hug and together we grieved our mum and dad. Life wasn't supposed to be this way.

Through tears we separated and said goodbye. My final words evoked more emotion as we carried on our lives without them.

'Love you Mum and Dad. Hope we're making you proud.'

Katie sat on Hannah's back verandah alone, aimlessly looking out at the backyard. She looked up at me as I opened the back door.

'Thought you might have been with Roy,' I said.

'He's okay. He's happily watching his third straight game of football... from 1998.'

On the mini drinks table beside her was a large potato chip packet.

'Thank God, Hannah does have some food in this house.'

But it was empty. Katie had eaten the entire pack.

'If I knew you wanted some...'

'You probably still would have eaten them all.'

'Probably.'

That was the problem with days like this – we didn't feel like eating at all during the morning and afternoon, but come nightfall, we were so hungry we could have eaten our own arm off.

'Mind if I sit?' I asked.

I thought she might have wanted to be alone but she was happy to have company.

'Hannah?' she asked.

'Brett's with her. I think they've both fallen asleep in their clothes.'

Hannah had gone to bed soon after we got back, and Brett was comforting her. The two boys had also been put down.

'You okay?'

Katie nodded, and after attempting to hide how she really felt, eventually let it out. 'I just hate it. I hate not having them here. I thought it would have gotten easier by now, but it still hurts. Everything reminds me of them; I look in the mirror and I see Mum, I see a sports game being played on TV and I think of Dad. I haven't gone to bed without them on my mind since the day they left.'

I'd been exactly the same.

'Love is supposed to fade and yet Dad was as madly in love with Mum the day he died, as he was the day they met one another. And Mum blushed every time he walked into the same room. And I think about it every night. I don't know how Roy puts up with it. I cry myself to sleep all the time and instead of telling me to shut up and get over it, he tells me he's there for me. And on days like this I treat him like shit and he still forgives me and cuddles me.'

Tears welled in her eyes again.

'That's love for you,' I said, visualising memories of Mum and Dad together. 'He loves you; he'd do anything for you, that's what makes him such a special guy.'

'I guess. I honestly don't know what I'd do without him.' She wiped her tears.

That comment saw her turn her attention to me – me who perhaps had it hardest of all; the youngest of the three daughters who hadn't had a husband or a boyfriend by her side since our parents had died.

'And that's why no one can begrudge you for putting yourself out there like you have. Just promise me, when he's in the same line as you at the bank, or on the same train carriage, or buying juice from the same café you go to, that you don't let him walk on by. Because he needs to see you, he needs to meet you, and he needs to know who you are.'

Of all those words she spoke, one stood out louder than the rest. *Juice.*

And for the first time that day, I stopped thinking of my mum and dad, and started thinking about someone else.

'Promise me,' she urged, shaking my arm and bringing my mind back to the present.

'I promise.'

I sat there thinking about him some more, and what Katie had said. She was right – I couldn't let him walk on by; he did need to know who I was.

Following a day of lethargy, I rose from the chair with renewed energy.

'You all right?' she asked.

'Yeah, there's just something I need to go and do.'

I jumped straight in an Uber, but only after doing so realised I had no idea where Max lived, so I texted him.

> **What's your address?**
> **Need to post you something.**

Thankfully, he replied thirty seconds later.

> 708/7, Balcombe Road Mentone, 3194.

708? What residence in Mentone could possibly have an apartment numbered 708, I thought.

But there was one; he lived in the apartment complex that was basically on the corner of Warrigal Road and Nepean Highway, in Mentone. I hated that apartment complex from the day they started building it – it replaced the ten-pin bowling alley I had my eighth birthday party at.

Truthfully, I was jealous of where he lived – on the ground floor were a pizza joint, a bottle shop and a Pilates studio. Anyone who lived there could eat pizza, get drunk, and then burn off the calories all within the space of fifteen steps.

I had to wait for one of the tenants to arrive home so I could get through the security door at the front of the complex. Once inside, I caught the elevator to level seven.

Standing in the elevator, a mix of emotions hit me I'd never experienced before. Adrenaline consumed me, yet I felt completely vulnerable – this was my all-conquering, glorious moment, yet I was convinced I'd be rejected again.

Of course Mum would give me all the answers on this very day, but what reason was there for Max to pick me over Shelly?

I reached room 708 and knocked but there was no answer. I knocked again but he wasn't home.

I thought about walking away with my tail between my legs but rallied against that mindset – that was what I always did. I was going to sit and wait this one out, and find out about he and I for good.

I sat down against the wall opposite the elevator. Again, my mind spun like a spinning top.

What if Max gets off the elevator with Shelly?

Who cares, you need to find this out one way or another.

What if he's kissing Shelly when he gets off the elevator? Then you being here will just look weird.

Then tell him you came because you've got a great idea for the project. But what idea?

I got my phone out and told myself if I was still sitting there at 7.30pm I'd leave. 7.30pm ticked by so I pushed it back to 8pm. I then pushed it back to 8.30pm. I then absolutely promised myself I'd leave at 8.45pm if he hadn't arrived home.

He arrived home at 8.49pm.

Fortunately, he got off the elevator on his own. He was in his work clothes and carrying his satchel. I stood as he walked out.

'Hey, what are you doing here?'

'Sorry, I know I said I'd post it, but I thought I'd come here instead.'

He smiled.

That smile, those eyes.

'That's okay, what is it?'

What was it indeed? My hands were empty, and I didn't have my handbag, so what on Earth had I brought that I couldn't post?

I hadn't gone to his apartment to lie, so there was no need to hastily think of something. It was time for me to come clean and tell the truth. About everything.

'I...'

He waited as I worked up the courage. With closed eyes and gritted teeth, I did so.

'I like you.'

A split second's silence scared me, and as a result, I blurted out an explanation to delay his rejection.

'And I know you're with Shelly and normally I wouldn't say such a thing to someone who's already with a greens keeper, but I've been holding these feelings inside me for so long and I can't keep going without telling you how I feel so I'm telling you... I like you.'

'I like you too.'

My beating heart and the fact I'd spoken at the speed of light left me breathing heavier, but I had heard right, *right?*

'You like me?'

'Yeah.'

'So, then... what about Shelly?'

'Shelly from the golf course?'

What other Shelly would I have been talking about?

'I haven't seen her since that day we ran into her at the café. She's just an old friend. Sure, we went on one date when we were in Year Eleven, but she made me play a round of golf with her, and, well, I hate golf.'

I chuckled; I hated golf too. He wasn't finished yet though.

'Plus it shouldn't come as a surprise that I like you; I've been trying to get in touch with you for weeks. I called you seven times to hang out again and you didn't call me back.'

Oh crap, I had done that; that had happened.

'I started working on your dating app project because I wanted to spend more time with you. I even said those things outside the Old Treasury Building when we played "Ellen and the Moon" and I let you win that last point.'

Silly Ella; all that had happened as well.

I suddenly knew what guys meant when they said they were getting mixed signals from a girl. But it wasn't all my fault; it was my stupid brain's fault.

I had completely over-read and over-thought a situation for the millionth time in my life. I saw Max with Shelly and the way they got along, and immediately convinced myself they were hot for each other. I didn't at all think they were a man and woman being friendly to one another as men and women could be.

'So you like me, and I like you; does that mean we can hang out?' I asked.

'It absolutely means we can hang out; how do you feel about pizza and beer?'

Nothing had ever sounded so good. After my day of malnourishment, I'd have traded both my sisters for a takeaway dinner.

'First drink's on me.'

20.

I bounced out of bed the next morning. I put my Ella's Awesome '90s Mix playlist on my phone and danced as I brushed my teeth, sang as I washed my hair, and tried to twerk after squeezing into my jeans. I fell over trying to twerk and ripped a giant hole in my jeans so changed them and decided never to twerk again.

Life was awesome; my Instagram and Facebook followers had grown again – thanks largely to Kye and the formal – and there was so much to look forward to.

I broached the topic of an official first date with Max the night before and suggested we do it twenty-four hours on. He declined, but only because he had a prior engagement. A prior engagement he wanted me to join him at, and not just me.

The toy store was open but unattended when I arrived. Elliot's normal routine after opening up was to be at the front register to happily welcome the first customer that came in for the morning. On this day, however, he wasn't there. I put my bag down and went for a wander.

I found him stocking shelves towards the back of the store. His response to my greeting was minimal and he didn't seem like his normal self.

'How do you feel about making some new friends tonight?' I asked.

'I have a lot of work to do.'

He told me he'd been having some headaches over the last few days and was finding them hard to cope with. Evie too had been sick and hadn't come into the store for a couple of weeks.

'Maybe she had a dog stuck in her belly,' I joked.

He didn't find it funny. Max's plans for that night would surely turn his frown upside down.

'But you and I normally do trivia tonight.'

Trivia was a ritual of Elliot and mine. We had missed the last few trivia nights due to me going on dates, which meant I owed him. But I really wanted to hang out with Max again.

'This will be even better,' I told him. 'Trust me.'

Elliot and I stood at a bus stop one-hundred metres down the road from my place. He looked at me like I was an alien. I didn't look far from it; I was covered in protective gear. As well as pants, boots and a jumper, I wore tea towels sticky-taped to my elbows and knees as elbow pads and kneepads, an old pair of ski gloves, an old empty weight vest I'd borrowed from Katie as a chest guard, a bike helmet and a cricket box I'd bought from a sports store. All the gear fitted except for the cricket box. I realised it moved around so much because it was made for a man, and, well, I didn't have anything to keep it in place.

Of course, I only realised that after I adjusted it feverishly at the bus stop for thirty seconds. Elliot observed me adjusting, as did an elderly lady who also stood at the bus stop. As if it wasn't weird enough that I was standing there dressed like a homemade medieval knight, I was fiddling with my bits in full public view. I eventually clocked the woman staring at me, slowly removed my hands from my pants and tried to cover-up what I'd been doing.

'Herpes,' Elliot said to the lady, which saw her turn away in disgust.

'Don't tell other people I've got herpes,' I whispered furiously but comically, at him.

'Then don't have your hand down your pants all the time.'

His response was more serious than my request. I got the feeling he still didn't want to be going out with us, but that changed when the bus arrived.

It wasn't your regular bus; it was an eight-seat mini-van, and a voice from the driver's seat yelled out at us.

'You know they provide protective gear?'

It was Max, and he had two black lines painted underneath his eyes. 'You'll have to take that stuff off.'

I reluctantly started to do so; I removed the weight vest with one hand and placed the other back down into my pants to remove the cricket box, but became aware of not just Elliot and the elderly lady looking at me, but five adolescent heads poking out of the windows of the mini-van.

'Maybe get into the van first,' Elliot said, 'Instead of undressing in the street.'

I was nervous; I'd never been paintballing before but I'd seen people that had, and they'd been covered in bruises for days.

'That's because they're not very good at it and they get shot a lot,' Max said.

It was safe to say I wasn't going to be very good.

Max called out to the back of the mini-van. 'Okay time to introduce everyone to everyone; everyone you all know Ella from that night at rehearsals, who's in the front seat with me. And in the middle seat with you guys is her best friend Elliot.'

They all said 'hi,' and then Max introduced them to us.

'Ella and Elliot, behind me is Chloe.'

He took his hands off the steering wheel momentarily and used sign language to communicate with her. She reciprocated.

Elliot smiled at her and she smiled back.

'Next to Chloe is Gloria, and in the back we have Phoebe, Finn and Owen.'

Gloria was blind, Phoebe had Down syndrome, Finn had cerebral palsy and Owen had an artificial leg. I looked back at all of them and felt privileged to have made new friends that were such special people.

'And that's pretty much us,' Max said.

'Aren't you going to introduce yourself?' Owen called from the back. 'Or should we do it for you?'

Max encouraged him to do so, but it was Gloria who introduced their fearless leader.

'This is Max, he plays really bad music on the bus radio, and has a serious case of road rage.'

'Hey!' Max responded light-heartedly, 'I don't have a serious case of...' To comically contradict himself, he paused mid-sentence, beeped the horn and entertainingly screamed at another driver that wasn't even there.

'... Get out my lane stupid; we've got paintball to get to.'

The entire van burst into laughter at Max's feigned displeasure.

The paintball course in Dingley looked intimidating; even with the sun still setting.

The course wasn't normally open at night, but Max knew the manager and he'd allowed us to have the whole place to ourselves.

Our paintball game was a face-off. We split into two teams – Max and I against Elliot, Chloe, Gloria, Phoebe, Finn and Owen. We stood in opposing lines and eyed each other off with dirty looks before the battle. I found giving a dirty look difficult, as on the inside my stomach was like a washing machine rumbling with fear. I wished I could have kept my bus stop padding on, as the gear the paintball people gave us seemed far less protective.

Max turned to me and studied my expression. 'Come on, put your mean face on; look angry.'

I thought I did have my mean face on; I thought I did look angry.

I looked down at the ground and then looked back up at the others and tried again.

'That's your mean face?' Owen asked. 'That doesn't look mean at all; it looks like you've got bad farts to push out.'

The others laughed at his inappropriateness, and – as they agreed with him – also laughed at me.

That was the final straw; I wasn't going to take crap from no one, not least these punks. I pierced my eyes, scrunched up my nose, and then in one final attempt to look even angrier, spat on the ground.

It was something I immediately regretted as the group looked at me in disbelief.

Being highly influenced young men and women, they were quick to change their minds however.

'Now that's a mean face,' Phoebe said, before she too spat on the ground.

The others then followed her lead and spat as well, but there was one person who didn't spit.

'Come on Max; what's wrong with you?' Owen asked.

Under severe peer pressure, Max leaned forward and half spat and half blew saliva out of his mouth.

'What was that?' Finn asked.

'Yeah, come on Max you've got to really hock it up,' Gloria added. 'Get it all gooey and mucusey and then unleash it like a paintball from your mouth.'

It was quite a descriptive demand from someone who was blind, but one Max obeyed.

He hocked up all the saliva he could muster and then spat it on the ground.

The kids loved it, he not so much. 'That felt awful.'

A red paintball then landed at his feet, close to where he spat, and shocked the two of us back into the moment.

'Enough of this gibbering nonsense,' Phoebe yelled. 'Let the war begin.'

The six of them turned and ran for cover while Max grabbed my arm and we charged over to the other side of the paintball warzone.

We reached a giant pyramid and crouched down behind it. The fear of being shot, the adrenaline running through my body as a result, and the way Max looked in his paintball gear made me aroused.

I could have made-out with him behind the pyramid there and then.

'What's our game plan?'

To make-out behind the pyramid.

With my mind in the gutter, I took a while to respond, so he asked a second question. 'Are you okay?'

Of course I wasn't; my erogenous zones were like a shaken bottle of lemonade ready to explode. I had to get my mind back on the job.

'Game plan?' he asked again.

'Not get shot,' I answered.

'Good plan, what else though? Split up or stay together?'

Stay together and make-out behind the pyramid. Damn it woman get your mind back on the job.

'Stay together.'

'Okay, you be the lookout and I'll be the shooter,' he said.

'Why do I have to be the lookout?'

'Fine, I'll be the lookout.'

'You'll be the lookout? What are you saying, I'm not good enough to be the lookout?'

'You said you didn't want to be the lookout.'

'Well maybe I do.'

'All right, you're the lookout then.'

'But I don't want to be the lookout.'

We were arguing, and I felt the sexual tension rising between us. He didn't feel it though. He lost patience with me and told me to stay put.

As he had lost patience with me, I felt it only necessary that I lose patience with him. I wasn't going to do what he told me to do.

I really should have though.

'You stay put, I'm the best shooter here, you do your thing and let me do mine,' I said.

I stood up from the cover the pyramid provided, dropped my guard for a single second and paid the ultimate price. Less than a second after getting to my feet, I was jolted by a massive thud and a feeling similar to that of hitting your knee against the corner of a table. The pain was excruciating and for some dumb reason, I didn't realise a paintball had caused it; I thought I'd been kicked by something. I held in a gigantic scream and then looked down at my pants to inspect the damage.

There it was – a giant green splat on the left leg of my body suit.

'Ha-ha, got you,' Elliot called from behind a cubby house-like feature on the other side of the warzone, rubbing salt into the wound.

That little...

So consumed by the stinging pain was I, that I was frozen on the spot. Moving would have caused my knee to hurt more, but as it turned out, standing still was worse. I took deep breaths to try and help deal with the agony, but soon felt the same stinging pain in my right leg, my abdomen, my shoulder and my forearm. Elliot shot me four more times, and laughed like an evil clown following every one of his direct hits.

'Ella get down,' Max said.

Standing still and taking deep breaths was no longer an option; on the brink of crying at the pain, I dropped back down behind the safety of the pyramid.

'I can't do this; it hurts too much, I need a Band-Aid™, or a surgeon.'

'Quitter.'

What did you just say?

Stunned by the shooting, I was no less appalled by Max's response to my agony. As the guy I liked and who liked me back, I expected nothing less than sympathy and support, but instead got an insensitive jerk.

'Did you call me a quitter?'

'Yeah, that's what you are if you quit. The way I see it is you can quit and they win, or you can pick up your weapon, stand with me and blow the hell out of those schmucks.'

He had dug himself out of a hole with the "stand with me" thing and inspired me to do just that. I had been pushed around too much in my life and was sick of it.

It was time to paintball the crap out of those disabled kids.

That thought wasn't the most considerate of my twenty-eight-year existence, but it was needed; it was time for payback.

I climbed to my feet and peeked out from behind the pyramid. I raised my weapon at Elliot who was out from cover high-fiving Phoebe and Chloe about fifteen metres away. I felt a moment's reluctance to fire a paintball at my best friend, but my hesitation dissipated when I heard him gloat.

'I got her good, so good.'

He grasped his gun to do so again but before he could engage in round two, I pulled my trigger and smashed him with an almighty thump right on the back of his shoulder.

The force almost knocked him to the ground and I was worried I'd hurt him badly, but he gradually picked himself up. Wilting in pain he reached around and touched the paint on his back.

He was stunned more so by the colour of the ball than the hurt it had caused.

'It's pink, she got me with pink.'

'I think it suits you,' Gloria said, making fun of her own blindness as well as Elliot's blow.

He stood and looked across the warzone directly at me; it was now my turn to laugh and give a high-five to Max.

Elliot, Chloe, Phoebe, Gloria, Finn and Owen stared at me and Max. Max and I stared back.

'You're going down punks,' Elliot yelled.

Both teams raised their guns – 'Ready, Aim, Fire!'

'I can't believe we didn't think to bring ice packs.'

Max could see the funny side of our injuries as he drove us home at the end of the night.

We were at war for thirty minutes and by session's end we looked like we'd fallen out of a giant bag of Skittles™.

Every square inch of my body was hit during the game, but the adrenaline that came with it was like a drug, and it quickly soaked up the countless aches caused by the paintballs hitting me.

After the game was a different story. There was no soaking up of anything – all I had was sore spots.

I checked the marks on my body; I'd never been so in need of a bath in all my life.

'I think I've got a bruise on top of a bruise,' Phoebe said.

'I think I need my other leg amputated,' Owen complained.

I looked around the van; everyone was observing and touching one another's bruises and laughing about it.

Elliot and Chloe were getting along like a house on fire. He'd certainly made a new friend, even though they couldn't speak to one another.

'Glad you came?' Max asked.

I was glad for a number of reasons; Max and I had been able to spend time together, but so too had me and Elliot. With everything that had happened with Tinderella, we hadn't been able to hang out as much.

Tinderella – and the sight of Elliot and Chloe – made me think about Max and my dating app project. A lot of disabled youths may have been missing out on this precious interaction; hopefully the dating app would make a difference.

'Maybe the next thing we do is just us,' he suggested. 'We make it something less painful and physically exhausting, like a dinner; a first date, if I could call it that.'

I liked that idea; a first date would be nice.

He looked at me, I looked back at him; we had a moment.

He shifted his eyes back onto the road and called out to the back of the van. 'How we all feeling back there?'

'Good,' they all called back at the same time.

'What about you Chlo'?' he asked, using sign language as well.

Chloe responded, and Max chuckled.

'What did she say?' I asked.

'She hates me for shooting her in the bum.'

I couldn't help but laugh; they sure did have a great sense of humour.

He yelled to the van again. 'So I'm thinking about what we're going to do next time. Should we do paintball again?'

'No,' came the response as the van erupted at his silly suggestion. Chloe leaned forward and playfully slapped him on the back.

One more bruise wasn't going to hurt.

21.

The house next door to Tiffany's was a reflection of my love life – bit-by-bit it was being put together.

In no time at all the property had gone from a vacant block to that with a wooden framework sitting on it. It made me think of the movie *Dear John*, the first kiss scene in the rain, and re-creating it with Max.

It wouldn't be happening that day because it was sweltering hot.

I wondered how Max and my first kiss might unfold. I then obsessed over it – all I could think about was kissing. Two blonde ladies sat next to each other on the bus and I thought of Britney Spears and Madonna kissing at an awards show, we went past the boats in Mordialloc Creek and I thought of Jack kissing Rose on the front of the *Titanic*, and I saw a ghost in my unit and thought of Demi Moore and Patrick Swayze.

The ghost was actually my own shadow.

Part of me felt – with things progressing with Max – I might not need to see Tiffany anymore, but I had a couple of sessions left and had paid for them, so thought I'd still attend. It would have been rude not to.

Her front door was open, and I could hear a piano being played. I walked through to her back room, suspecting it was she, and it was.

'Hello, darling.'

I had no idea she played the piano, and she was good too.

I was eager to tell her of everything that had occurred since my last visit and my anxieties about what lay ahead, but it would have to wait, as she wanted me to do something first.

'There's a carpenter putting up some wood next door; go and make an approach.'

Another game?

'I think I'm past that.'

I really was; the "approach" was no longer an issue. My first date with Max was going to be that day and I needed assistance making the right moves, and knowing what I should do when it was time for the first kiss. But she wasn't changing her mind.

'Approach please.'

I dropped my bag, headed back out the front door and walked over to the house-to-be next door. I had a couple of nerves but nothing like I used to.

I didn't hesitate; I walked straight up to the tradesman and said hello.

'Hey,' replied this sombre voice.

Under the hat was Liam.

I had to do this with her son again?

'Being made to dress-up as a tradie, huh?' I asked. 'That's harsh in this heat; hope you've got sunscreen on.'

'Actually, I am a tradie. Mum bought the land and I'm building on it. Remember a few weeks ago when I went to the hardware store after you wanted to strawberry cream your pants?'

I did remember that.

'Well I did go to the hardware store.'

'So your mother has sent me out here to help you build?'

'She's sent you out to make me feel better.'

'Why, what's happened?'

'My girlfriend broke up with me.'

He kept working as we talked. He measured something and drilled something else. It was hard labour but something that seemed therapeutic as well.

Our chat was like therapy too.

'Nothing happened; neither of us did anything wrong; she told me she didn't like me anymore and that was it. Mum kept telling me all this crap about me being young and how there were other girls out there, but I don't want to hear it.'

If his dating coach mother couldn't make him feel better then what hope did I have? It was best I told him that.

'You know how many times I've been dumped?'

'How many?'

'None, because I've never had a boyfriend before, so it makes it hard for me to understand.'

'Then I'm glad you're out here.'

He was being sarcastic.

'But I've learnt over the last few weeks – and not just with your mother – how important perspective is. For so long I went on dates and they didn't work out, and I'd think it must have been me, that I was the worst person in the world, and no one could ever love me. But then I changed my perspective. Lately, when dates have been horrible, instead of thinking there's some huge problem with me, I've looked at things differently.'

He stopped measuring and listened, 'And how's that?'

'That he's rejecting me because he knows there's someone better in my future, and if he stays around when he shouldn't, he'll get in the way of me meeting them.'

'That's a little bit mental.'

'Sure, but it's helped, and when the day comes that I do meet the right guy, I'll be glad the other ones said "no", because if they'd said "yes", I might not have met him.'

He thought about it for a second and then changed his mind, 'That's actually not a bad way of looking at it.'

'All relationships are different but perhaps you should look at this one in a similar light. If your ex-girlfriend stayed with you out of pity, she would have gotten in the way of the next girl that comes along. The next girl that comes along might not just be your future girlfriend, but your future wife.'

I could see he felt better having heard those words, and was in a better headspace.

'I guess you're right. Why are you seeing my mother? You seem to know this relationship stuff better than she does.'

'That's just it, she's the one who taught me.'

I returned to Tiffany's house. She was still sitting at the piano.

'Thank you,' she said.

How did she know I'd had any success?

'I was watching from the window. He's barely made any progress with that frame in three days.'

That's why she was thankful? Because he was once again making progress with the frame?

'What else should I be thankful for? You making my son happy again?'

It was her way of letting me know her son's happiness was what she was thankful for.

She stood, closed the piano lid, moved into the living area, and moved the conversation to me. 'Now, what's been going on in your world?'

'Max.'

She was proud I'd got on the front foot and told Max I liked him, despite the possibility of him having a girlfriend. She was also of the opinion the first date and the first kiss were a piece of cake compared to the approach, especially when I knew the guy quite well.

Our discussion, which was relative to the notes in my folder, largely surrounded that of being myself and how "less is more".

'Even with the kiss, keep it brief.'

Katie had often told me to always leave them wanting more.

'No, I didn't mean that,' Tiffany disagreed. 'Mature men and women don't play games; you have to respect his feelings as well, but don't go diving into his mouth like you would a packet of peanut M&Ms.'

Like pretty much everyone else in my life, I'd told her about the peanut M&Ms.

I arrived home in the early afternoon to find Max waiting for me.

'Sitting outside people's apartments, I thought only I did that,' I joked.

'How do you feel about spontaneous getaways?'

I loved them, but probably preferred an hour's heads up.

'I'll give you ten minutes to pack a bag and meet me at my car.'

He wasn't agitated, but this spontaneous getaway seemed less like a bright idea, and more like he was trying to avoid something. I wanted him to talk about it, but only having ten minutes, didn't want to hit the road without a change of clothes.

22.

'Probably best to check the weather map ahead of any spontaneous getaway.'

That afternoon, and the following forty-eight hours, was close to the most rainfall the state had had all year.

'What? It's just a little rain.'

It wasn't just a little rain at all; it was bucketing down, and it was the pits.

Max's demeanour lifted the moment his foot hit the accelerator outside my place. I asked him if there was anything wrong, and he said everything was fine.

He was being honest – the longer the day went, and the heavier the rain got, the happier he became.

Everything wasn't fine with me; as I stood and held a tent pole on a site at Wilson's Promontory, I wished like anything I was changing into a fancy black cocktail dress and getting ready for our incredibly special first date. In fact, forget the special date, I would rather have been anywhere other than where I was.

I looked down at the site number on a peg below me. We were on Site 155, on Fourth Avenue at Tidal River, which was the camping section situated on the southwest coast of the 505-squared kilometres Wilson's Prom was made up of.

Unsurprisingly, there was not one other person camping on our avenue.

'That's the best way to camp,' Max said.

'Are you almost done?' I asked.

Not that it mattered; after standing in the same spot, holding the same pole for twenty-five minutes, I was that drenched I looked like I'd taken a bath in my clothes.

'There, finished; you can jump inside now.'

The inside of the tent was cramped, and even more so when Max pumped-up two inflatable mattresses and put two doona covers on top of them.

He lay down and let out a relaxing 'ahh.'

'So do we go to sleep now and hope that when we wake the rain will be gone?'

I was being cheeky, but he took it well and then one-upped me.

'No, we have our first date.' He flicked a packet of rice crackers over to me.

'Are you serious?'

I was disappointed he'd seen the biggest moment in our romantic lives to that point as something trivial, but he quickly redeemed himself.

'I'm sorry, I know you pictured tonight being something completely different, and I really do thank you for coming here with me, knowing I needed an escape. But you should know – whether we're fine-dining or eating dry biscuits in the rain, I'm just happy doing it with you. Come here, lie down.'

I didn't really want to lie down in my wet clothes, but being out of my comfort zone anyway, decided to do so. He put his arm around me and I fell a mile into his gaze. I joked about it, but I could have fallen asleep there and then, and not woken until the rained stopped.

Typically, he had other ideas.

'You know what? Grab your coat; I've got somewhere we can go.'

Wilson's Prom had an open-air cinema that showed a different movie every night of the week through summer and autumn. It was the last viewing night of the season and due to the inclement weather, Max and I – and three others – were the only people in the cinema. It was billed as Classic Film Night. I anticipated that meant *The Wizard Of Oz*, *Gone With The Wind* or even *Grease*, but it didn't. The film they showed was *The Blair Witch Project*, which was made in 1999.

'How is 1999 considered classic?'

'I think by "classic" they mean cult,' Max said, as he paid for the tickets.

My issue with the choice of picture wasn't just the year it was made but it's genre as well. I had never had a relationship with horror. Not at midday inside a sunlit room with the sound down and coloured balloons everywhere. It took just five minutes for me to bury my head into Max's shoulder and look away from the screen. Every so often I checked to see what was going on and each time someone was having the wits scared out of them in a dark forest.

There was an intermission forty-five minutes into the film and I asked Max if we could please leave. I thought he'd prey on my fears and say no, or tell me I could walk back on my own, but thankfully he didn't.

'We'll even take the shortcut back to our camp site,' he said.

With it being dark and the two of us only having one torch, I had no idea of my bearings. After climbing a small hill, we reached the start of a narrow dirt pathway, which looked frighteningly like the one in the horror movie.

'It's fine. Our campsite is three hundred metres at the other end of this path; we'll be home in no time,' Max reassured me.

The pathway was surrounded by dense forest. The tree branches intertwined above, which created something of a tree-tunnel, and the branches made eerie sounds as they blew in the wind.

I gripped onto his arm from the moment we stepped foot on it. I was terrified, and was taking the smallest, slowest steps in case I stood on a wombat, or a skeleton.

'Why don't I tell you a story; to help take your mind off it,' he suggested.

'Yes, please, tell me a story.'

He thought about it for a second and then begun. In taking my "mind off it", I anticipated he'd tell me a story that involved beaches, and palm trees, and hammocks.

Not of other scary pathways.

'The scariest track I ever walked was called Biddy's Trail. The first time I walked it I was thirteen and I was told of its origins by a park ranger.'

He spoke slowly and calculatedly, as if not wanting to overlook a single detail.

'The park ranger told me hundreds of years ago, white sailors kidnapped an aboriginal woman named Biddy. She tried to escape but the sailors recaptured her and killed her. From then on, Biddy's ghost haunted the track every night, and spooked those who sauntered along the path, in the same, very particular way.'

'What way was that?'

'She approached those who walked it and tapped them on the shoulder. I thought the park ranger was being funny but the first time I walked it, sure enough, I felt a tap on the shoulder and the ghost of Biddy appeared. It scared me more than I've ever been scared before.'

I swallowed a thick and anxious swallow and continued to hold onto Max with all my might.

'Thank God we're not on Biddy's Trail then,' I said.

He paused a moment, and then in a deliberate frail and fearful voice, spoke the final detail of his story.

'That's just it – this is Biddy's Trail.'

I felt a freezing cold chill shoot up from my feet into my legs, and up my spine. 'We're on Biddy's Trail?' I asked with growing terror.

'Sure, but don't worry, Biddy doesn't come out on nights like...'

At that moment I felt a hand fall onto my shoulder, and I screamed like I'd never screamed before. I turned and swatted in every direction, fearing the ghost of Biddy was right beside me. She wasn't, but no longer was Max either. The torchlight lay on the ground and shadows were all I could see. Max had dropped it, but what had happened to him?

I was so scared I was on the precipice of crying. I picked up the torch and called out to Max. But there was no response.

I quickly turned to my left and there was nothing. I turned back to my right and there was still nothing. I shined the torchlight into the bushes but couldn't see Max at all. I called his name out again.

A hand then grabbed my shoulder again.

'Argh! Argh! Argh!'

I screamed as loud the second time as I did the first, and only stopped when I turned and saw it was Max who was connected to the hand.

He laughed.

'Why the hysterics? You called my name; I was letting you know I was here.'

He so was not.

My heart beat fiercely and I breathed heavily. I'd had enough; I'd been so badly petrified I was not far from needing a therapist.

I begged. 'Can we just walk the rest of the path and get back to our camp site please?'

He nodded again, and then walked back in the direction we'd come.

'Where are you going?' I asked.

'Oh, didn't you know? This isn't a shortcut at all. Our camp site is back this way.'

Suffice to say I didn't sleep very well. The softest noise saw me grip my pillow in fear a giant echidna was going to enter the tent and eat us both.

I eventually did fall asleep, and when I woke, the rain had stopped, and outside sitting on a log was Max, waiting with a coffee and an egg and bacon roll.

'Where'd you get that?'

'From the local store; I can drink it if you don't want it.'

I would have fought him to the death for that coffee.

'Need to get your energy levels up for what I've got planned today.'

'Let me guess, another walk?'

'Supposed to be a nice day for it.'

After breakfast and a shower, we caught a transport bus ten minutes out of the camping grounds to a car park located halfway up a mountain called Mount Oberon. Even at the halfway mark, the peak looked impossible to reach.

'It's only five hundred and fifty metres high.'

550m high but a 3.5km walk to the summit. A walk made all the more difficult by another downpour that set in at that exact moment.

'Nice day for it huh?' I complained.

Twenty-five minutes into the walk and I trudged along like a drowned rat. A drowned rat with lower back soreness.

'How about a game?' Max suggested.

'How about you carry me?' I countered.

I was only kidding but he stopped and squatted down. I meant for him to carry me in his arms, but a piggyback was better than nothing.

'Is this the moon game again?'

'No, this is a game I only play when it's raining. It's called, "Where are we getting married".'

The title intrigued me, but it needn't have, as there was no intrigue to it. It was a simple question and answer game he'd made up on the spot.

'You're asking me that now? Like already?'

'Come on, surely you've thought about your own wedding; haven't most girls?'

Yes, I had, but if he was going to mess with me on this trip, I was going to mess with him.

'Where are we getting married? Vegas.'

'What?'

'I want to gamble at The MGM, get drunk at Caesar's and then get married at the Little White Chapel, all while slurring my wedding vows.'

Unable to see my face, he couldn't tell I was playing around. 'Okay... that's um... that's interesting.'

'I'm kidding. Maybe at the Botanical Gardens, or at a vineyard down the peninsula with magnificent flora everywhere and a cellist playing to the side. What about you?'

'Venice.'

Woah.

He had clearly thought about it as well. Venice would be nice but definitely out of reach.

'Don't worry I won't make your dad pay for the whole thing.'

Cue awkward silence.

I didn't know how to respond. I hadn't told him of my parents, and wasn't ready to, so – after an awkward pause – moved the conversation on in another direction.

'Good game, should we play another?'

'Wait, that game's not finished – what kind of house are we going to live in?'

'Um... a brick one.'

'Nothing else? Interiors?'

I was still a little bit thrown by his "dad" comment. We'd passed it now and I needed to relax and continue with the game. Whatever the game was – us planning our future, or something.

'You have thought about it, yeah?' he pressed.

Of course I had.

'The main bedroom will have an en suite, the kitchen will have a walk-in pantry and there'll be a small garden with an outdoor setting, but a courtyard with grass for our dog to run around in. What about you?'

'Happy with all that; needs a juice room though.'

'A what?'

'A room dedicated to just drinking juice. Nothing else happens in it, just juice; I'll call it Max's juice room.'

I knew he was now playing, and it made me relax.

'That's weird; I'll buy you a vintage bench chair for the backyard and you can drink all the juice you want on it. What's next?'

'How many kids are we having?'

'Two – a boy and a girl.'

'Too cruel; has to be three, one of them has to have a best friend to play with, while the odd one out gets more attention from his or her parents.'

'I'm not pushing three babies out; two's enough.'

'Okay, what are their names?'

'Grace and Maggie.'

'Maggie for a boy?'

'What, no, they're both girls.'

'You just said a boy and a girl.'

'I change my mind. Women are allowed to change their minds you know. What are your three names?'

'Steeler, Rabbitquest and Buck.'

'What the hell is that? Characters from a video game?'

'No, they're names I like.'

'Hell will freeze over before any one of my kids gets named Rabbitquest.'

Mount Oberon wasn't far from freezing over itself, as the rain came down even heavier. Our conversation couldn't have been more contrasting to our actions. Each step Max took with me on his back brought us closer to the clouds that created the storm. Yet the words we spoke were of a bright and sunny future.

'Where are we honeymooning?' he asked.

'We're having kids first and honeymooning with them second?'

'No, I forgot to ask it before the kids question and now I'm going back to it.'

'You go first,' I told him, changing it up.

'Sports tour of the world – England for soccer, America for basketball and baseball, and Sweden and Norway for curling.'

I had never heard of curling, nor had I seen Max have anything to do with sports. I was curious to find out what his real answer was.

'Come on, really, where are you going to take me?'

'St Lucia, then maybe spend the second week travelling the other islands like St Barts, Jamaica and The Cayman Islands. I visited a cousin who's worked in the Caribbean for the past five years. The whole setting is incredible. What about you?'

I needed a second to check St Lucia on my phone because I didn't know what it looked like. Max wondered what I was doing as I rummaged in my pocket.

'Have you ever tried to get a phone out of your pocket, while receiving a piggyback in a cyclone?' I asked, cheekily.

Keeping the phone covered and "Googling" the Caribbean was just as difficult.

My whole life I'd thought a honeymoon to Santorini would be perfect but looking at photos of the places he suggested, I conceded, 'St Lucia, I suppose I could put up with that.'

'So we agree on something. Not sure we'll agree on this last one though – which celebrity did you have a crush on through high school?'

That was a question much different to the others but one he had a reason for – he wanted to make sure he didn't have my high school crush as one of his groomsmen in case I left him at the altar.

My answer was Zac Efron.

'Fair enough; guy has abs and stuff.'

Max's answer was Rachel McAdams. I admittedly liked that answer, but after doing the sums, couldn't help but investigate why.

'Didn't *The Notebook* come out when you were in high school? Is that when you got a crush on her?'

He denied it, of course.

'No, never saw it, I think I just saw her on a poster somewhere.'

'Are you sure? You didn't see her during a viewing of *The Notebook*, while you were crying and pleading for Noah and Allie to get back together?'

It felt good, me teasing him for once, and he went along with it.

'Noah and Allie were meant for each other! They needed to be together.'

I laughed; he made me laugh.

I liked the name Noah. I did have my daughter's names locked in, but if one of them came out a boy, then I could have easily named him Noah.

'I told you – Rabbitquest.'

'Definitely not Rabbitquest.'

'Okay, how about Wanda then?'

He laughed this time.

Oh good God.

He'd remembered how I'd talked about my fake Aunt Wanda when playing theatre games the night I visited him at Shirley Burke Theatre.

That was a conversation I didn't want to have.

'Come on, walk faster now, my back is starting to hurt.'

'*Your* back is starting to hurt?'

The view at the top of Mount Oberon was incredible. The rain stopped as we closed in on the summit and the sun began to peek through the clouds. I could see the surf beach, the nearby river and even faintly the area in which our tent was located. The weather had been poor, and the walk had been strenuous, but I was glad Max had taken me to the top.

'Maybe we can build our first house up here,' I said.

He nodded.

'So long as it's got my juice room.'

Standing beside me with an arm over my shoulders, he turned and faced me, and looked into my eyes.

'Speaking of firsts... you look really pretty.'

He then leant in and kissed me.

The kiss caught me a little by surprise, but that was good – it didn't allow me to think or become nervous.

It was a slow, soft kiss that was amazing. He then placed his thumb and his index finger on the tip of my chin, which sent an amazing, tingling chill down my body. His lips were so delicately perfect I could have allowed them to massage mine forever, but then, just at the right time, he slowly pulled away. He kissed me on the cheek and then gave me a hug. Only then did the gravity of the moment hit me; had I just experienced a little slice of heaven? Yes. Was I proud of myself for not ruining a truly romantic moment like I always did? Kind of.

In his arms I thought of what best to say next, but – determined to prolong such perfection – decided not to say anything.

Max eventually looked down at me and smiled, 'I think we should take a photo.'

He took out his phone and did so, and I handed him mine for the same. I looked at the photos and was happy with what I saw. In fact, looking wet-hot in my active-wear from the soaking the rain had given me, I couldn't pass up the opportunity for a solo photo. I hadn't updated my social media for a couple of days and it was the perfect time to do so.

When I asked Max to take a picture of just me however, he didn't appear so keen.

'Ah... yeah, I suppose I can do that.'

'Just for my sisters,' I explained.

I got the feeling he knew the real reason I wanted a solo shot.

He took some snaps and nonchalantly handed me back my

phone. I felt bad, like I'd just wrecked our perfect moment.

Fortunately, Tiffany's training came to hand just when I needed it to, and admiration once again replaced awkwardness.

'My turn to carry you down?'

'I think I'd be too heavy; maybe we can just hold hands.'

Dinner was fish and chips from the local store. I showered again in readiness for bed, but as I left the toilet block the rain began pelting down again. So I rang Max.

'Can you come and pick me up?'

'Our camp site is eighty metres from the toilet block.'

'I've washed my hair.'

While I'd been showering he'd prepared yet another game. I was getting over all the games but he'd secretly packed Guess Who into the car, so I relented.

'Why don't we make it interesting,' he suggested. 'And play Strip Guess Who instead.'

Strip Guess Who was the same as normal Guess Who™ but whoever lost each game had to remove an item of clothing. We hadn't been dating that long, which meant I was still a little body conscious, but finding the right guy meant stepping outside my comfort zone so that's what I was going to do. Plus, only having torch light meant it was quite dark.

The first two games went exactly the way I thought they would.

'Are you Anne?' he asked.

'Am I Anne? Yes, Anne I am.'

He won them both, easily.

I revealed Anne as my card and removed the sock from my left foot, having removed the sock from my right after losing the first game. I still had eight cards standing on my board but was determined to guess which card he had.

'Are you Peter? Are you Robert? Bernard? Susan?'

He answered no to all of those.

'Are you Phillip? Are you Charles? Are you Eric?'

The answer was still no.

'That means you've got to be Herman and you can't be Herman.'

'I am,' he revealed, flicking his card over to me.

The card hit me on the arm but that didn't bother me. Him cheating however did.

'Herman?' I questioned. 'You were Herman in the first game.'

'So?'

As a woman who owned a toy store, board games and the rules of board games were my specialty. I wasn't going to let him get away with cheating.

'It's a well-known fact in Guess Who that you can't use the same person two times in a row.'

'You can so.'

'No you can't.'

'You can.'

'Can't.'

'Read the box, it says nothing about not being able to pick up the same card twice.'

'Fine I will.'

I picked up the lid but because we sat in near darkness, I couldn't read a thing. Not that that mattered – it was common knowledge you had to change cards in between games.

'So the creators of the game are wrong, and you're right?' he jested.

'Yes.'

'I didn't knowingly pick up Herman twice; it was an accident.'

'Doesn't matter, you did, which means you broke the rules, which means it's two-nil to me.'

It should have been one-one technically, but as he'd cheated, I felt he should forfeit any previous points he'd accumulated before the cheat and pass them over to me.

'I want to take this to an appeals panel.'

'And with you and I the only one's here, who do you suggest makes up this appeals panel?'

He eventually yielded and allowed me the two points; confident he'd still win anyway.

Three games later he sat opposite me in nothing but his briefs.

I deliberately took my time choosing my next card, so I could glance at his chest. A man's body had never meant that much to me – a kind face, nice eyes and someone who made me laugh were much higher on the agenda, but his physique was a pleasant surprise. His shoulders weren't overly broad, he didn't have abdominals and his chest wasn't without body hair, but he did have some definition, and really nice skin.

Game six saw him take a risk and it paid off. A lucky guess right off the bat saw him successfully select Frans and that was the card I'd picked up. I slid my arms out of my sleeves and lifted the body of my jumper up to my head, but got it stuck around my jawline. I couldn't see anything and yanking it to try and get it off my head would hurt.

'Here, let me help.'

Max crawled over and gently raised the jumper above my eyebrows and my forehead. He handed me the jumper and while I clasped it, he didn't let go. On his knees, less than a foot away from me, he stared into my eyes and swallowed nervously. I knew what he wanted, and I wanted it too. I let go of the jumper with one hand and placed it on his, to let him know it was okay to continue.

He kissed me, let go of the jumper and I threw it off to the side.

He helped me lift my t-shirt over my head, leaving me in just a bra and the cotton tracksuit pants I had on. And then he pushed a few strands of hair behind my ear, lowered his hand to my jawline and kissed me. It started off like the kiss on Mount Oberon, but this time became more passionate. It wasn't overbearing; he knew what he was doing. He kissed me on the neck and gradually worked his way back to my lips again. He then stopped and looked into my eyes. I could almost feel his heart racing, but it may have just been mine.

'Are you okay?' he asked.

It was his way of asking if I consented. Kissing him back was surely a sign I did, but I respected him for asking.

I nodded.

'I'll take care of you I promise.'

I nodded again, and this time initiated the kiss. We slowly leant back onto the mattresses and undressed as the rain continued to fall. I never imagined enjoying such heightened sensations.

With each kiss I fell more and more in love.

23.

Sleeping in my own bed in my unit in Aspendale was a real comedown. Even more so when I was woken by an early morning knock at my front door.

It was Hannah, and it was the first time she'd ever come to my flat.

'Where the hell have you been?'

I was going to tell her, but she didn't let me.

'I've had editors and publicists calling me telling me they've been trying to get hold of you for the past two days. Why don't you answer your phone?'

'Because I had no reception.'

That was the truth, not that it made her go any easier on me.

'No reception where?'

'Didn't you see the photo I put up on the mountain?'

'Ella, Katie takes care of all of that crap, I do the important stuff.'

Her phone rang before she could tell me what that "important stuff" was. She answered it. 'I left his dummy in the bag; I said only call me if it's an emergency.' She put her phone back in her handbag and expressed a humph, 'In-laws. I've got a meeting to get to. What are you doing tonight?'

She turned and walked back up the pathway. We shouted back and forth at one another as she left.

'Trivia with Elliot.'

'Cancel it.'

'I can't; we do it every week.'

'Well then take somebody else; I need you on a date tonight. It's non-negotiable. I'm happy to line someone up for you, just let me know by lunchtime.'

She didn't have to; I already had someone. Not that that made me feel any better about it.

The next person to knock on a front door was me.

I'd earlier put on the huskiest voice I could and called in sick to work. If I spent the day at the toy store in full health and then cancelled trivia on Elliot, it would have seriously dented our relationship. Being told on the phone I was sick saw him accept my cancellation more easily.

The second task was convincing Max to come with me. He'd been unreachable on the phone all day, so I had to go to his front door at 6pm and proposition him.

'Sorry, left my phone at home and was going to call you back now. You're all dressed up.'

I was, and I needed him to be in less than fifteen minutes. 'I've booked a table at trivia tonight and Elliot's sick, so I need you to come with me.'

'How long have I got?'

'Not long.'

'Aw, that's a shame.'

I suddenly realised why he was asking, and I was keen for it as well. But I couldn't; there wasn't enough time to re-shower and re-dress and still make it to trivia on time. And I couldn't do the Katie thing and head straight there after doing the deed. All those trivia players would have smelt me for sure.

'We'll do it after trivia,' he suggested.

'I'm holding you to that.'

Trivia was at The Bridge Hotel in Mordialloc. It was aptly named The Bridge Hotel because it was positioned right beside Mordialloc Bridge.

Max and I sat down at a table for two, the quizmaster greeted us and handed us an answer sheet.

'Different partner tonight, Ella?'

He was one of those observant types.

I feigned a smile and felt the guilt I'd been trying to bury for the past hour rise in my throat again.

There were two rounds of twenty questions and a three-question jackpot worth three hundred dollars at the end. The quizmaster also left us with a pen, and Max wrote our team name down at the top of the page – Max and Ella.

He put a lot of thought into that one.

He went off to get us drinks and I changed our name to – Max and lady friend.

I removed the Ella part so other regulars wouldn't discover I was there without Elliot, when the quizmaster read our team name out aloud.

The questions during the first half were relative to events of that week, while the second half was general knowledge. We were behind the eight ball from the beginning; having spent three of the last seven days inside a tent, we had no idea when it came to recent news and current affairs. We didn't make up any ground in general knowledge either, however the jackpot round was ours.

The first two questions of the jackpot involved information technology and the Caribbean, and having studied one and visited the other, Max knew the answers.

With question three pending, my phone rang. It was Hannah and she couldn't have called at a worse time. I knew what it was about and that I had to answer it. Only, I couldn't answer it around Max.

I apologised to him, moved over to a window and put the phone to my ear.

'Can you make it quick?'

'Ah, sorry to bother, just doing a favour for you,' she said, sarcastically.

'Sorry, what is it?'

'Go to the pier.'

'Great, bye.'

The jackpot round was done by the time I got back to Max. He looked at me like a sad puppy dog. 'We can go now, yes?' he asked.

No way, I wanted to stay and find out if we won.

'We didn't win.'

A walk on Mordialloc Pier followed trivia. It was a walk taken for many reasons – to enjoy the night sky and to get some fresh air, but also to stop me making a scene inside The Bridge Hotel.

Why? He got the last jackpot question horribly wrong.

'Oprah? Are you kidding me?' I growled.

The final jackpot question was - Name George Clooney's wife.

And he wrote down Oprah.

He tried to explain.

'I knew it wasn't right, but I didn't know what else to write.'

'You take an educated guess. Even the dumbest person in the world knows George Clooney and Oprah aren't married.'

I was being semi-serious but serious enough to make him feel guilty. He did, after-all, cost me three hundred dollars.

'A hundred and fifty – we would have gone halves.'

'No way. I was team captain, so I would have got it all. You have to give me something worth three hundred dollars now to make up for it.'

I was fully teasing him.

'I do, do I? And what would you like?' he asked.

'A dinner; a really fancy dinner.'

'I did have that in mind.'

That came as a nice surprise – the proper first date I so longed for.

What followed, however, was a surprise that wasn't quite so welcoming.

'Maybe a dinner where you could introduce me to your parents?'

We still hadn't spoken about it. It was something I knew I had to talk to him about at some point; I just needed more time.

With the rawness of their anniversary still deep-seated, my emotions began to spill over and I got upset.

Max was naturally sincere. 'Hey, it's all right; what's wrong?'

I felt silly crying about it, but it was one of those moments where I wasn't in control. I'd only talked about my parents with my family and one other person – Elliot. I truly believed Max was in my life for good however, as a boyfriend or friend, so – despite our relationship being in its infancy – I decided to tell him the truth.

'There's something I need to tell you.'

He nodded, with the kind of fear in his expression that struck when sensing a relationship was about to end.

Of course, it wasn't that.

'I don't have a mum or a dad.'

He didn't say anything. I was sure he wanted to ask how or why but he remained quiet out of respect; he knew the importance of listening to something that, for me, would be incredibly hard to say.

'They died in a car accident when I was twenty-one. It's just me and my two sisters. I don't tell many people, and I was waiting for the right time to tell you, but it's hard. You'd think after all this time I'd be able to tell people my parents died without getting emotional, but it still makes me sad.'

I wiped away tears and – feeling considerably vulnerable – looked up at him. He looked solemn. An apology followed.

'I'm sorry, I should have been more sensitive.'

He needn't have apologised; how was he to know?

A thank-you then followed. 'That was incredibly brave of you to tell me something so personal.' And then came a promise. 'And I'll respect your right to talk about it whenever you're ready.'

He brought me in closer for a hug. It felt good to be held tight, but his grip loosened quicker than I thought it would...

'Sorry but, can you give me a sec'?'

... And then he walked away. I turned to see what he was doing. He strode back to the start of the pier and approached a man. I couldn't hear what he was saying but he looked to be speaking quite sternly. I noticed the man had a camera by his side and from that moment knew exactly what was going on. I hurried over to extinguish the flames that were starting to burn between them.

Max had his hand out and with each demand his voice grew louder until he was shouting. The cameraman finally surrendered something into his hand as I got to them. 'Max, it's okay.'

'What? This guy was taking photos of you while you were crying; how is that okay?'

'It's fine, I promise.'

I placed my palm onto his, which held the cameraman's SD card.

The subtext to my promise became clear to him – the cameraman was supposed to be there. I took the SD card from him, handed it back to the cameraman and apologised. He accepted my apology, but I wished he hadn't.

'It's all good, Ella.'

His use of my name made things in Max's mind even clearer. With the cameraman gone, he put his hands on his forehead with embarrassment. For the first time in a long time I didn't know what to say to a guy.

Didn't know what to say to Max.

He on the other hand knew just what to say, and for the first time, he said something to me that really hurt.

'So, was that Ella hanging out with me tonight or was it Tinderella?'

I thought of how best to answer that, but he didn't give me the chance.

'I have to go.'

There I stood, alone on the pier, ashamed of myself and petrified we were over.

The night wasn't supposed to end like that.

24.

All four seasons in one day – Melbourne was known for it, but with so many emotions flowing through my veins, I was beginning to think it was a fair description of my heart as well.

I fully expected Hannah to rock up on my front door step the next morning yet again. This time however, she woke me with a phone call.

'Are you trying to cause me as much grief as possible?' she asked.

She'd received a phone call the night prior from a publicist at the newspaper complaining about the treatment of one of their photographers, and was relaying the message onto me.

I knew it was coming.

'Fair enough if he'd been stalking you for an hour but I rang them and organised it. You knew exactly where he was going to be, and you still let the guy you were with walk over to him and almost bash him. She threatened to stop all her camera guys from taking photos of you. How do you think I felt having to plead with her not to? Get out of the way idiot.'

She was driving, which caused her last outburst.

I apologised – it was an innocent mistake Max had made and it wouldn't happen again.

'Wow, that was quick; I suppose it shouldn't surprise me considering they ran a pic of him making you cry.'

It took me a second to figure out she'd misunderstood – I meant it wouldn't happen again because I wouldn't allow it, whereas she thought I meant it wouldn't happen again because I'd dumped him already.

'Don't worry; all is not lost; I've got something else in the works.'

I should have explained what I meant by "wouldn't happen again", but didn't have the time or the patience. Plus, I wasn't one hundred per cent convinced Max and I *were* still together.

It was something I'd rectify later; first I had to get to work.

The autumn leaves metaphorically falling off with the publicist's threat and Hannah's disparagement was nothing compared to the coldness I met with after arriving at the toy store later that morning. I thought Elliot's despondency was due to the fact I was twenty minutes late...

'It was Hannah's fault for calling.'

... But that wasn't the reason at all.

He handed me the newspaper with a glum face.

'Turn to page twenty-seven.'

I did as he asked, wondering what it was he wanted me to look at.

I should have known. Hannah was right – the photo the paper had run was of me crying, and Max standing nearby. The heading wasn't too harsh – *Tinderella Heartbroken Again*, but it revealed to Elliot what I'd been doing at the time, and he was angry about it.

'Sick yesterday, huh?'

I had no option but to come clean and tell the truth. 'I needed to stage a photo with a man, so I took Max to trivia instead. I'm sorry.'

'You cancelled on me and took Max to trivia?'

I thought Max and I standing on Mordialloc Pier made that obvious, but Elliot hadn't figured that out, and I'd just given it away.

He dropped eye contact with me and looked confused and upset. I didn't think it was that big of a deal; I hadn't traded Elliot for just some random – it was Max. Max was a good guy and Elliot knew that. In Elliot's eyes however, whom I'd taken made no difference.

'It's the principle, Ella; if you told me the truth I wouldn't have minded, I would have told you to take Max because I know how much fun trivia is. But you told me you were sick. You lied.'

He walked off towards one of the aisles, not giving me a chance to explain.

'Elliot, I made a mistake.'

He called over his shoulder but I didn't quite make out what he said.

I told him as such and he stopped and repeated himself.

'I said, you've made a lot of mistakes lately.'

What? How so?

That remark was unfair; nothing else I'd done had impacted negatively on him. Had it?

'You've been missing work to go to the dating coach, you've been missing work to go on dates and on other days you turn up late. It's been really hard having to be here and do everything on my own.'

The strain on his face was clear; my actions hurt, but so too did it hurt telling his best friend off.

What followed was something that hurt me like nothing he'd ever told me before.

'You haven't been a very good friend lately.'

That couldn't have been further from the truth – I'd been working on a project with Max to help his love life. I was remorseful from the moment I found out he knew about Max and trivia, but now I was angry. There was good reason for my absence – Tinderella – and I wasn't going to back away from the fact I was putting myself first for the first time in my life.

My sisters and past female friends had found love and neglected me. I resented it but came to understand it was natural for other relationships to change as a result of someone finding love. Now it was my turn. That didn't mean I'd forgotten about Elliot; it meant my priorities had changed and he had taken a back seat momentarily to my quest to find love.

'And have you?' he asked.

'Have I what?'

'Have you found love?'

I didn't want to answer. I knew the answer but was too fearful to say. Hearing Elliot ask, however, helped me recognise he did love me, as a friend, and he had my best interests at heart. I couldn't be angry with him anymore.

'I don't want to fight with you. Not even on the paintball battlefield. Truce?'

After a ten-metre shouting match, Elliot walked back over to me and shed his bitterness. 'Truce.'

'I'm sorry I wasn't a very good friend.'

'I'm sorry too; not seeing you made me think I was going to lose you.'

There was no chance that was going to happen, but I understood making Elliot feel that way was horrible enough in itself. 'You will never lose me. From now on I'm going to be more reliable at work and include you more when it comes to me and Max. Hug?'

He wrapped his arms around me. 'And invite me to the next cool party Hannah throws?'

If not for being a last-minute thing, he would have been invited to the first one. We broke from our hug.

'How do you know about that?'

'Saw it in the newspaper as well.'

I looked back at the newspaper sitting on the front counter. The open page and the photo of me crying told me what my next move needed to be.

And who it was I needed to make peace with next.

25.

'Hey.'

'Hey.'

'I've got a confession to make.'

'So have I.'

Standing at Max's front door, that wasn't the response I was expecting from him.

He welcomed me inside his apartment demurely, which made me more nervous. If his confession needed to be said in private, then surely it wasn't good.

I began to analyse everything to figure out what was coming my way. His clothes mirrored his mood. He wore a hoodie and jeans and had a five o'clock shadow, which I felt was a bad sign. But the blinds were open, and some sun shined through, which I took as maybe a good sign.

His laptop and a thick, navy-blue textbook were on his dining table and we sat down beside them.

'Working from home today; hence the lazy outfit,' he explained.

I smiled in acceptance.

'Drink?'

I declined.

Things were so sedate it was like we were settling a debt.

'Visitors first,' he suggested, referring to our confessions.

I was happy to oblige. 'I'm sorry about what happened on the pier the other night. It was something I wish didn't happen and I promise it won't happen again.'

That was pretty much my confession.

He nodded, which gave me no indication of whether he was accepting of my apology or not.

'And I'm sorry for it,' I repeated.

'Thanks' was all he gave me.

'Now your turn.'

His hesitation almost had me shaking and I began to prepare myself for the worst. Surely, he wouldn't though; surely one little indiscretion wasn't going to see him break-up with me.

He bit his bottom lip, took a deep breath and confessed. 'I'm not sure about us.'

My heart started racing immediately, a lump rose in the bottom of my throat and tears started to well in my eyes. All I could muster in response was, 'Okay.'

I was certain, "I'm not sure about us", really meant, "I want to break-up", and knowing as such hoped his confession was as short as mine, so I could get the hell out of there.

But it wasn't short at all.

'I was really looking forward to wining and dining you on our first date. But the morning of, someone I'd never seen before followed me around in the city for an hour. Everywhere I went he bobbed up and took photos of me, and it freaked me out. Eventually I figured out why, and when I did I panicked. I packed my car, drove straight to your place and made you come on a weekend away with me.'

I sensed his apprehension when he came to meet me, but never knew that was the cause – the paparazzi had followed him around all day. I was a little upset he didn't tell me the truth on the way to Wilson's Prom, but respected it was his turn to confess, and let him continue.

'I knew this Tinderella thing existed; I'd seen the newspapers and magazines and my stupid receptionist was always talking about it on the phone. But after what happened between us at Wilson's Prom, I thought you'd cancel it all. I thought you'd tell the magazines and newspapers you were finished, that you'd found the guy you were looking for.'

The tears that welled in my eyes trickled down my cheeks. Emotion began to take over him too; he took another deep breath and ran a hand through his hair as if to distract himself from crying.

'Less than twenty-four hours on, and I began to think none of that would happen. You changed our trivia name from "Max and Ella" to "Max and lady friend", as if to portray us as friends and nothing more, then when I saw some guy taking our photos on the pier, I just lost it. And when it became clear you'd set it all up, I felt like the next bit part, lover-boy in your personal reality show. Someone who gave your social media followers something to talk about, until you moved on to the next guy.'

I completely understood the way he saw things. I was desperate to clarify why I changed our trivia name and was desperate to tell him things would change from now on. But the change I envisioned and the change he did wasn't the same.

'I can't be that person who lives his life in the public eye,' he said, more stoically than before. 'The guy who's grilled online for accidentally littering in the city, or whose private life is front-page news for every stranger to see. I'm not going to condemn you for wanting that; you need to be who you need to be, but if you can't stop being Tinderella, then you have to stop being with me.'

I wiped the tears away. I hated being given an ultimatum but had learnt from my angry reaction to Elliot earlier, and had to respect Max's position.

But what was my position?

I did have strong feelings for him, but I didn't want to give up Tinderella. Having one million Instagram followers and having my photo online and in the magazines on a weekly basis made me feel awesome. For the first time in a long time it made me feel valued.

For the first time in my life however, I felt loved, and that was what I wanted most.

Wasn't it?

So many questions with such few answers – and probably the crying as well – made my head hurt. Maybe it was time to take a break.

The stress on my face must have been evident, as Max suggested the same thing. 'Go home and have a think, and don't put pressure on yourself; just do what you want to do. I want you to be happy, and if being Tinderella is being happy, then that's okay.'

He took the blue textbook off the dining table and held it out to me.

'And if you need more answers... then you'll find them in here.'

It was his diary.

Was he sure?

He offered it again. I took it from him. We stood, and he put his arms around me. 'Safe travels home.'

I walked out of his apartment and he closed the door behind me. I pushed the button for the elevator and – intrigued by what I was holding – opened his diary to a random page while I waited.

There on the page were drawings of a whole bunch of animals, an old boat and an elderly man with grey hair. At the top was a heading that read – *Noah's Ark Set-up.*

The reason for them dawned on me; *the stage play he's doing.*

I went to turn the page but noticed more writing and an unusual character in the bottom corner below the animals. It was a woman with red hair and the caption read: *New girl came to rehearsal tonight. Was there an angel on the ark? Might have to make one.*

He was writing about me.

The elevator doors opened, and a girl stood there staring at me, wondering if I was going to get in. So entrenched in the diary was I that I would not.

'Sorry, I'll get the next one.'

I walked over and sat down against a wall; it was the same spot I sat when I waited for Max to get home on the night of Mum and Dad's anniversary.

The next few pages of his diary were full of magazine cut-outs, letters from a newspaper heading rearranged and the neatest handwriting I'd ever seen. The newspaper letters read S H E M A K E S M E S M I L E, and underneath was a handwritten poem that read –

A night of paintballing and we were on the same team,
If only I'd known she had a little scheme,
She shot me in the leg so bad I couldn't stand,
Said, 'It was an accident,' but I knew it was planned.

That made me chuckle as it had actually occurred – I had shot him at paintball and claimed it was an accident, even though it wasn't. The writing continued and described many happenings of the night. It wasn't in rhyme except for the last two lines.

The bruise was so big; I should have been carried away in a wheelbarrow.
But the feeling was so nice, I felt like I'd been struck by cupid's arrow.

Other pages had little poems about work, his family and spending time with me. And then I came across a page filled with a proper diary entry. Being well into the night and having sat in the same spot for two hours, I considered resting my tired brain and reading the last few pages at home.

I changed my mind however when I noticed the date at the top of the next page, and my name in the first sentence below it. The diary entry was from that day, written about events from the previous night.

I had a dream last night about Ella that was all-too real. And now I wish it was.

As soon as I read those words I became unresponsive to anything else around me. *A dream about me he wished had been true?* I couldn't have read on any faster.

I had a dream last night about Ella that was all-too real. And now I wish it was.

I was sitting on a child's wooden stool reading a picture book. The page I was on had four ducks on it. Two big ducks leading two small ducks in a pond. I couldn't see the words because there weren't any. I was on the last page.

I closed the book and looked up. I was sitting in a child's room next to a cot. There was a baby asleep no more than two-months-old. She was a girl as she was wearing a pink baby suit, and the room was decorated with fairies. I put the book down and crept out not wanting to wake her. The thought crossed my mind – "I must be babysitting."

Outside the door I noticed another door. There was a name written on it with wooden letters, but I could only make out the vowels "A" and "E". The door was ajar, so I walked across and peeked through. There was a little girl asleep in a bed in the corner. The bed cover had unicorns on it. She had shoulder length brown hair and looked about two-years-old. I started to feel nervous as I didn't know whom these kids were, and that I might have been in a stranger's house. But then I saw a photo on the bookshelf... it was her and me.

"Do I babysit these kids a lot?" I thought.

There were more photos of us on the chest of drawers. One of the frames read, "I love my dad".

I couldn't believe it. I was in my daughter's room.

I started to check myself. "Do I look any different?" No, my hands looked the same and so too did my arms and my legs. I couldn't see my own face, so I took a pocket mirror from the bookshelf. It looked like me. Normal me. "What?"

I pulled the doona over the little girl's shoulder and kissed her on the forehead, before leaving quietly.

The hallway was dark. I couldn't find a light switch, but as I got further and further down the hallway, it lit up more and more. There were all these photos on the wall. I was in a suit, and it looked like my wedding day, but I couldn't see anyone else; everyone else in the photos was blurred out. In most of them, there was just a puppy at my feet.

"What is going on?" I thought.

As I got closer to the end of the hallway, someone spoke to me from around the corner, "Dinner is served, darling."

I recognised the voice but I couldn't figure out where from. I was worried now as I walked slowly towards an open sliding-glass door that lead to the living room. I entered and looked down and I saw... that it was you. You had long red hair, wore a dark grey cardigan with jeans and socks on, and you were sitting in front of the couch with an empty bowl, and a packet of peanut M&Ms.

'Dinner is served,' you said to me again.

I felt more at ease knowing it was you; actually, I felt stupid. I looked around the living room again and noticed two things. There was a dog at the side window looking in at us, and all the photos in the room now had a face, and it was yours – it was you and I.

'I wanna watch TV.'

I'm not sure where that came from, but I said it.

'We're not watching TV, we're playing a game,' you told me. 'The girls are asleep, role models we need not be until they wake. We can eat peanut M&Ms for dinner.'

I sat down in front of you and you continued. 'You have to close your eyes and pick an M&M. You then have to guess the colour; if you get it right, you get to eat it. If you get it wrong...'

'No,' I interrupted, 'I'm not taking my shirt off.'

'No silly, as if I'd make you do that,' you said, grinning. 'If you get it wrong you have to tell me one thing you love about me.'

I began to speak more freely, 'We could be here all night,' I said.

'Why, because there's a whole packet of M&Ms to get through?' you asked.

'No, because there are a lot of things I love about you.'

The game began, I picked an M&M and I guessed... purple.

'You're an idiot,' you told me. 'There's no such thing as a purple M&M. Guess again.'

I guessed red. I opened my eyes and found that it was brown. My response followed a slight pause...

'I love the way you make me laugh,

'I love the way you look,

'I love your eyes; I love your smile,

'The way you read me like a book.

'Your honesty, your kindness,

'Your patience and your fears,

'I love you when you're happy,

'More so when you're in tears.

'I love the way you take on life,

'When you tell me it's okay,

'I love that when I'm with you,

'You take my breath away.

'I love your cheekiness,

'Miss you when we're apart,

'Love the way when I'm alone,

'You fill the emptiness in my heart.

'I love the way you touch,

'The way you light up my life.

'I love the way you love my kids.

'I love that you're my wife.'

You didn't blink for the whole time I was talking. When I stopped you simply stuttered, 'You were only supposed to say one thing, but that was good.'

It was then your turn to pick a peanut M&M, and to no surprise the rules changed. 'If I get it wrong, I have to eat it,' you told me, 'But if I get it right, you have to take your shirt off.'

I'm not sure why, but I agreed, maybe because I knew you'd get it wrong. With your eyes closed, you reached into the bowl, but as you did, the dog barked, and I turned and looked at him. As soon as I looked at him he seemed satisfied. I turned back as you guessed, 'Yellow.'

You opened your eyes and then the palm of your hand to reveal a yellow M&M. And you smiled. And the dream froze on your smile, because that's when I woke.

And the dream hit me straight away.

It hit me not just because you're the first person I want to see when I wake up, but because at that very second, I realised I'd woken with no shirt on. I must have taken it off in the middle of the night.

While that seemed certain, there was one thing I'll never know – looking back on the dream, tomorrow, next week, or next year, I'll never know if you snuck a look at your yellow M&M, when I turned to look at the dog.

A tear of happiness trickled down my face; I'd never read something so powerful in all my life and it was about me. He wrote my voice perfectly, remembered I'd told him I wanted two daughters and even hinted at one of their names with "A" and "E" – Grace.

More tears ran down my face and I had to wipe them away to stop them from falling on the pages of the diary.

So this was what it felt like?

It felt like relief; it felt like unbridled joy; it felt like a key had opened my heart and allowed the full extent of life's bliss to enter all at once.

This was a life free from uncertainty; this was the reason for the chase, the heartache, the rejection and the crippling doubt.

This was love, and I had to tell Max about it.

I had no idea how late it was but climbed to my feet and belted loudly on Max's door with my fist. I kept hitting and hitting, and then he answered. From that moment, I aired my feelings with a level of intensity and passion that matched the actions of my fist just seconds earlier.

'I read it and I get it and I'm sorry I made you wait so long for an answer, and I'm sorry I did all those terrible things with the photographer, but I know what I want and it's you.'

I was out of breath but wasn't done. I knew the neighbours could probably hear me, but I didn't care – I wanted the world to hear me.

'I'm giving up Tinderella, I promise, I swear, she's never coming back, you have to believe me. And you have to believe me when I say... I love you.'

I'd never said those three words to anyone outside of my family before.

Strangely enough they later brought back brief memories of my dad. He and I had three serious chats when I was a teenager. The first was about sex, the second was about drugs and alcohol, and the third was about love. He taught me the words 'I love you' were never to be thrown around. Boys threw them around a lot he said, because they knew of their power and how persuasive they could be. I was to wait until someone I truly did love came along. That time was now, and that person was Max, and only in saying those three words to him did I realise how powerful they really were.

'I love you,' I repeated.

He bit his bottom lip again, but unlike the last time he did it, what followed was what I wanted to hear.

'I love you too.'

I leant forward slowly and kissed him. It was the best kiss ever, and because it was the first time I'd ever initiated a kiss, it made me feel even better.

'And I love that I love you,' I said.

We conversed between kisses as we made our way back into his apartment.

'Were you thinking about going to bed soon?' I asked.

'I can stay up a little longer.'

'No, I think you should tell me you're thinking about going to bed soon.'

'Oh yeah, I'm thinking about going to bed now.'

26.

The most common question asked over the next four days was, 'Can we do it again?'

Every spare minute of my life was taken up by love making, and it wrecked my body clock, but I loved it.

I felt free. I started work at 9am on two-and-a-half hours sleep, went to Max's post-work, ate bacon slices for dinner and stayed up until 3am again.

An afternoon nap in Max's arms was one of the sweetest things I'd experienced.

Being behind closed doors all day and all night meant the paparazzi weren't able to snap me, which meant Max had no way of finding out I hadn't stopped being Tinderella yet. I was going to do it, I was, but I just wanted to hold on to my 1.6 million Instagram followers a little while longer.

I wanted to hold on to Max a little while longer as we napped as well, but my phone rang, and then beeped to signify someone had left a voice message. It was Hannah, and I slowly rose and excused myself to the bathroom.

She wasn't happy – she'd once again been bombarded by phone calls from the press. They were this time complaining about my whereabouts. She wanted me to get my butt over to her place within the hour. I was happy to do so, but being so blithe and in love, decided I was going to play a prank on her as well.

For that, I needed Katie's help.

'Why, what for?' she asked, on the phone.

'Because Brett's been away for two weeks and because it'll be funny.'

'But it's not finished; we haven't even put the roof or the door on yet.'

'I don't care, and neither will Roy, just be at Hannah's in an hour.'

I hid in Hannah's front garden waiting for Katie to arrive. Thankfully, she walked up the drive only a couple of minutes after I did. I whispered to her, 'Psst.'

'What the hell are you doing?' she asked.

'Shhh,' I ordered.

'What the hell are you doing?' she whispered.

'You go in first and then I'll walk in thirty seconds later. Just don't tell her it was my idea.'

She took me for a giant weirdo but did as I said – progressing through Hannah's front door and into her living room. Within moments I heard Hannah going ballistic.

'Are you serious? Do you want a beating? You have sex with Roy in another caravan you've finished, and come straight to my house again?'

'Actually, this time we didn't even finish the caravan.'

'So what are you doing here?'

I walked in the front door before she could dob me in.

'Ella, thank-god. Would you kick this shag-addict out before I drown her in the pool?'

I walked over and stood on the other side of Hannah, 'Why? What's she done?'

'She's...'

Hannah went to answer but was overcome by my smell before she could. She put her hands over her mouth and nose, and spoke through them.

'What on Earth...?'

'What?' I asked, pretending I had no idea what she was reacting to.

'You've been doing the deed as well? Is this some kind of joke?'

'Yes,' I replied.

'What?'

'Yes, it is a joke and a pretty funny one as well.'

Motioning sickness, she kept her hand over her mouth and rushed into the kitchen for a glass of water. Katie and I weren't going to let her escape that easily, so we followed, and I continued to bait her.

'We wanted to make you jealous; with Brett away for the last fortnight we figured you haven't been getting much of late.'

'I'm going to kill you both.'

Katie and I laughed and high-fived, but as we did so, Katie too dropped her hand down over her nose.

'Woah, Ella, you do smell pretty bad.'

Hannah stopped the kitchen tap, dropped her mug in the sink and yelled at us like a drill sergeant in the army.

'Get out the back, both of you. What I've got to say can be said out there.'

Hannah locked Katie and I in her back shed where all her gardening equipment was stored and spoke to us through the glass door.

'Is this really necessary?' I asked.

'Yes, that shed already smells awful, so I don't care that you're in there. Plus, I'm hosting another party for you in a couple of weeks and don't want my backyard smelling like bums.'

'Another party?'

'Yes, which is why I need you to stop hiding and get yourself photographed so we can build some publicity. The money we're making on the side...'

'I can't.'

My response knocked both Hannah and Katie for six, and they simultaneously asked, 'What do you mean you can't?'

I told them about Max, how we'd fallen in love and why I needed to quit Tinderella. They were disappointed – the "side" money we'd split three-ways from the many photos taken, articles written, and products plugged on Instagram had been quite a lot. Tinderella had also brought a different sense of vitality into their lives as well, and I was taking that away.

I thought they'd both breathe fire, but they didn't. They understood my decision.

'You can't put a price on love,' Hannah acknowledged.

'And it is ultimately why we started this whole episode in the first place,' Katie added.

I didn't expect them to respond that way, but was relieved, as I'd gone around to Hannah's with a motive of my own.

'I was hoping to bring Max around on Sunday.'

'Sure, I'd love to meet him,' Katie said without thought.

'Sunday?' Hannah questioned, with thought.

She knew exactly what Sunday was. 'Sunday's Mother's Day; I don't think so.'

That response I did expect, but I had a rebuttal ready to go.

Mother's Day, like Father's Day, like Mum and Dad's birthday's and like their anniversaries, was our day – the day we sisters got to be miserable and not have anybody bother us. But I'd given it a lot of thought and decided that needed to change. Celebrating on those days may not have been the right thing to do, but we still needed to live those days like we lived every other day of the year. Mum and Dad would have wanted us having fun with Justin and Brody, and Brett and Roy, and they would have wanted me to bring Max around for a barbecue and have him meet my wonderful sisters. We despised those days for what we didn't have, but Mum and Dad wouldn't have wanted us to be like that. They would have wanted us to appreciate those days for what we did have – fond memories, a bright future and a loving family.

My speech, which wasn't intended to be a speech, brought Hannah to tears.

'Okay, you can bring Max around on Sunday.'

She unlocked the glass door, slid it open and brought the two of us in for a hug.

My silly prank ended in tears but for all the right reasons. Hannah, though, still couldn't shake the smell, and questioned me about it one last time.

'Is it weird that I can smell chocolate as well?'

'No. I ate chocolate while Max and I did it.'

I walked across the railway, showered and dressed at home, and then returned to Max's later that day. He was freshly showered as well. Like me, he was bouncing around in seventh heaven, and like me, was glad to see me for one main reason.

'I've got something I want to talk to you about.'

'I've got something I want to talk to you about too.'

I could see a pattern developing, but a quick joke from him eased any rising anxieties.

'It's okay, it's not a confession this time, just an invitation.'

He welcomed me inside and pulled out a seat at his dining table. We sat down, and he revealed what the invitation was to.

'My mum and dad's house on Sunday for lunch.'

Our physical desires were uncanny, but they had no match on our mental desires.

'Oh,' was my response.

He picked up on my hesitation to accept.

'It's okay, you can say no, I'm sure it's a really hard day for you, but I just thought if you'd like to do something then the offer is there.'

'Actually, it's not that; I mean, yes, it normally is a tough day, but Hannah's organising a Mother's Day lunch and I asked if you could come and she said, yes.'

This time he struggled to muster a response.

'But you can say no as well, I mean, you can spend time with your family and I'll spend time with mine; we can spend a day apart for a change.'

He looked me adoringly in the eyes and answered the way a man in love should. 'No, it's an important day for you, and if you're inviting me to your sister's for lunch, then I'll be there.'

He leaned forward and gave me a hug.

Dad always told me the key to a good relationship was compromise and Max compromising reaffirmed I was in just that.

He leaned back, 'Actually there's something else I want to talk to you about as well.'

He swung around to face the table and opened the lid of his laptop. He signed in, opened a random computer program and slid the laptop in front of me.

'I have a few more numbers to code, but I thought you might be curious.'

It only took a moment for me to realise what it was – our project. There was a design of Elliot's profile page. The colours and the layout were flawless, it looked easy to use and conveyed the one message I wanted it to – it was safe. I scrolled across to the settings page. It didn't describe the software as being a dating app but instead a friendship square. I loved that. The third design was the homepage, complete with the cartoon kitten and the magic wand, and the friendship square's title.

So many things Max had done that week had taken my breath away, but the title of our project was equal to any of them.

'Koolish,' I read.

The gesture yet again showed the size of Max's heart. He had spent weeks working on *Koolish* without getting a single penny, and had done much of the work before we declared our love for one another.

'You like?'

'I love; it's perfect and I'm sure Elliot will think so too.'

For all he had done for me, I knew it was time for me to do something for him. I put a gentle hand on his knee.

'How do you feel about dinner?' he asked.

'How do you feel about Sunday lunch at your mum and dad's?'

27.

Mother's Day eve should have been harder than what it was.

I should have lay awake, unable to sleep, looking up at my bedroom ceiling for hours, but instead I was asleep less than twenty minutes after my head hit the pillow.

I'd never met my boyfriend's parents before yet there wasn't a single vein in my body that carried anxiety. Better still, there wasn't a single vein in my head that carried bitterness, which was normally the case on Mother's Day.

To help things, both Hannah and Katie were accepting when I told them I was cancelling on them. I knew Katie wouldn't mind, but even Hannah told me she was fine with it. She said that, despite me not being there, they'd still have a really fun day.

I ate breakfast calmly, showered calmly and got dressed calmly, and sat on the front fence outside my unit and waited for Max to pick me up.

I couldn't force myself to worry, that's how happy and relaxed I was. Such happiness needed to be documented, so I got my phone out and took a selfie. I didn't put it on Instagram or Facebook, but rather kept it, as a reminder of how good life could be.

My casualness billowed into vivacity as Max pulled up to the curb.

'Sorry, sorry, no excuses, I didn't manage my time well.'

He was five minutes late, but a compliment upon arriving quickly made up for it. 'Wow, that dress looks amazing, and flowers too?'

The sun was out, and I'd decided to wear a summery dress, even though it was autumn. The dress had flowers on it, but he spoke of the flowers I carried as a gift for his mother.

'You didn't have to do that.'

'Yes I did; your mother is important to you, so she's important to me too.'

He had a gift of his own and reached into the backseat to get it. It was an envelope. *Ella* was all that was written on the outside of the envelope, but in it I could see a hand-written note.

'It's not for now but for later; it's nothing special; just a letter I'd like you to read.'

'You wrote me a letter?'

'Not quite.'

'So it's a letter for someone else you want me to read?'

'No, it's a letter for you but not to you.'

That didn't make a lot of sense, which made me even keener to open it and find out what it was, but he wouldn't let me.

'You can read it at the end of the day, promise.'

I buried it deep into the bottom of my handbag as he pulled out from the curb. I continued to wonder what it could be. I wanted to talk about it, but he changed the subject.

'So I have to word you up just so you don't burst into laughter when you first meet my parents. It's about my mum – her name is Jill.'

I wasn't sure why he needed to word me up on that.

'Because my dad's name's Jack.'

Really? His parent's names were Jack and Jill? I did laugh a little.

'It gets worse,' he added. 'They met on a hill.'

Max's parents lived in a timeless family home in Regent Parade, Cheltenham that looked untouched in the twenty-eight years they'd lived there.

Timeless, or perhaps ageless, was a fair description for his father as well, who looked more like his older brother when he answered the door.

'We had him at twenty-one,' Jack explained. 'Plus, Jill's had me on this anti-ageing moisturiser rubbish for years. Come in.'

The interior of the house was just as endearing as the exterior. As we walked through the hallway however, Jack told me he'd done plenty of repairs on the place, due largely to Max's growing sense of adventure as a teenager.

'Cricket bat put a hole in the wall there, football put a hole in the wall there, and I think a skateboard did that one.'

A skateboard, how was that possible?

'I built an indoor ramp and tried to do a 360 off it when I was twelve,' Max said.

What I also loved were the so many photos that documented memories, all over the house. Sure enough, there was one of Max with his skateboard next to a homemade ramp. It had been perfectly placed between the hallway and the kitchen so everyone could see it.

'Nah, that photo's just covering a wound as well,' Jack said, before turning to Max. 'Think your mother came home drunk one night and did that one.'

Unsurprisingly, Jill came out of the kitchen in protest, 'You can keep some things a secret you know.'

She was naturally stunning, and youthful-looking like Jack; I could have easily traded Hannah for her, as my older sister, and no one would have known the difference.

'Mum, this is Ella,' Max said.

'The girl I've heard so much about.'

That was nice to hear.

I handed her the flowers and gave her a hug. She, like Jack, was very welcoming.

'These are beautiful, and that is a lovely dress. Max would you put these in some water for me?'

Max obliged.

Lunch wasn't far away, but Jack was cooking it, which allowed Jill the chance to show me the rest of the house.

'Drink first though?' she offered. 'I bought a bottle of white and red because I wasn't sure; we're not very big drinkers in this house; it's normally blended juice for us.'

I couldn't help but grin at Max – juice, perhaps that was the secret to their youth. If so, I was happy to copy it.

'Juice will be just fine for me, too, thanks.'

Jill and I carried our juices through the rest of the house to where I presumed we'd be eating lunch. I expected the blend to be hard to swallow, but it was actually really nice.

'Jack makes a mean juice,' she joked.

'Nice that he gives you a reprieve in the kitchen too,' I smiled. 'My mum cooked even on Mother's Day.'

She stopped for a moment, 'Reprieve? Jack cooks every single night; has done so since the day we met. Tell me Max has been the same?'

Chocolate, ice cream and peanut M&Ms had been the most regular dinner we'd had, although that was due to a lack of cooking motivation in between sex sessions.

I didn't want to denigrate Max to his mum, nor tell her I was sleeping with her son, so I lied, 'Oh absolutely, Max is a great cook.'

We eventually made our way to the back of the house where Jill opened a door. I thought it might lead to the back verandah but it didn't. 'You don't know how long I've been dying to show someone this.'

It led to Max's old room.

No way.

I felt like I'd been given a ticket to Willy Wonker's chocolate factory. His doona cover had a big wave surfer on it, there was a pair of horribly worn skate shoes under the bed, and there was a pet rock on the bedside table. I sat down on the bed and picked it up.

'This is too cute.'

'He made that when he was eight; he threw it in the bin but I took it out again and kept it. He still doesn't know.

Mothers.

Then there were the photos.

Braces in Year Eight, a mohawk haircut in Year Nine...

'I think that was around the time David Beckham had a mohawk.'

... And blonde tips in Year Eleven.

'Beckham again?'

'No, I think he did that because he thought it would look good.'

It didn't look good at all.

His homework desk had all these items on it that screamed the mid-2000s. There was a Season One DVD of *Prison Break*, an empty tub of Homebrand™ hair gel, and a number of rubber charity wristbands with Livestrong and Make Poverty History written on them.

'I got those for him,' Jill said. 'He wouldn't wear a watch in summer because he didn't want to get a watch tan, but bare wrists didn't look cool, so I brought them home from work one day.'

'You work with charities?'

'I did, now I'm a part-time canteen worker at a local high school and a part-time youth worker.' She laughed and picked up the photo of Max with braces. 'What can I say? Max terrorized me so much when he was a teenager, I became addicted to it. I'm kidding, he was a good teenager, he was a horror baby.'

It came as no surprise she worked with underprivileged kids. She had a kind and generous nature, like that of a nurse, a paramedic or a teacher.

That high quality of character I'd become quite used to; while Max looked a lot like his dad, much that shone from within came from his mum.

That very thought coincided with the door creaking open and Max sticking his head in. 'You are in here. Mum, really? Did you have to?'

He was embarrassed but not surprised by Jill showing me around his old room.

'This is the first girl you've ever brought home; this is a big moment for me; I'm going to talk about you and show you off Maxwell.'

I giggled on the inside; his mum called him by his full name just as my dad called me by my full name, "Elizabeth".

Being the first girl he'd ever introduced to his parents made me feel pretty special too.

'Well, I'm not going to stick around and listen, and neither should you,' he said, pointing at me. 'Lunch is served.'

He ducked away but returned at my request.

'Oh Maxwell, who's this guy?' I held up the pet rock.

He looked at it and then stared at his mother. 'I threw that in the bin.'

She laughed.

He feigned shame, answered quickly, 'his name's Rocky,' and left just as hastily.

How original.

'He never was good with names,' Jill said.

'I know; he wants to name our first child Rabbitquest.'

'Ooh, grandchildren, that sounds nice.'

She was joking, well, at least she spoke in a way that made it sound like she was joking.

She surveyed the room again. 'You know, Ella, for the longest time I never had a sister, and for the longest time I never had a daughter. I love that boy and I do love this room, but I envy not being able to do the girly things in life.'

I could identify with that – for the longest time I didn't have a mother to be able to do the mother/daughter things with.

Neither Jill nor I were complaining, but rather acknowledging the potential start of a very special relationship. An acknowledgment verbalised when she took the words right out of my mouth.

'I feel like that might have just changed.'

No one would ever replace my mother, but I couldn't help but feel that too.

We exited the bedroom and found Max a few feet outside the door.

Jill kept walking, whereas I stopped in front of him. He pushed a runaway hair behind my ear. 'Are you going to break up with me now?'

'Trust me, I like what I see.'

A group of thick clouds saw lunch moved from the verandah to the family dining room. Having cooked up a storm, it was Jack's turn to tell stories of Max. It was clear that once told, those anecdotes were the lead in to a more important story – the day he and Jill met.

Max had warned me in the car, and true to that warning, Jack didn't leave out a single detail. But it was the first detail that roused a smile on my face and helped me understand why Max had taken me to Wilson's Prom on a weekend away.

'Have you ever heard of Mount Oberon?' Jack asked.

I darted my eyes to Max – 'Actually I have, Jack.'

'Well you'll be able to picture this story like it was yesterday.'

Nineteen-year-old Jack was on a summer trip with school friends and they'd decided to climb The Prom's highest peak – Mount Oberon. Dropped off by the bus at the car park halfway up, he'd locked eyes on Jill, who was about to embark on the walk with her parents. In his eyes and words, 'she was the most beautiful girl I'd ever seen.' At the time, Jack simply told his friends, 'we have to follow that girl up.'

Easier said than done, he told.

'I was breathing heavily, probably due to my lack of fitness, but also because of nerves. She looked like an Olympic runner; so athletic did she look in her sports clothes. I was in a pair of torn sports shorts, and wore sneakers that had holes in them. Still, there was no way I was going to lose sight of her and lose the chance to find love.'

He'd been too nervous to say hello at the top of the mountain, but managed to find the courage to approach her on the way down. Twenty metres in front of her parents, under the watchful eyes of her father, the two young adults walked back down Mount Oberon and from then on, never left each other's side.

'Jack and Jill went up a hill and both fell on the way down,' Jill said. 'Jack didn't break his crown and Jill didn't come tumbling after, but they instead fell in love with each other.'

There was a slight pause before Jack added one final detail. Jill and Max however were quick to cut him off.

'A few nights later Jill came over to my tent on site 155...'

'Ah, Dad, that's enough.'

Site 155? That was the site we stayed on.

Max falling in love with me at the same place his parents had was cute, but staying on the exact same site they had, and completing the same activities, was slightly disturbing.

With his daring sense of humour, Jack had no issue taking the joke further. If in fact it was a joke.

'Okay, okay, we won't talk about the night you were conceived. We'll just skip straight to the birth.'

'No we won't,' Jill said, 'Not living through that again.'

'Yes, how about we stop talking about Jack, Jill and Max altogether and start talking about Ella,' Max suggested.

'Good idea; how's the toy store going?' Jill asked.

'And this project you two are doing is going well?'

'Tell us about this young fella, Elliot,' Jack said.

They spoke of Max's work with the disabled and expressed admiration after hearing how important I'd become in Elliot's life. Their praise evoked a unique feeling – a combination of gratitude, satisfaction but mostly love. Jack and Jill didn't ask these questions and listen to my answers out of etiquette, they did so because they genuinely cared and wanted to learn about me.

Max had only introduced me to them an hour earlier, yet I felt like I was part of their family already. Seemingly, they were also willing to become part of mine.

'What about your family Ella?' Jill asked.

I told them of Hannah, Brett and the boys, and of Katie and Roy.

I didn't go into great detail other than to say I 'couldn't imagine a world without them.'

'Well it's good you're all so close after what happened,' Jack said.

I took his observation as a compliment, but quickly wondered what he meant by those last three words.

'After what happened.' After what happened? Was he talking about... surely he meant something else?

I became nervous, knowing how my emotions faltered whenever I spoke of that topic. I was going to ask Jack to clarify, but my perplexed expression must have given that away, as he didn't need prompting.

'I'm sure they're with you in spirit anyway.'

I nodded in agreement however struggled to look him in the eye. He could, of course, have only known this information because of one person.

A lump rose in my throat, and knowing that normally led to tears, I excused myself from the table. 'Where's the bathroom?'

'Just to your right, down past the laundry,' Jill said.

I stood, tucked my handbag over my shoulder and briskly walked away from the table with my head down. That alone might not have been enough to let Max know something was wrong, but me going left towards the front door, rather than right towards the bathroom, certainly made him aware.

I made it onto the front lawn before I heard the front door open and close again, and Max call out to me. 'Ella, is everything all right? What's the matter?'

I was in tears, unwilling to talk about it, and desperate to get out of there. I reached the top of the driveway and felt a hand on my shoulder.

He'd run after me.

'Hey, wait up; talk to me, what's wrong?'

He ran around in front of me and turned to face me, not allowing me to escape. That only heightened my level of disappointment and frustration.

'You told your parents about my mum and dad, that's what's wrong.'

His response was an expression only – he was surprised my parents' death was what caused my distress.

'My mum and dad dying, that is a big thing for me; it is the biggest thing for me. It was impossibly hard for me to tell you that night on the pier, heck I struggle to talk to anyone other than Hannah or Katie about it, and yet you go and tell your parents like it's nothing?'

He tried to find a way out but stumbled through his reasoning. 'I thought it would be okay; I thought we loved each other.'

None of that mattered; what mattered was it was my sisters and my business to tell and no one else's. We had gone through the pain and anguish and it was up to us who knew, and who we wanted supporting us.

Anger boiled within me. I wanted to yell, I wanted scream, but I did my best to remain respectful.

'You told me on the pier you respected my right to talk about it whenever I was ready. My right to tell people, not your right to tell your parents.'

He didn't argue, but instead asked a simple question. 'So what now?'

'I need to be on my own; I need to figure out if I can still trust you.'

I lowered my gaze from his to the ground, stepped onto the footpath and headed for the bus stop.

'Trust me? Come on Ella, really?' he called. 'You don't think you're overreacting?'

His last question stopped me dead in my tracks. All he had to do was show me some sympathy, accept we saw things differently, or at the very least just let me walk away.

But he couldn't even do that.

I turned back and released my burning fury by way of a verbal grenade. Seven brutal words, the final two those I thought I'd never say in my entire life.

'You broke my one rule – we're over.'

28.

'Nice dress; what are you doing here?'

I caught the bus back to Hannah's where I wished I'd spent the entire day.

Katie lay back on the couch in the living room staring at the TV Guide graphic on the television. Roy lay asleep on the couch opposite her, while I could see Brett and the two boys playing in the backyard.

'What happened to the barbecue?' I asked.

'Couldn't do it; piece of shit day doesn't deserve a barbecue,' she answered.

It made me upset my sisters couldn't muster the energy to carry out our plan, but in truth, I half expected it. 'I'm sorry, I should have been here.'

'Don't be sorry; if you get the chance to squeeze some happiness out of this day then go for it I say. God knows the rest of us should be.'

I'd squeezed nothing but sorrow out of the day, and felt the need to be honest and tell her.

'You all right? Do you want to talk about it?'

I sat on the end of the couch she was lying on, and dropped two bags at her feet.

'Is that food?' she asked.

'Our favourite takeaway. Just in case Roy burnt the sausages.'

'Or you brought a bribe, so I'd listen to you.'

She knew me too well.

'Should we get Hannah in on this?' she asked.

'Where is she, in bed?'

'She was, for about four hours. She's now pulling weeds out of the cracks in her driveway. I thought she was doing it out of frustration, but she told me it was therapeutic.'

'Son of a bitch, why won't you come out?'

Hannah's weed pulling didn't look too therapeutic. Her hands and knees were that dirty and crusty, she looked as if she'd crawled ten miles through a mineshaft. She looked up at me with disdain, 'Nice dress; what are you doing here?'

There was a reason we were all sisters.

'My day's been crap too; I broke up with Max.'

'And you're not crying?'

'It doesn't really feel like we've broken up.'

'Weird.'

'Plus, I cried on the bus the whole way over here.'

'Even weirder.'

She kept yanking at the weeds; it was her way of telling me she didn't wish to discuss nor hear of my problems. I got down beside her; I thought the two of us being on the same level might see her engage. 'Do you have any gardening gloves?' I asked.

'Don't be a sissy; just start pulling,' she said, as she wretched a different slice of grass with her bare hand.

My knees started hurting the moment they touched the pavement, and worse, my floral dress was going to get ruined. 'Got an old pair of jeans I could borrow?'

'You want me to listen and you want my jeans?'

She was sometimes unpleasant and often self-centred, but she was my biggest sister, and being that – with respect to Katie – it was her advice I always needed the most.

Katie crouched in front of the two of us and gently clasped Hannah's chin with her pointer finger and her thumb. 'We were hoping we wouldn't have to bribe...'

Hannah mumbled through Katie's hand, 'Nothing you have could make me...'

'Two bags of hot chips and sauce.'

Hannah sat back on her knees and Katie let go of her chin.

Like Katie, I knew Hannah's weak points and yet again used them to my advantage.

'Bring the chips out and my attention is all yours.'

We pulled a weed out, put the same hand in the bag of chips, and fed our mouths with the same dirt covered hand. Hot chips were unhealthy at the best of times, but I couldn't help but think of the health risks eating with such unsanitary hands might cause. My stomach had started to cause me some discomfort, although that may have been due to the fact I was now in a pair of Hannah's old jeans. They were two sizes too small for me and I could feel the belt line leaving marks on my stomach, but I gritted my teeth and got on with it.

While the three of us gardening in the driveway may have looked unusual, defeating the little suckers was strangely therapeutic. Although it may have been the debrief.

'... And I said, "we're over".'

'Good,' Katie exclaimed, as she tossed another weed by the side fence.

Good she ripped another weed out or good I told Max we were over?

'Good you told him you're over. So you should drop his arse. How dare he tell his family about what happened to Mum and Dad.'

Hannah agreed, at least with the second part, but she was more meaningful in her response. 'I can tolerate many things but I can't tolerate someone passing on someone else's private information. You've known each other how long?'

That was one of many things I needed to weigh-up. Max was a great guy who'd made a mistake. But what was to say it wasn't the beginning of a pattern; that he'd continue to do untrustworthy things if our relationship continued.

While I was thinking that, Katie and Hannah were saying it.

'They always start out kind and loving but they change,' Katie said.

I found that comment a little odd, seeing as she'd only ever been with one guy herself. But understood she was only trying to support me.

She continued. 'And there's no guarantee he won't break-up with you anyway.'

'Plus, you have a lot to gain from being Tinderella,' Hannah added, as she climbed off her knees and sat back on her haunches.

Katie and I did the same.

'You are still hot property; you've reached one million Instagram followers and who knows, you might one day score a high-paying role writing for a prominent women's blog.'

Money had never been something I'd had a great desire for; I'd always wanted my toy store, a place to live and a family. It certainly was tempting however, particularly the way Hannah sold it.

'Everyone – me included – focuses too much on their career and forgets about living life. I'd kill to be in your shoes; photo shoots, fans, dating lots of men.' She paused and grinned, 'If only for five minutes.'

Of course she loved being a wife to Brett and a mum to Justin and Brody. I knew what she was trying to say though – life was about experiences and my Tinderella experience was one I would look back on and cherish.

'So it's decided then; glad we could help,' Katie said, munching on another chip. She turned to Hannah, 'Good thing you never cancel a party.'

'What party?' I asked.

'The party I was telling you about last time you were here,' Hannah reminded me. 'It's Hollywood themed, and it's next weekend; I've got the invitations printed on my desk. By party's end, you'll have stopped thinking all about that last guy.'

Knowing how her last party turned out, and how much I had to drink, she was no doubt going to be right. The problem was I knew I'd spend a lot of time thinking about him before it.

29.

I placed an envelope down on the front counter.

It was mid-morning and the toy store was quiet. Elliot sat behind the counter writing down some stock-take.

'Actually, I'm writing down my top ten favourite matchbox cars we currently have in stock,' he said, somewhat drained, holding up a notepad. 'What's in the envelope?'

'It's an invitation to my next Tinderella party, hosted by Hannah, and it's fancy dress.'

He looked at me like I was kidding, 'you're having another party? What about Max?'

I hesitated in answering; I hoped some time would have passed before telling him, but it wasn't going to be. 'Max and I broke-up.'

My swift delivery did nothing to blunt the force of such news. Our break-up left Elliot shattered, for in Max he'd found a friend. All he could simply utter was, 'What was his reason?'

It was reasonable for Elliot to presume Max had broken up with me given my abominable history with men, but it hadn't happened that way and I couldn't lie to him, 'Um... I broke up with him.'

I reached for the invitation, set on watering down the break-up news and spicing up the magnificent party news, but it didn't work. Elliot's disappointment continued to grow colder and colder.

'Is he all right?'

'I don't know; it was only yesterday.'

He stared down at his notepad and then picked it and his pen up off the counter and trudged towards aisle one. I feared him verbalising his displeasure, considering the connection he'd made with Max, but what came was worse – silence.

He said nothing.

He never said nothing, and it made me dread where things were at between us. 'Elliot, I'm sorry.'

He stopped and looked back at me. 'Sorry? You don't need to be sorry. It's your life, you're allowed to choose who you do and don't love.'

I would have believed him if his tone matched his words.

He kept walking.

The real world following that encounter was a place I didn't want to be in, so I visited the Ladies Of The World, and escaped into their world. Not even they helped.

After a while it became less about playing with them and more about waiting for Elliot to come over and talk, but he didn't. After an hour I put the ladies down and walked around the store looking for him. He was nowhere to be found, so I headed towards the front entrance. The front counter was unattended but as I got close to it I saw something sitting on it. It was Elliot's notepad, open, with a letter written on it – to me.

Dear Ella, it's hard for me to say but breaking up with Max was not a nice thing to do.

It's hard for me to say but you not leaving the store and going to see him, was also not a nice thing to do.

It's hard for me to say but I've been doing a lot of work here lately and you've been away and never noticed.

It's hard for me to say but things can no longer be this way.

It's hard for me to say but I don't want to work here anymore.

My mind raced like a canine chasing its own tail.

He's leaving me? He's left me? He's gone? Oh my God, what have I done?

I was then hit with a feeling of constriction; the same harrowing physical restraint that overcame me the day my parents died. My arms and chest went stiff, my throat tightened, and I felt like I was breathing through a straw. It wasn't a panic attack but an unbreakable grip of self-hate and an unshakeable dread things would never be the same again.

At that moment, I couldn't have cared less about love, Max or Tinderella. They paled in comparison to what was happening then and there.

The greatest person in my life didn't want to be a part of it anymore.

There had to be a way to fix things. There had to be.

30.

I knocked on the door frantically and waited but there was no answer.

I could hear noise coming from the house next door, so I went over and knocked frantically on that front door.

Thankfully she answered.

'Ella, our final session isn't until next week.'

The outside of Tiffany's neighbouring house was complete. She was inspecting the inside – which remained bare – when she heard my knock and saw the remnants of my tears.

'Come next door love; I'll put some coffee on.'

Liam and I sat on her lounge aimlessly staring at the TV Guide graphic on the television.

'You'd fit in well with my family.'

He didn't get it, because he wasn't there the day prior when Katie was doing the same thing.

'Couldn't convince your girlfriend to get back together huh?'

He shook his head.

'I broke up with my boyfriend too.'

'What are you doing here then? Mum's only going to make things worse.'

'I heard that,' Tiffany said, as she entered with a mug in each hand. She handed me one and moved over towards Liam.

'You're sitting in my seat.'

He grumbled, 'See? You *are* making things worse.'

It was her way of asking for some alone time with me.

He stood and walked towards the front door but not before telling me, 'When she gives you a choice between the red and the blue pill, take the red pill, for the love of God take the red pill.'

The front door slammed.

What pills?

'He's kidding.' Tiffany turned the television off and took Liam's vacated spot. 'He's off to keep fixing up that house. It's been rather soothing for him; I don't know what it is about home maintenance and gardening that's so therapeutic, but there's something.'

That coincidence brought a rare smile out of me – he would fit in well with my weed-pulling family.

'And it seems you need to fix something as well,' she added, sipping from her mug. 'Max?'

'No, not Max. Elliot.'

'Ah, the rock star that is; the only person outside your family that truly understands you.'

That was correct – Elliot was that person.

She had spoken to him on the phone when he booked my first appointment. I had also told her about him in sessions gone-by, and how our friendship came about. The words 'rock star' I had used myself. While he didn't possess the look of a conventional rock star, Elliot certainly had rock star looks. I had no trouble describing his eye-catching features, despite only being his friend. What I also had no trouble doing was conversing with him the very day he came in and applied for a job. I should have been a mess, as I always was with men, but I quickly learnt he and I both held an aching within that had been caused by the same circumstance.

Elliot's life had been turned upside-down by a car accident, and so had mine.

'And that's why you can't lose him from your life?' Tiffany asked.

'Part of it, yeah.'

Tiffany's belief was that Elliot's resignation and overall discontent with me stemmed from my relationship with Max. Specifically, how I'd spent all my time with Max, and none of it with Elliot. Elliot had reached his limits following the news of our break-up.

'Sad it was over? Yes,' she said. 'But angry you stopped hanging out with him for nothing? Probably that too.'

So I had to get back together with Max to fix everything with Elliot?

'You don't have to get back together with Max, but you do have to do the respectful thing and put a full stop at the end of the relationship. Right now, it's a comma, but find the courage to talk to Max, and allow him closure. Once Elliot knows you've done the admirable thing, hopefully he'll come around.'

She stopped short of saying he'd return to the toy store, but said that came a distant second to maintaining our current friendship. 'And who knows, maybe you'll manage to stay friends with Max as well.'

'I haven't completely decided if Max and I are over for good anyway.'

'Well, that's something else for you to consider.'

I couldn't help but think how far I'd come with Tiffany in such a short space of time. I gave myself no hope of repair in the beginning, and yet by the end, had not only eradicated my anxieties, developed charisma and attracted the guy, but managed to lose him as well.

'Love can be hard,' she said. 'I guess you're finally learning that. Come with me, I want to give you something.'

I followed her into her garage, which doubled as her office. Being our last session, I was expecting some kind of sentimental speech about choices, how I had to figure out what the right choices were to make, and how only then would I find true happiness.

She instead walked over to her desk, picked up a piece of paper and handed it to me.

'Congratulations on finishing the course; you're now a seeker, not an avoider. Actually, considering what you did to Max, there's still a little bit of avoider in you, but it'll disappear eventually.'

Very funny.

What she'd handed me was a picture of a bikini model that had been pulled from the middle of a fitness magazine. On it were printed the words...

Yay, you've graduated, congratulations.

And Tiffany had signed her name at the bottom of it.

She leant down, opened the door of a bar fridge I hadn't noticed, and handed me a beer.

'Sorry, it's normally a better brand but it's all I've got; Liam in all of his heartbreak has been hitting the "bevos" most weekends.'

It wasn't exactly the uplifting final speech from my dating coach I was expecting, and as a result, I didn't really know what to say.

'Thanks, I guess.'

'Just on Liam,' she said, as she drank her beer from the bottle. 'He's my son but he's not actually my son. I've been infertile my whole life.'

I wondered why she was telling me this, but after we both drank, I realised this was her uplifting final speech.

'I had the man of my dreams leave me because I couldn't have a baby, twice. Two different men, not the same man twice. And then I realised I had a choice to make...'

There it was – the bit about choices.

'I could spend my whole life trying to find the guy or I could spend my whole life trying to find the child.'

She didn't need to keep going; I knew what happened next – she chose the child.

'I spent the next six years trying to find the guy but couldn't, so I changed my priorities.'

Okay, I didn't know what happened next.

'I conceded there was a chance I might not find him, so put my effort into finding a son or daughter instead, and then Liam came along. He was a teenager who'd been in and out of foster homes because his parents had died when he was a baby, so I adopted him. It was the best decision I ever made. He completely filled my empty heart and brought a great deal of love into my life that never would have been there without him. I didn't become a dating coach because it sounded cool, I became one because I wanted other women to obtain what I never could. I'm not a miracle worker or some kind of magic love doctor, at best I'm a friend, but I hope in the short time we've known each other, you've realised what's most important in your life, and how you can go about achieving it.'

Those last few words struck a chord with me – what's most important in life and how you go about achieving it.

She raised her bottle and clunked it against mine. 'Cheers.'

I walked out of Tiffany's place and back towards the bus stop but stopped outside her house next door.

The front door was slightly ajar, so I pushed it open and stuck my head through. Liam was carrying a piece of wood through the unfinished hallway.

'Pretty cool house,' I said.

'Given to me by a pretty cool person.'

'This is yours? I thought it was Tiffany's.'

'Mum bought the land for me. Mum's can be pretty cool.'

That was an understatement.

'You know, older sisters can be pretty cool as well.'

Watching the TV Guide graphic in Tiffany's living room earlier, the remark Liam would fit in with my family well was a throwaway one. Learning of his upbringing however, sparked a desire not to let our fleeting acquaintance end.

He walked back over towards me with another plank of wood and placed it on top of a pile of wood planks that lay up against a wall, 'Last session, eh?'

I nodded and took a few steps closer to him. 'What do you say we stay friends?'

I held my hand out for a handshake but instead of shaking it, he raised both of his hands and faced his palms towards me. His hands were filthy.

I left my hand exactly where it was, not put off by his lack of hygiene. 'Believe it or not, I ate chips with hands that dirty just yesterday.'

He smiled, lowered his right hand and shook mine. 'See you around, friend.'

I did as Tiffany instructed and attempted to resolve things with Max first. I called him minutes after I arrived home, but his phone rang out and it went to message bank.

'Hey, it's me; I'd like to meet, can you call me please?'

I sat on the couch, watched television and waited. Seconds felt like minutes and minutes like hours. I was impatient but had to give him time to reply.

He didn't.

I rang again shortly before going to bed, but it rang and went through to voicemail again. I didn't leave a message.

Where was he?

That and two hundred other questions kept me awake for hours. I hardly slept a wink.

Elliot didn't come into work the following day. His mum rang and said he hadn't slept well of late, had become rundown as a result and was battling the early stages of a virus.

Knowing his illness came from being overworked – which was my fault for never being at the store – twisted the dagger more and more.

Elliot being unwell made me more determined to talk to him, which saw me more urgent to get in touch with Max.

I rang Max three times from the store, but there was still no answer. After work I killed time by going through newspaper cut-outs I'd featured in. I then trawled through dozens of my own Instagram posts and read the hundreds of positive comments. I then progressed to my Hot, Hot Ella Folder and looked at the photos in there. In the folder was a selfie of Max and I at the top of Mount Oberon. It was one of the few photos that fitted the description of the folder – despite having incredibly wet hair due to the rainfall on the way up the mountain, I really did look Hot, Hot.

It didn't take me long to figure out why. I looked Hot, Hot because I was happy. In fact, I wasn't just happy, it was the happiest I'd been since before Mum and Dad died. That photo and those thoughts brought a tear to my eye, and no longer did I see talking to Max as something I had to do for the sake of my relationship with Elliot, but something I wanted to do.

Under a night sky and a moon three-quarters full, I caught an Uber over to Max's apartment.

A resident allowed me to enter the front security door and then helped me catch the lift to level seven. I knocked on his door, but he wasn't home. I suspected he was in there and just not answering so I called him, but there was no sound of a phone ringing from inside his apartment. I sat down against the wall in my normal place. With no diary of Max's and just three per cent battery left on my phone, I waited without entertainment. I changed seating positions, walked a few laps of level seven and then lay down to rest.

I waited for him for hours, but he never showed.

Starving and dehydrated, I thought about going to his workplace or his mum and dad's house, but then thought better of it. It was clear he didn't want to be found, so I caught a bus back to Hannah's house. Katie walked out the front door as I walked through the front garden. 'Hey, I called you like three times; where have you been?' she said.

'Battery died. I need food and water.'

I went to enter the house but she stopped me. 'Ella, it's 9pm; Hannah And Her Sisters is over. Brett and the kids are home, Hannah's going to bed; she'll hit the roof if you walk in now, especially after she cooked for you and you didn't show.'

She could see I was mentally and emotionally drained and hadn't arrived intent on causing commotion. 'You can come over to mine; I'll get you some food there. Where have you been anyway?'

'I've been trying to find Max but I can't. I know I told him we're over but the way he's hiding, it's like he's telling me he's breaking up with me.'

Katie looked at me like she knew something I didn't. She then turned and slipped back inside Hannah's front door.

What was she doing?

She came back out with the newspaper and gave it to me. 'I gather you haven't seen this?'

It was a photo of me in my floral dress on Mother's Day. I was sitting on my front fence waiting for Max to pick me up. Excited by the impending lunch with his parents, I hadn't noticed a photographer taking snaps of me from across the street.

He was taking photos because I'd forgotten to contact the newspapers, magazines and paparazzi and tell them I'd found love and was quitting Tinderella. What made it worse was that the published picture showed me taking a selfie, and no doubt led the reader to believe I was about to post it on my Instagram account.

'Might this have something to do with it?' Katie asked.

Of course it did, I told Max I was done with Tinderella, and yet here I was a short time later, appearing to joyfully display my singledom to the world.

At that moment, I knew why I hadn't been able to reach Max. I had told him outside his parents' place I could no longer trust him. Having seen this photo, he was now sending me the same message.

He couldn't trust me anymore, and because of that, we were over.

I raised the newspaper over my face, unwilling to face the world.

Where was I to go now?

Even with Katie's arm around me, I didn't know how I could carry on.

Any chance of reconciling with Max was gone, which meant so too was any chance of reconciling with Elliot.

For the second time in seven years my life had changed forever, and there was nothing I could do about it.

31.

Tiffany had said it – "realise what's important in your life and go about achieving it."

I'd lost Elliot and Max, and neither was coming back. I thought Max was "the one", and it turned out he wasn't – he was just like every other guy – come in, play around with the girl's heart and body, and then clear-off with no accountability.

Love was all a crock anyway.

Finding "the one", falling in love and living happily ever after didn't happen to all people, it only happened to some. Those lucky ones had it fall in their lap, while the rest of us put in so much effort for zero result. The quicker love's enemies – a-la me – realised we were the leftovers, the quicker we could accept it and concentrate on the other stuff on offer.

And boy was there plenty of "other stuff".

The minute it became apparent I was part of the lonely-hearts club was the minute I jumped straight back on Tinder and went looking for my bad boy. Someone who didn't care about feelings but who was hot, and I could fondle.

Frustratingly, my first three matches all declined because they were looking for love. Losers.

Then along came Romeo.

How ironic; he who was named after the male lead in arguably the greatest love story of all time, was looking only for a good time.

Perhaps it wasn't ironic; *Romeo and Juliet* was, after all, a tragedy, and so too was my life.

If there were one hundred boxes for everything I hated in a guy, then Romeo ticked them all.

His lifestyle choices were horrible. His profile photos consisted of him shirtless on boats, smoking cigars and flexing his muscles, with numerous women. He had piercings, tattoos, and an undercut with a crop of hair that looked like a giant leaf. He also had a horrible dress sense; he wore a pair of jeans with tears in the knees and one of those tank singlets that hung far too low around his rib area – on our date.

Looking at him as we drank beer at a random pub in Frankston, I didn't really care about any of those things, as he was there to serve a purpose.

He looked at me in the same light – I was the girl with the public profile who would enhance his reputation with his mates and increase his chances of getting more women in the future.

I knew it and he knew it, so I said so.

'I say we screw drinks and get straight to screwing each other.'

Never in my twenty-eight years on planet Earth had such revolting words come out of my mouth.

But I didn't care.

Sure, I had despised Aaron the Canadian for thinking all he wanted was a one-night stand, but the goalposts had moved. I'd never had a one-night stand before and swore I never would, but spiralling around in an emotional tornado, all I wanted to do was rebel.

I wanted to treat love and life the way it had treated me.

I wanted revenge.

Hot, steamy, zero inhibitions, so rough you break things nearby, revenge.

'Here in the bathrooms?' he replied. 'Or in the back of my Ute?'

I really had picked a gem this time around, and one who obviously didn't have the wealth he promoted on his profile.

How the hell was he on a million-dollar boat in his pictures when he drove a shoddy old ute?

'Bathroom first, then Ute,' I said.

I drank the rest of my beer, as did he his. We then stood, and he adjusted the front of his jeans as if readying his downstairs area for what was to come. It was pathetic really, but kind of understandable; with no kissing and no foreplay, I guess he had to wind himself up somehow.

We walked over towards the toilets but halfway there a hand from a nearby table reached out and grabbed my arm.

'Linda?'

It was a voice I didn't recognise from a face I'd never seen. It was a case of mistaken identity, and the woman immediately went red and apologised.

'Sorry, I thought you were someone else.'

She let go and I moved off, but I stopped again when I overheard her tell her friends, 'Should have known, Linda would never go for a guy like that.'

Romeo, who was ahead of me, turned back to see where I was at, and why I'd halted. 'What's going on?' he asked.

'You go ahead,' I told him. 'I've just got to kick the shit out of someone.'

The cold evening wind at Frankston Beach stabbed my skin like ice needles, but I deserved it.

With Romeo in the toilet waiting for me, I left the bar and walked to a place where I could ask for forgiveness.

The person I wanted to kick the shit out of was me, for straying so ridiculously far from who I really was. The whole night I'd been blinded by bitterness and hatred, but the girl who grabbed my arm allowed me to see how much I was still loved.

I wasn't Linda, but my mother was, and the woman who grabbed my arm was right – my mother would never have approved a guy like that. Worse, she would have been disappointed in me for pursuing him and having lively intentions of sleeping with him twenty minutes after we'd met.

She would have cried with disappointment.

It was times like this I really suffered. I suffered because I didn't have my mother around to guide me, I didn't have my mother around to hug me, and I didn't have my mother around to tell me the right thing to do.

I didn't have my mother around, so I picked up my phone and called the next best thing.

'Katie, it's me. Can you come and get me?'

32.

My spirits began to lift in the week following.

I took a few days off work to clear my mind. I closed the shop for forty-eight hours, and when Elliot was better, let him manage things on his own. There was only two weeks before he finished up. I hadn't spoken to him since he quit, and knew I had to go to work on Monday to try and restore what was left of our friendship. But it was the weekend, and it was time for some fun first.

Katie picked me up and drove us to Hannah's for my Hollywood themed Tinderella party. We had no trouble finding a car park close to Hannah's house second time around, as we'd arrived three hours before the party was due to start.

Hannah again turned her house into a festival. Apart from the Tinderella signage, and another champagne tower, everything else was new. She also organised a professional hair and make-up artist to beautify us. Once our make-up was done, it was time to dress, and reveal the costume we'd wear for the night.

'I like it,' Katie said, as I exited Hannah's bedroom.

I was in Marilyn Monroe's white cocktail dress from *The Seven Year Itch*, and I felt amazing.

I was also relieved; despite me being a redhead and Marilyn a blonde, Katie had no trouble identifying me. If she knew who I was, the party guests would too.

'That's the most iconic dress in the history of dresses. Your hair could be pink, and we'd still know who you are,' Hannah said, as she came out of the kitchen.

'You're just jealous Ella's outfit is better than yours,' Katie said.

'Says she who's dressed as an overweight crow.'

Katie didn't look like an overweight crow. She was dressed up as Natalie Portman from *Black Swan*. She hadn't quite been able to pull it off though. While Portman's character in the film was pale and thin, Katie was tanned and burly.

'I'll peck your eyes out and make you blind if you don't watch it.'

'Going by the last party, we all know who's going to be blind by the end of tonight,' Hannah quipped.

Katie widened her mouth to argue back, but then agreed, 'True.'

As if to validate Hannah's point she then headed for the champagne tower.

Hannah – like me – had gone for a more classic look. She was Rose from *Titanic* in that red Edwardian dress and those white opera gloves that helped make Kate Winslet so memorable.

'And if Brett tries to climb aboard my floating raft, I'm going to push his butt off just like she did Leo's.'

Neither Brett nor Roy was invited to my first party, but both were going to be at this one. They were security guards for the night and had been given one strict instruction by Hannah – 'No sneaking off to watch football.'

The atmosphere compared to my first Tinderella party was on another level.

I'd always thought people had reservations about dress-up parties and played things on the safe side, but not this crew. These partygoers had one aim in mind – to outdo one another. Mary Poppins held a small umbrella in one hand and a cocktail in the other; Alf from the TV show *ALF* drank bottles of scotch through his headpiece, and Chris Hemsworth danced with Wednesday Addams. He wasn't dressed as *Thor*, but just as Chris Hemsworth. I had to take a second look, as this guy looked so much like Chris Hemsworth I thought he actually was.

Not everybody's costume was of a high standard however; some guy came dressed as a truck and parked himself near the fireplace, and there was this dark-haired tattooed woman who I thought was going for Catwoman, but looked more like a female stripper.

'Wait, is that Nude Nellie from the newspaper ad?' I asked Katie.

'Yeah I think so.'

'How did she get in?'

'Probably showed Roy her boobs.'

Hannah was quick to clutch my arm and lead me around the room. Much like the first party, she put a fresh glass of expensive champagne in my hand and introduced me to numerous men. While the party potion remained the same, the guys she nudged me in front of didn't – the last crop of wealthy entrepreneurs had been replaced by a whole new bunch.

'The last crop are now all in relationships, which means there's no point having them here. Which also means there's no time to waste.'

No quicker had she said that, did she place me in front of a guy dressed as a pirate.

'Ella meet Beau, he's an executive with one of the major banks. Beau, meet my youngest sister Ella, she's famous.'

Her introduction wasn't what I was expecting but things had changed; unlike last time I didn't need to sell myself with lies; every guy knew me as Tinderella and that's all I needed to be.

'I like your pirate costume.'

'Actually, I'm Prince Eric from *The Little Mermaid*.'

Following a second look I could see that he was.

Beau was sweet, smart and funny, and so too were the other guys Hannah introduced me to. And their costumes were impressive also. But they all had the same attribute that made me want to run a hundred miles – they were more desperate than a bunch of housewives from Wisteria Lane. They either grovelled, invaded my personal space or revealed information that made them sound like a frenzied prowler.

'March 23, you posted a photo on Instagram of you shopping with your sister. It was so good; I messaged you with fifteen thumbs-up emojis. I follow you on Instagram.'

Right. Stalker alert.

Their desperation was actually ruining my night.

I wanted to tell Hannah and ask her to introduce me to guys similar to the first party, but she was preoccupied. I walked out onto the back verandah and spotted her standing at the top of the backyard pool, with a champagne glass in one hand and her necklace in the other. A number of her drunken female groupies stood around her and yelled, 'Do it! Do it! Do it!'

She was recreating the scene at the end of *Titanic* when elderly Rose threw her necklace into the ocean. She tossed her necklace into the pool, screamed with delight, and then screamed in horror.

'Shit, that necklace is worth six grand, and the pool monster's going to scoop it up. Brett!'

The "pool monster" was the pool cleaner, and Brett was upholding his job as security out the front, which meant there was no one to get the necklace.

So she jumped in the pool herself.

She dived down, picked it up and resurfaced to a rapturous round of applause. She swam over to the side of the pool but couldn't climb out, so – with the help of some of the other girls – I reached my hand out and pulled her up.

'I think you need some water,' I said.

'But there's heaps of water here.'

'Not water you can swim in, water you can drink.'

The second party certainly didn't go the same way as the first. Hannah – not Katie – was drunk, and not a single guy in attendance had charmed me.

I got a towel from the linen closet and walked over to Hannah, who sat with Katie away from the party. No matter where I looked, guys ogled me and didn't even try and hide it. It was becoming overwhelming, so much so I considered getting drunk and throwing my pin pearl earrings in the pool to the raptures of a group of women myself.

'Is that one of my new towels or my old towels?' Hannah asked, as I sat beside her.

I had no idea.

'It's one of your new-old towels,' Katie said.

'Good,' Hannah replied.

She dried her face with the towel, but did so weirdly, like she was massaging her cheek with it.

'You okay?' I asked.

She wondered why I was asking.

'It's just that, you've drunk half as much as the last party, and yet you were much more sober then.'

'No one has spiked my drink you nuffy; I was more sober last time because those champagnes were watered down.'

I knew it! Sneaky little thing.

She finished drying herself off and asked after Brett.

Justin had been having trouble sleeping at Brett's parents' place, so he went around to look after the two boys. He'd be back in the morning.

'What a man; best man at this party,' she said.

That was something I wasn't going to disagree with; not that he or Roy had much to compete with. As I sat with my sisters, making Hannah warm again, I decided I was done talking to any more men for the rest of the night.

It wasn't long before I changed my mind however.

In the front door walked a young man with a kind face and the best outfit at the entire party. He was Russell, the young wilderness explorer from the animated movie *Up*, and I couldn't help but want to talk to him.

'Can you girls excuse me for just a minute?'

I got up, cautiously approached and then just as cautiously said hello. 'Hey. I didn't expect you to come.'

'Well, someone gave me an invite and I figured I couldn't miss the party of the year.'

It was Elliot, and while playful verbally, he was guarded emotionally. After what had happened the last time we were together, he didn't initiate a hug or a kiss on the cheek.

'So how have you been?' I asked.

'Good. What about you?'

'Good.'

It was the kind of conversation you'd expect from two people who had fallen out. Following niceties, neither of us knew what to say.

'I like your outfit. I remember the day we watched *Up* at my place. I remember you saying you wanted to tie a hundred balloons to the roof of your mum's house to see if it would float away.'

He broke into a slight laugh. 'I actually did do that, but I only got three balloons in before Mum caught me and yelled at me to get off the roof.'

Again, silence fell over the two us, and in the midst of it, the guy dressed as a truck came to life right near us and motored away.

He was a Transformer™, and he scared the daylights out of both of us.

Eventually our hearts stopped racing and Elliot's opened up. 'I didn't come to party.' His hands shook as he worked up the courage to say what he'd come to say. 'I came here to tell you I'm no longer quitting the toy store.'

'What? Really?'

'Yeah.'

I was so glad to hear him say that; never in my life had I been so thankful. The feeling of relief was so overbearing I couldn't help but close my eyes and exhale. And then a tear trickled out from underneath one of my closed eyelids.

I was getting my best friend back.

The reason for his change of mind was something I also didn't expect.

'Max came to the store today; he showed me this.'

He got out his phone and handed it to me.

It was *Koolish*, my Friendship Square app for the disabled, and it was complete. Complete with Elliot's profile right there in front of me.

'Scored three matches already,' he smiled.

I scanned through it – the video and photos captured Elliot's personality perfectly, as did his tagline – Tea and biscuits are my specialty.

Evie could verify that.

His profile was as perfect as I'd imagined it would be, and he felt exactly the same way, with a touch of regret.

'All that time you spent away from the store, you were creating an app to help me find love? When I got mad at you, why didn't you tell me?'

'It was Max's and my secret. He also did most of it, and when we broke up, I wasn't sure if we'd finish it.'

'Funny... He said you did most of it.'

Elliot told me Max came into the store and together they spent half-an-hour hanging out in the cubby house. Max was aware of the many times I'd called but knew of my photo in the newspaper and needed time to contemplate his feelings and his future.

'Plus, he told me he's been really busy. The matinee of *Noah's Ark* is tonight.'

The play, of course.

I'd forgotten all about it; I would have liked to have seen it.

'And he asked if you'd read the letter. Mind if I use the bathroom?'

'Sure... Wait, what letter?'

'The letter he gave you on Mother's Day.'

I'd completely forgotten about that too – the envelope he gave me in the car on the way to his parents' place.

The envelope he'd asked me not to open.

I hadn't read it, but I also hadn't moved it from the place I'd originally put it.

Elliot moved towards the hallway and I rummaged through my handbag right to the very bottom. I found the crinkled envelope, opened it, and read the opening line.

What Max said to me in his car that day was true – it wasn't a letter written to me but one written to someone else – my mother.

Dear Mrs Bang,

My name is Max Hatheway and I wanted to say hello.

They say in our lifetime we're likely to meet 0.001 per cent of the Earth's population. How lucky should I consider myself to have crossed paths with your youngest daughter, Ella. I'm a Catholic, not a very good one, but I believe despite being in a better place, you are still with Ella, Hannah and Katie; watching over them with care and love.

It's no secret I have a deep love for Ella. She is perfect in every single way. But in thinking about this, I realise she is this way in large part because of one person – you. To be such a beautiful person, she must have had one incredibly beautiful mother.

You should be extremely proud of your youngest daughter. She is kind, she is smart and she is funny, she's courageous and she's patient. One of the things I love about her most is how selfless she is – she's always putting others before herself, and that's a rare trait in this world.

It makes me sad knowing how much I love my own mother, and how much she sacrifices for me, that Ella has missed out on all of this over the last seven years. But I hope you can take comfort in knowing I will do my utmost to take care of her in yours and Jacob's absence.

I can only imagine how proud you must be looking down on her. Ella is the perfect daughter and the most perfect partner anyone could ask for, and I'm certain that, just like you, she will one day become the perfect mother too.

God bless you and Jacob, and thank-you for creating such an amazing human being.

And happy Mother's Day.

I hope one day, some day, I can say hello for real.

Love, Max x.

By the end of it I was sobbing. No words had meant more to me than those which lay upon that crinkled piece of paper, and at that moment, no person meant more to me than the man who'd written them.

How was he able to find such feelings and express them on a page?

I was snapped back to reality when the DJ cut the music, but realised he'd done so out of concern for me, having seen I was crying. While his intentions were pure, his actions saw a hushed room full of partygoers stop and stare at me.

So, too, did Elliot stare when he came back from the bathroom. 'Tears of joy, yes?' he asked.

He didn't mean to sound funny, but I chuckled through those tears of joy at how he said it.

My entire adult life I'd wrestled with my confused head and heart. My cluttered mind created a constant stream of frustration and self-hate, and my cowardice heart stopped me from going after what I really wanted in life.

But the contents of Max's letter made all that disappear. My head had never been clearer, and – finally feeling worthy of love and all the good things life had to offer – I knew there was only one thing left to do.

'I need to go.'

Elliot looked at me with a beaming smile. 'I was hoping you'd say that.'

I shoved the letter back into my handbag, handed the bag to Elliot and made a beeline for the front door. The eyes of the partygoers followed me as I made a hasty exit. Hannah and Katie also watched and wondered what on Earth was going on.

I ran through the front garden and out to the top of the driveway. For a moment I stopped and considered whether catching an Uber was the right move, but quickly concluded the fastest way there would just be to run. It was, after all, only two-and-a-half kilometres.

Two hundred metres down the road however and my high heels were hurting my feet, so I stopped and took them off. As I unstrapped the second of my heels I noticed of a wave of people hurrying out of Hannah's driveway and coming my way. They were all men, and they were running.

Running after me.

Oh my God.

I looked at my heels and my Marilyn Monroe dress and realised what was happening – my daydream was coming true. All these men were running after me, desperate to find out where I – the most beautiful woman in the world – was going.

I wasn't waiting for them to catch me, so threw my heels onto the nature strip and ran on.

Every fifty metres I looked back to see if they were gaining on me and saw glimpses of my daydream. Chris Hemsworth pounded the pavement in all his glory, the entire shirtless cast of *Magic Mike* did the same in all their glory as well, and Eric from *The Little Mermaid* was right behind them. A man walking his dogs joined in, a fire truck pulled out of a side street, as did a limousine from the bottle shop at The Bridge Hotel – the hot Prime Minister of Canada no doubt sitting inside of it. All these guys were desperate for a chance at love with this woman, but she only had eyes for one man.

The run up Main Street Mordialloc was adrenaline-charged, so much so I forgot to take Como Parade West, which would have been the shorter route. The journey down Nepean Highway towards the toy store felt like something out of a movie, and leading a group of intoxicated desperadoes over the railway crossing at Parkdale Station was probably not the best move. But finally, I reached my destination – the Shirley Burke Theatre on Parkers Road.

Trying to catch my breath, I greeted the blind, elderly, Mother Teresa-like lady who again stood out the front with her Labrador guide dog Daisy.

'Daisy doesn't like Noah's Ark huh?' I asked.

'She's scared of the lions.'

That response was predictable.

I pushed through the front door, ran through the foyer area, up the side steps and stopped in the aisle between the rows of seats. Ten rows in front of me, on the stage, Max and the rest of the cast performed.

'Can the one-legged frog join us on the Ark?' Max, as Noah, asked Chloe, as a giraffe.

Chloe responded with sign language.

'What did she say?' called Owen, who was dressed as the one-legged frog.

Max went to answer—

'Is there any chance you'll take me back?'

The cast looked around, unsure of where the response had come from. It hadn't come from anyone on the stage, because it had come from me.

With adrenaline still trickling through my veins, I ran down the aisle that separated the audience, climbed up on stage and stood in front of Max.

With my Marilyn Monroe dress dishevelled, my forehead covered in sweat and my feet black from running, it came as no surprise my appearance wasn't a welcome one.

'Ella, what are you doing? You're interrupting.'

I looked behind him and saw Gloria dressed as a horse. She looked so cute, but also so very disappointed I was ruining their performance.

All the men that chased me from Hannah's swiftly and noisily entered the theatre. Elliot, Hannah and Katie also arrived. They pushed their way through the men and discovered me standing on stage with Max.

Max wondered what was going on.

I looked over at Elliot in search of reassurance. He nodded at me – the stage was mine and I should say what I came to say.

I turned my attention back to Max and faintly asked again, 'Is there any chance you'll take me back?'

He didn't answer.

I swallowed a thick and anxious swallow. After countless dating nightmares and rejections, I thought I knew fear and vulnerability, but I'd never known it like this.

I was petrified.

I'd discovered first love meant doing many things for the first time. There on stage, I understood for the first time in my life, I had to bare my heart and soul.

So I did.

'I made a mistake. I didn't mean to say those things on Mother's Day, but I was angry. I thought you told of my parents' death out of gossip, not out of pride. I read your letter to my mum and now I get it. I get why you told. And the photos, I promise I gave up Tinderella, I just forgot to cancel the photos. I didn't even know the photographer was there.'

I was drowning in my own explanation. Characters in films always expressed their regret with flawlessness despite their overflowing emotion. I couldn't proficiently find the words and felt I was only making things worse. Still, there was one last thing I needed to say.

'I'm sorry. You just need to know I'm sorry for what I did to you, and I'm sorry for interrupting your play. But I love you to the moon and back, and I hope one day, *some day*, you'll give me another chance.'

Max's reaction was nonchalant; a blank expression on his face gave little away as to how he felt.

Finally, he reacted.

He turned to Chloe and with sign language asked her a question. 'Do we have room for a human woman on the Ark?'

Chloe gave her answer in sign language.

'What did she say?' Owen called again.

Max turned back to me and relayed her answer. Only it wasn't her answer, but his. 'She said, I'm sorry too. I made mistakes as well and I lost sight of what was important – you and me. I don't want to be anywhere else than by your side; I'll give you another chance, if you'll give me one.'

My mind and body flooded with a rainbow of emotions; I was relieved, I was excited and I was grateful.

He stepped forward to give me a kiss but was halted by a demanding Owen.

'That's not what Chloe said, what did she really say?'

'She said as long as she's not carrying a paintball gun, Ella can happily come aboard.'

Those on stage laughed at Chloe's instruction, as did many in the audience. Elliot chuckled as well. He stood next to Katie and Hannah. Hannah was still drunk, but beaming with pride all the same.

Max led me onto the Ark. It was made out of cardboard and wood, and had been painted. Once on it, the two of us stood in near darkness, away from the eyes of the audience. He kissed me softly, and after several kisses, spoke at the same time.

'Who are all those guys dressed in costume?'

'Just friends of Hannah's.'

'You know we're not going to have enough room on the Ark for them.'

'The way I see it, there's only enough room here for you and I.'

He kissed me through a smile.

I kept kissing him through a smile.

Ella Bang was back in the arms of her perfect match.

3 3 .

A large blob of ice cream went splat on Hannah's kitchen floor.

'Ah crap,' cursed Katie, as she reached for something to clean it up.

'What are you doing? That's one of her good tea towels,' I said.

Days after the Tinderella fancy dress party, we were all back at Hannah's for Hannah And Her Sisters. Only for once, Brett, the kids, and Roy were also present.

Hannah had cooked dinner, so I was in charge of dessert. I'd also engaged Katie for her own benefit – she was in the bad books with Hannah after using the magnetic letters on her fridge to write *Necklace in Pool.*

Of course, the necklace wasn't in the pool – Hannah had dived in and got it out – but Brett hadn't known it was ever in there, until he saw the letters.

'Dessert's here!' Katie said, as she re-entered the dining room and greeted everyone at the table. 'I brought Hannah's favourite that's going to see me forgiven for all past indiscretions.'

'Still hate you forever,' Hannah sniggered, before feigning excitement for the benefit of her children. 'Wow, ice cream, we love ice cream, don't we boys?'

Justin said, 'Yeah,' while Brody said nothing, much to her disappointment. He still wasn't saying a lot, which proved Katie right.

'No "I love you, Mumma's" yet? I guess he'll start speaking after dessert.'

'Shut up.'

I passed bowls of ice cream to Roy and Brett and joined them at the table.

'Not eating any yourself?' Brett asked.

I didn't really feel like it; dinner had been more than enough for me.

'Even though you only ate half of it,' Hannah said.

She did give me a huge plateful.

'Suppose that means you don't post photos of food on Instagram like Katie does?' Roy asked.

Katie told him to 'piss off', and Hannah wasn't happy about her language around the children.

I told Roy I didn't post photos of food, but that I had started posting the occasional photo of my new boyfriend.

Max and I had talked about Tinderella. He said it was okay for me to keep my social media profiles active; he understood 1.6 million followers was a lot to give up. I appreciated that, and while I didn't post too many snaps of him, I did alter the theme of my photos from desperate and dateless to family, friends and being happily in love.

'We should take a photo now,' Hannah suggested. 'One with all of us at dinnertime; let me get something to wipe Brody's mouth clean.'

As toddlers do, he'd put more ice cream over his face than he had in his mouth.

No sooner had she gone into the kitchen did she yell, and then charge back out.

'Katie, Ella! What the hell did you two do to my good tea towel? God Katie, you throw-up in my bathroom sink and now this? I'll be banning you from the house soon if you don't watch it.'

Katie looked over at me to signal it was my turn to even things up. She hadn't thrown up in Hannah's bathroom sink, I had. I had a minor bout of gastro and didn't want to suffer from Hannah's disdain at the same time. The illness probably came from eating hot chips with dirty, weed-pulling hands. Katie took the blame for my sickness, so it was my turn to repay the favour.

'Sorry Han, that was me, must have just forgot.'

She grabbed her phone, ordered us all to squeeze in closer and took a group selfie of us. She wasn't overly pleased with the end result; she wanted a nice family photo and Brett wasn't looking at the camera and Roy was pouting. She ordered another, but just as she took the shot, Brody sneezed a mouthful of ice cream all over her.

She froze in horror, while the rest of us found it hilarious.

'That is definitely a keeper,' Katie said.

I was certain she'd want to clean herself up and have another photo taken, but the sound of a car horn came from the front drive, which meant I had to leave.

'Can't keep lover-boy waiting,' Katie said.

'When do we even get to meet lover-boy?' Brett asked. 'Why don't you invite lover-boy in now?'

Brett describing Max as "lover-boy" sounded just plain wrong.

None of them had officially met Max yet and they were due to do so, but I didn't want it to be there and then. Thankfully Hannah agreed.

'He's not coming in with me looking like this Brett. Ella, tell him we'll have dinner soon. Without the kids, or the partners.'

Without partners?

The reason quickly dawned on me – she wanted to grill Max; she wanted to make sure he was the perfect guy for her little sister.

That made me feel kind of special.

Three heads hung out of Max's car as it sat in the front drive; Max was one, and Elliot and Chloe were the other two. We were going on a double-date of sorts. Elliot and Chloe had of course been friends for some time but had both created profiles on *Koolish* and deliberately matched with one another.

'Can't be late,' Elliot called. 'With four of us we'll have twice as much chance of winning.'

We parked in the car park at The Bridge Hotel and headed to the entrance for trivia.

Elliot and Chloe walked ahead of me and Max. Elliot was showing her how he'd set up a specific folder in his phone for his *Koolish* profile photos.

'Max,' he called back to us. 'How do you say Hot, Hot Elliot Folder in sign language?'

Max demonstrated, Elliot copied, and Chloe grinned.

'I'd like to learn how to communicate with Chloe,' I told Max. 'Do you think you could teach me?'

He feigned a look of reservation. 'I'm not sure; I feel like you two would talk about me behind my back.'

'No we won't.'

He looked at me with a stone-cold expression as if to say, "Oh really?" and then disagreed.

'She told me yesterday she knew about the George Clooney/ Oprah thing.'

I couldn't help but laugh at the way he said that, and also couldn't help but lie about how she found out. 'I didn't tell her; must have been a lucky guess.'

'Well let's hope she's full of lucky guesses tonight, seeing as I'm no good with celebrity marriages and you're no good with... pretty much everything else.'

It was a low blow, despite his cheekiness, and he deserved to be punished. 'No cuddles for you; you're sleeping on the floor tonight, mister.'

He donned his puppy dog face and puckered up to me. 'I'm sorry, I didn't mean that, please don't ban me from cuddles.'

The cuddle ban was a game I'd created and was like that of "Ellen and the Moon". I'd enforced the cuddle ban three times but caved each time because I couldn't keep my hands off him.

'Okay, cuddle ban has been withdrawn, but know that one day, I might be able to find the willpower to enforce the cuddle ban and go through with it... maybe.'

He accepted that and gave me a cuddle.

We approached the entrance door; Chloe had already walked through, and Elliot held it open for us. Max and I went to walk in when my phone vibrated.

'Hang on, I just got a message.' I checked it, expecting it to be Hannah or Katie, but it wasn't a text message at all – it was a Tinder match. *How ironic.* 'I'll be in in a second.'

Max nodded, and he and Elliot walked inside.

Tinder had been a fun, learning experience, but with my soul mate now in my life, it was time to close it down.

I went to, but hesitated. It would have been bad karma to turn it off before telling my latest match the truth. So I wrote him a quick message and he messaged me back straight away.

Thankfully, he was really accepting of what I had to tell him.

Ella

Hi. I've fallen in love and forgotten to delete my Tinder profile. Hope you find your one true love as well. From Ella.

Chad

Hey, I want to have sex with strangers who are skilled and very intimate in bed. If you are of the same interest like mine meet me at http://seeXX99sexed45 and we will have intimate and unforgettable bed experience.

THE END

ABOUT THE AUTHOR

Matt Kelly is a Melbourne born and bred 30-something who has lived in Sydney, Brisbane and Perth. Inspired by award-winning scriptwriters Nancy Meyers and Richard Curtis, Kelly studied screenwriting at RMIT University alongside fellow author Graeme Simsion, before working on script teams for *Packed To The Rafters* and *A Place To Call Home*. A qualified journalist and romantic at heart, Kelly enjoys spending time with friends and family, and listening to iconic 90s pop songs.

ACKNOWLEDGEMENTS

Mary Rennie, Sarrah Le Marquand, Julie Postance, Fiona Wainrit, Luke Devenish and Sophie White.